He'd known she was pretty, suspected that Heather could be beautiful in a soft, delicate fashion. He'd had no idea that she could be stunning, breathtaking even.

"Talk about hiding your light under a bushel!" Ethan didn't realize he'd said it aloud until Heather gusted out a nervous laugh.

"That's what my mom always says," she admitted shyly.

"Listen up, boss lady. When I tell you to walk, I want long, fluid strides. Walk forward. Look up. Stop. Half turn."

Heather had been around enough photo shoots to know the drill, so he wasn't worried. Click after click, he shot two rolls in rapid succession, moving from one camera to another.

"Ladies and gentleman," he muttered to himself, "a star is born."

* * *

DAVIS LANDING:
Nothing is stronger than a family's love

Books by Arlene James

Love Inspired

The Perfect Wedding #3
An Old-Fashioned Love #9
A Wife Worth Waiting For #14
With Baby in Mind #21
To Heal a Heart #285
Deck the Halls #321
A Family To Share #331
Butterfly Summer #356

*Everyday Miracles

ARLENE JAMES

says, "Camp meetings, mission work and the church where my parents and grandparents were prominent members permeate my Oklahoma childhood memories. It was a golden time, which sustains me yet. However, only as a young, widowed mother did I truly begin growing in my personal relationship with the Lord. Through adversity, He blessed me in countless ways, one of which is a second marriage so loving and romantic, it still feels like courtship!"

The author of over sixty novels, Arlene James now resides outside of Dallas, Texas, with her husband. Arlene says, "The rewards of motherhood have indeed been extraordinary for me. Yet I've looked forward to this new stage of my life." Her need to write is greater than ever, a fact that frankly amazes her, as she's been at it since the eighth grade!

ARLENE JAMES

BUTTERFLY
SUMMER

Steeple
Hill®

Published by Steeple Hill Books™

To Kathryn Springer, Irene Hannon, Valerie Hansen,
Patricia Davids and Lenora Worth, a great group
with whom to work. Your creativity, dedication
and cooperation are much appreciated.
God bless, Arlene.

STEEPLE HILL BOOKS

Steeple
Hill®

ISBN-13: 978-0-373-81270-7
ISBN-10:   0-373-81270-1

BUTTERFLY SUMMER

Copyright © 2006 by Deborah Rather

www.SteepleHill.com

Printed in U.S.A.

Bless the Lord, O my soul, and all that
is within me, bless His holy name.
Bless the Lord, O my soul, and forget not
all His benefits: Who pardons all your
iniquities, Who heals all your diseases.
—*Psalms* 103:1–3

The Hamiltons of Davis Landing

Nora McCarthy – m – Wallace Hamilton

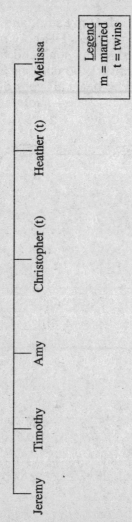

Jeremy   Timothy   Amy   Christopher (t)   Heather (t)   Melissa

Legend
m = married
t = twins

Prologue

Heather stuck her nose into the elaborate bouquet and inhaled deeply, but not even the beauty of the flowers or their heady aroma could dispel the anesthetic odor of a hospital, however well-appointed the room. Decorated in jewel tones with dark cherry furnishings, the spacious suite where her father had taken up residence and endured test after test had become a place of tension and worry for her and the remainder of the Hamilton family.

She closed her eyes and sent a silent prayer heavenward. *Gracious Lord God, please don't let it be serious.*

She had uttered or thought the words so often over these past few difficult days that they had become a private litany, and still she could not quite fathom the idea that Wallace Hamilton might actually be seriously ill.

Tall and urbanely handsome, with his thick silver hair, dark eyes and long, patrician face, he had always seemed larger than life. At fifty-nine, Wallace was still a force to be reckoned with, not only within the Hamilton family but also within the publishing world, at least that part of it centered here in Tennessee.

Now his expensive, expertly tailored suits had given way to silk pajamas and his lean, fit frame had begun to appear gaunt. Yet Heather could not believe that he wouldn't soon rise, button on one of his famously pristine white shirts, knot his silk tie and stride off to once again control Hamilton Media, the family company that he'd built into a small empire from the weekly newspaper established by his grandfather.

Her mother, Nora, entered the sitting room from the bedchamber beyond, pulling the heavy door closed behind her. Petite and elegant, Nora looked more like Heather's sister than her mother, despite the silver threading the shoulder-length gold of her hair and the new shadows around her enormous hazel eyes.

While Heather herself looked older than her twenty-seven years, her mother could easily pass for forty rather than fifty-five. Heather accepted without question the fact that she had not inherited her mother's pale beauty. It was more important to her that she take after her mother in other ways, because there was no one in the world whom she admired more than Nora Hamilton.

Her mother might appear tiny and elfin, but she possessed a backbone of steel and a fiercely protective nature, which any mother of six required. She routinely placed herself between the world and her family, shielding them all with prayer, showering them with love and guiding them with pragmatic wisdom. She could not, however, protect them from illness. Only God, in His infinite mercy, could do that.

Today they would learn whether Wallace had been spared the worst or if God would allow the specter of death to hover over him.

Nora folded her arms and looked around the room at her grown children, hugging herself tight. "The doctors are with your father now. He wanted to hear the news alone. They'll be out to speak to us next."

"It's going to be all right, Mom," Amy, Heather's older sister, said from the sofa.

Melissa, the youngest, promptly rose from her seat on the arm of the sofa and shoved her hand into the pocket of her frayed jeans, asking, "Anyone want a cola?"

"You just finished a cola," Timothy, the second-oldest brother, pointed out, pushing away from the wall and bringing his hands to his hips.

Tim was the Hamilton most like Wallace. As vice president of Hamilton Media, he had little time or patience for anything that took him away from the business *except* family. Unfortunately, he seemed to resent that their oldest brother, Jeremy, who had a more mellow disposition, had been handed the reins of the business when Wallace had entered the hospital. It didn't help that they'd recently uncovered an embezzlement scheme by one of their most trusted employees, who also happened to be a good friend of Jeremy's.

"Yeah, well, I'm having another," Melissa retorted, striding rapidly from the room, ostensibly headed for the vending machine down the hall.

Heather suspected that she just couldn't bear the pressure any longer. Melissa resembled Amy in looks, both having inherited their blond hair and enormous, doelike eyes from their mother. But unlike Amy, who at thirty was senior managing editor of the family-owned *Nashville Living* magazine, twenty-three-year-old Melissa was something of a wild child.

Christopher, Heather's twin brother, rose to his full six-foot height and crossed the room to their mother, whom he enfolded in his muscular embrace. With his dark, wavy hair and burly build, he couldn't have looked less like Heather if he'd tried, especially when wearing his policeman's uniform. Something about that dark-blue suit of clothes, with its gun belt and tools, added consequence to his already impressive stature, especially when he was standing next to their petite mother.

"Amy's right," Chris told Nora. "No matter what the doctors have to say, everything's going to work out for the best."

Nora nodded. "God takes care of His own."

"No doubt about it."

The door opened at Nora's back. She and Christopher stepped aside to allow the doctors into the room.

One of them, an older man with thinning steel gray hair, Heather had never seen before. He had to be the specialist Luke Strickland had called in from Nashville. Dr. Strickland himself was well-known to them. In his midthirties, with dark hair and eyes, the tall, handsome, charismatic physician had quickly won the respect and trust of the entire family.

It was Dr. Strickland who swept his gaze over the family. "I've just spoken with Wallace, explained our diagnosis and outlined our treatment options."

Heather glanced at Amy, a knot of dread coiling tight in her stomach.

"How bad is it?" Tim demanded, but Jeremy stepped forward, forestalling any reply.

"Hold on a minute, Luke." At a lean six feet and two inches, Jeremy was the tallest of the three Hamilton brothers. He had the same dark, wavy hair as the other two, but instead of brown eyes, his were a vibrant, piercing blue. The eldest at thirty-five, his calm, confident manner and quiet, even-handed leadership had made him a favorite at Hamilton Media. Yet he and Tim seemed eternally at odds. "Melissa needs to hear this, too. Give me a minute to get her in here."

Tim rolled his eyes, obviously impatient with the delay. Fortunately, Melissa walked into the room just then. She took in the heavy atmosphere and threw out one hip, a soft-drink bottle clutched in one hand.

"Are we having a wake or what?"

"Melissa!" Tim scolded.

Melissa immediately colored. "I didn't mean it like that."

Jeremy tossed Tim a look and laid a hand on Melissa's forearm, effectively quelling both before nodding at Dr. Strickland.

The younger doctor folded his hands and spread his feet slightly, balancing his weight. "I want you all to understand that the treatment options for your father's condition have greatly improved in the last few years."

Nora closed her eyes at that foreboding announcement. Jeremy immediately crossed the room to stand beside her and Christopher. Amy rose from the sofa, the fitted jacket of her stylish suit pulling taut across her slender shoulders as she folded her arms protectively. Heather tucked her hair behind her ears and hid her trembling hands in the voluminous folds of her full skirt.

Please, God, she prayed. *Please. Oh, please.*

"How bad is it?" Jeremy asked softly.

Luke Strickland swept the room with his dark, compassionate gaze before nodding to the other doctor. The specialist took one small step forward, lifted his chin and changed all their lives.

"Your father has leukemia."

Chapter One

The door into the corridor opened and Dr. Luke Strickland strode through it, bristling with purpose. In the weeks since Wallace's diagnosis, Heather had come to greatly appreciate the good doctor's utter devotion to his profession and his deft bedside manner. She couldn't help thinking that the Hamiltons and the Davis Landing Community General Medical Center were blessed to have him, despite the fact that he again wore that carefully blank expression which she had come to dread.

"Is everyone here?" he asked without preamble.

Timothy stopped his pacing long enough to frown. "All but one—as usual." Tossing out his hands, he demanded of no one in particular, "Where is Melissa?"

"You didn't seriously expect her to show up, did you?" Jeremy asked mildly.

Tim fixed his brother with his intense brown gaze

and lifted an eyebrow imperiously. "Today, considering what's at stake, yes."

The pair were often at odds, but these days they just couldn't seem to keep from butting heads, whether over Hamilton Media or the family itself, and Heather quickly moved to intervene in her own mild-mannered fashion.

"I called her cell before I came up in the elevator. No answer. I don't think she's coming."

"Well, that's just great," Tim grumbled, folding his arms.

"It's probably for the best, actually," Heather offered quietly. She glanced at her twin, Chris, expecting and receiving his silent support. "You know Melissa doesn't do hospitals well."

In truth, Melissa had been edgy and distant ever since their father's diagnosis. More often than not, she seemed to try to escape her problems rather than face them head on, and that appeared to be the case today. That was an issue that would have to be addressed at another time, though. Heather decided that she would have a private talk with her baby sister as soon as the opportunity presented itself.

"I suggest we just get on with it," Amy said pragmatically.

Her senior by three years, Amy was also Heather's boss at the magazine. Unlike Tim, though, Heather didn't mind yielding authority to an older sibling. Amy was everything that Heather herself was not, a high achiever, self-assured, even forceful, not to mention well-groomed, stylish, graceful. In many ways, she was Timothy's female equivalent, except that she had been blessed with their mother's beauty and was blond and blue-eyed, whereas Tim was dark like their father.

Heather, on the other hand, was just…Heather. Mousy, meek and quiet, stuck in the middle, always living too much inside her own head and content to be there.

It had always been that way. Even in high school, Heather had been the sister who'd disappeared into the woodwork, while Amy had been elected homecoming queen and most popular. Heather had persecuted herself with envy back in those days. Eventually, however, she'd come to accept that God had a different role for her.

As a result she'd managed to avoid jealous feelings for their beautiful blond, but troubled, baby sister. The others considered Melissa overly dramatic and rebellious, which she could be, but Heather sensed a deep well of pain in her, especially lately. Then again, their father's illness had shaken them all.

Dr. Strickland led the way from the sitting area into the bedroom of the hospital suite, with Jeremy, Tim and Amy following in that order. Heather and Chris crowded in behind them. Their mother stood at their ailing father's bedside, looking decades younger than her husband of thirty-five years, which just pointed out how very ill he was. Heather went straight to Nora's side and squeezed her hand.

During the weeks of her father's hospitalization, Heather had grown even closer to her mother. She supposed it was natural since she and Nora were often the only ones rattling around the house these days, especially after Vera Mae, their housekeeper and cook of many years, went home for the evening. The longer Wallace was ill, the more Melissa seemed to stay away. The other four Hamilton siblings had moved out years ago, keeping apartments and penthouses around town.

Nora momentarily laid her head on Heather's shoulder in a gesture of affection, then lifted her cheeks to receive supportive kisses from her other children. She slid a look around the room.

"Melissa?"

Heather gave her head a slight shake, feeling her long brown hair ruffle against her shoulders.

"Did you call the house?" Nora asked.

"She wasn't there when I left, so I called her cell instead," Heather said. "No answer."

Nora sighed and smiled wanly at Dr. Strickland, gripping her husband's hand. "Go ahead, Luke. What do the latest tests say?"

"Have we beaten it?" Wallace demanded, cutting straight to the heart of the matter.

His silver hair had thinned over the past weeks and would soon begin to come out in clumps if they had to continue the chemotherapy.

To Heather's dismay, Luke Strickland shook his head.

"I'm sorry. The leukemia has not responded to treatment."

Nora gasped, and Heather closed her eyes. Standing behind them, Chris lifted protective hands, resting one upon her shoulder and the other upon their mother's.

As a police officer, Chris alone had not gone into the family business, finding nothing at either *Nashville Living* magazine or its sister publication, the *Davis Landing Dispatch* newspaper, to spark his interest. Tall and dark like his brothers and just as intelligent, Chris was somehow more *physical* than either of them. He was also devout in his faith, though his work schedule made regular church attendance more difficult for him than for Jeremy, whom Heather could always count upon to join her and their mother for services.

It was Amy who asked the pertinent question, "What can we do, doctor?"

"The next step is the bone marrow transplant, isn't it?" Jeremy said.

The doctor nodded. "Yes. In fact, it's our only other option at this point."

"Then what are we waiting for?" Tim demanded impatiently. "I assume that the sooner it's done the better."

"That's true," Dr. Strickland agreed, his gaze moving purposefully around the room before coming to rest on Wallace himself. "Unfortunately, none of you is a perfect match."

Heather covered her mouth with a trembling hand as Nora swayed before abruptly stiffening her spine.

"What does that mean?" Amy asked quietly.

"That we have to go to the national database for a suitable donor," the doctor explained.

"How long will that take?" Tim wanted to know.

Dr. Strickland shook his head. "That's impossible to say. We'll match him as quickly as possible, though."

"People wait years for transplants," Amy murmured, frowning.

"That's true," the doctor informed her, "but your father's condition is sufficiently grave to put him at the top of the list. I have to warn you, though, that if we don't find that perfect match soon, we may have to go with our second choice and hope for the best. Time is our enemy here."

"But we do have some time, don't we?" Nora asked with obvious desperation.

"Some. We're not beat yet, and while we're looking for that perfect donor we'll keep him comfortable and support him with appropriate treatments."

"Meaning more needles, I suppose," Wallace groused.

Unruffled, the doctor smiled compassionately. "As if a little thing like a needle ever intimidated you."

Wallace humphed. "Entirely beside the point. No pun intended."

"We're going to beat this," Nora declared insistently, ignoring her husband's weak attempt to inject some normalcy into a nightmarish situation.

"Goes without saying," Wallace retorted, waving his free hand dismissively, but Heather noted that his knuckles were white where they gripped her mother's fingers.

"Mom's right," Heather said softly. "We'll just keep praying and trusting God. He knows how much we need you, Daddy."

"Thank you, dear. Now, if that's all, doctor, there are more important matters to consider at the moment."

Heather bit back a groan, knowing what was coming, just as did everyone else in the room, including Nora. Well or ill, Wallace would always be about Hamilton Media. Heather took comfort in knowing that nothing had changed in that regard. Nora, whose primary concern would always be the well-being of her family, obviously did not.

"Wallace, I forbid you to worry about business at a time like this."

He sent her an affectionate, amused glance. "Might as well forbid me to die, sugar, which, by the way, is something else I have no intention of doing anytime soon."

Tammy Franklin entered the room just then through a second door that opened onto the corridor. Busily efficient, the petite, pretty nurse checked the bedside monitors and the IV line at the patient's wrist, her blue eyes flicking intently from equipment to patient. Wallace ignored her, fastening his dark gaze on his eldest child.

"Jeremy, I want to know why you haven't signed that contract with the new accounting firm."

Jeremy squared his shoulders and calmly replied, "Because I don't believe it's in the best interest of the company. Why pay to have done what we already do so well ourselves?"

"Well?" Tim echoed disbelievingly. "How can you say that?"

The whole family knew that Curtis Resnick, a trusted employee, had betrayed both the company and the family—and Jeremy, in particular—by embezzling thousands of dollars.

"We have adequate oversights in place now," Jeremy insisted.

"Nevertheless, doing our own accounting is what allowed the problem to develop in the first place," Wallace stated sharply.

"What makes you think an outside accounting firm will be any more honest than our own employees?" Jeremy countered. "The people left in that department are faithful and loyal. They had no part in what happened. They deserve to keep their jobs."

"Jeremy's right," Chris put in. "It's not fair to punish a whole department for one person's malfeasance."

"You have no say in this matter!" Wallace snapped. "Since you opt to put yourself in danger every day rather than take your place in the company—worrying your mother sick in the process, I might add—you have no right to comment."

"I'm sorry you feel that way, Dad," Chris said carefully. "Nevertheless, I agree with Jeremy."

"You would," Tim muttered.

"Meaning what exactly, Timothy?" Jeremy asked, sounding genuinely perplexed. "That he takes his faith too seriously for your comfort?"

"Please, boys, that's enough," Nora pleaded. "Now is not the time. Your father is too ill for this."

"I am not too ill to look after the welfare of the company!" Wallace insisted. "My father and grandfather devoted their lives to Hamilton Media, and I simply will not allow a momentary physical weakness to harm it in any way!"

"Please, Daddy," Heather interjected softly. "If you can trust God with your health, surely you can trust Him and your sons to take care of the company for a while."

Wallace grimaced shamefacedly. "You're right, you're right. It's just that…" He passed a hand across his forehead, and Nora followed it with one of her own. "I feel so helpless, stuck here in this bed."

"All the more reason you should rest and let us take care of things," Tim said.

"Good advice," the doctor agreed.

"Have a little faith, Dad," Jeremy put in. "We won't let you down."

"Not that faith is an adequate substitute for hard work and dedication," Tim muttered, and Heather inwardly winced.

Jeremy immediately bristled. "Are you implying

that I'm not dedicated, that I don't work hard enough?"

Tim had the grace to look abashed. "I didn't say that."

"You might as well have, so let me remind you, little brother, that I hold the reins at Hamilton Media now."

"Then do what you should," Tim demanded. "Bite the bullet and sign that accounting contract!"

"It's my decision, Tim, and I'm not bound by your opinions."

"I have a right to my opinions!"

"Please!" Nora interjected sternly. "Now is not the time."

"We're all too upset at the moment for this discussion," Amy interjected reasonably.

"Confound it, this is important!" Wallace bellowed, turning red in the face.

"That's it," Dr. Strickland interrupted, placing a quelling hand on Wallace's chest. "Take it outside, if you please. And you…" He wagged an admonishing finger at the patient. "Calm down. You need to rest."

Amy stepped up to the bed and bent to press a kiss to Wallace's forehead.

"At least try to follow the doctor's orders," she urged, a wry smile curling her pretty mouth.

"And don't worry," Jeremy said. "Everything's going to be fine."

Wallace nodded curtly, his jaw working.

"I'll walk you out," Nurse Franklin said politely but firmly, herding them all toward the door.

Chris was the first to move toward it, saying, "I'm picking up a little overtime tonight, so I'll see you tomorrow, Dad."

"Call if you need anything, Mom," Amy said, following on Christopher's heels.

"Yes, of course, sweetheart," Nora murmured. Then she abruptly lifted a hand, stopping everyone in their tracks. "If you talk to your sister," she dictated firmly, "go easy on her. Melissa is still very young, you know."

Tim huffed but didn't argue. Chris traded looks with Heather and went out. Amy nodded, smiled and, with a final wistful glance at their father, followed Christopher.

Jeremy hugged Nora, whispering, "I know you'll take care of him. Just be sure to take care of yourself, too."

"Don't worry about me," she returned, cupping his cheek with one hand.

Heather squeezed her mother's delicate shoulder and kissed her father, while Tim stood glowering at the foot of their father's bed.

"It may be his right to make the decision," Tim said to Wallace, "but we both know that signing that contract is best for the business, and I don't intend to let him forget it."

Wallace slowly blinked his eyes in acknowledgment but said nothing until Timothy had left the room. Heather moved to follow him, hearing her father murmur what sounded like, "Maybe Jeremy shouldn't have the right."

Nora gasped, and Heather immediately halted. "I'm sorry, what did you say?"

Wallace shook his head, but then he blurted, "It's still my company! Jeremy's only in charge temporarily, Nora." Frowning, he muttered, "And maybe I made a mistake with that."

Obviously shaken, Nora whispered, "Wallace, what are you saying? Jeremy's the eldest, and just because he does things differently than you, doesn't mean he isn't capable."

"I know, I know," he mumbled, his great energy and strength of will abruptly waning. "It's just that knocking on death's door makes you rethink some things." His head fell back against the pillow, and Dr. Strickland reached for his pulse.

"I really must insist that you rest now. Nora, that goes for you, too."

With a last tender kiss, Nora turned from the bedside and ushered her middle daughter into the sitting room, pulling the door closed behind her.

"Oh, Heather," she whispered. "He's so weak."

"In body, perhaps, but not in spirit."

Nora smiled wryly. "True."

"Dad isn't really having second thoughts about Jeremy taking over the company, is he?"

Evading her gaze, Nora turned away. "Your father knows that Jeremy deserves to be president, but in

Wallace's mind I suppose he'll always be the CEO of Hamilton Media."

Even had it been characteristic of Heather to press, concern for her mother would not have allowed it just then. Yet something about the way her father had looked and sounded had disturbed her as much as it obviously had Nora.

"I'm sure you're right," she murmured, trying to believe that it wasn't more than that.

"Your father's so very ill," Nora whispered. "I'm afraid he's not thinking clearly."

Heather reached out and gathered her delicate mother into a warm hug. "It's going to be all right, Mom. One way or another, it's going to be all right."

"It has to be," she said fervently, her eyes closed tight. "I'm trying so hard to trust God to heal him." She pulled back far enough to give Heather a reassuring smile. "We have to keep holding on. Now is not the time to relinquish our faith."

"We'll keep praying," Heather promised, "and we'll keep trusting God, no matter what happens. Now, let me take you home."

Nora stepped away then. "No, no. I want to stay close by." She gestured toward the sofa. "I'll lie down here for a while. Besides, you need to get back to work, and my car's in the parking lot."

Heather knew that her mother was right. The office couldn't seem to get along without her for more than an hour or two. Still, after such devastating news, it was difficult to leave her parents here on their own. It just seemed to be one thing after another lately.

"If you're sure."

"Absolutely," Nora said, stiffening her spine. "I'll see you at home later." She kissed Heather's cheek. "I'm so glad that you and Melissa are there. I couldn't bear coming home to that big old house all alone."

Heather smiled. She knew that few twenty-seven-year-olds still lived at home with Mom and Dad, but there was plenty of room and the time had never felt right to leave. She'd almost done it after college when her boyfriend of two years had proposed marriage, but that would have meant not just leaving her parents' home but moving away from Davis Landing and Tennessee for Florida, where he'd had a job waiting in the aerospace industry. She'd known that wasn't right for her.

Now, six years later, she seemed stuck, but as much as she prayed about it, she couldn't convince herself that it was time to strike out on her own. This, obviously, was the life that God meant for her. If the very worst happened and her father died, her mother would need her more than ever. No, now was not the time to be thinking about moving out.

Nora smiled indulgently. "You go on, darling. Don't worry about me. Or anything else."

"That goes for you, too," Heather said, moving away. "Get some rest."

"I'll try. Tell Vera Mae not to hold dinner for me, will you?"

Heather stopped. "Mom."

"Please don't say it. I'll eat here, with your father, and be home later. Besides, the pastor is coming this evening, and I don't want to miss him."

Heather sighed. She understood Nora's need to spend as many waking moments at Wallace's side as possible, but these past weeks had taken a toll on her, too. She had started to look brittle and fragile. Still, convincing Nora Hamilton not to give her utmost to her family was easier said than done. In the end, Heather left her mother just as Nora wished.

She knew that staying busy would help keep her own mind off her father's health. Nevertheless, once she was alone in her car in the hospital parking lot, with the air conditioner humming against the mid-June heat, Heather took the time to formulate a cogent and purposeful prayer, one that included family unity during this difficult time.

Her family truly loved one another, but Wallace's illness had upset everyone and exacerbated their differences, especially those between Jeremy and Tim. It didn't help that this crisis had come just after Curtis Resnick's embezzlement had been uncovered.

Heather agreed with Jeremy's decision not to prosecute Curtis and to demand restitution instead. Tim, however, did not. Amy claimed not to care so long as the money was recouped. Chris had taken no position, and only spelled out the likely consequences of prosecuting Resnick when asked to do so by Jeremy.

Thankfully, Wallace had left the decision to his eldest son, who seemed determined to be generous as well as fair. After all, he and Curtis had been very good friends at one time.

Whatever opinion any of them held, however, no one wanted to be dealing with the aftermath of embezzlement while Wallace was fighting for his life. It was added stress that none of them needed just now. Yet, they'd get through it.

They were Hamiltons, and Hamiltons might bend, but they didn't break. If Heather hadn't learned anything else from her father, she'd learned that much. It was one more reason why going on without him was almost unthinkable at this point.

"Oh, Lord," she prayed aloud, "I don't know what Your purpose is in all this, but I do know that You have one. I just hope that when all is said and done, it includes healing my father and bringing our family closer together. I won't ask for things to be the way they were before. We'll never be the same after this, but we can be better. Isn't that what You always want for us, Lord, to be more like You? Use this, then, toward that end."

She went on with her prayer, fervently seeking God's will and claiming His mercy. Afterward, as always, she felt better, strong enough to face whatever awaited her at the office.

As features editor of the magazine, she was always dealing with some crisis, stepping in to settle differences and adjust priorities, choosing projects, making sure all the i's were dotted and the t's crossed—whatever it took to get each feature and column brought in under deadline. She just never dreamed that today of all days *she* would become the feature.

Chapter Two

Heather walked into the stately three-story brown brick building on the corner of Main Street and Mill Road in the very center of the city and smiled at the elderly pair sitting behind the reception counter in the small lobby.

The Gordons had been with Hamilton Media since the days when the *Davis Landing Dispatch* had been a weekly, rather than a daily, newspaper. Since then they had each "retired" from one position to another, finally winding up as self-proclaimed "gatekeepers."

Stooped and gray, they resembled nothing so much as someone's great-grandparents, which they were. They were also sweetly formidable, and as such had earned the nickname "The Gargoyles." It was virtually impossible for an outsider to get past either one of them and into the building without an appointment, let alone into the offices of the newspaper on the ground floor, those of the magazine on the second or those of the corporate center on the third.

Without missing a beat, Mr. Gordon hopped up from his stool and swiftly crossed the polished marble floor to the elevator, punching the up button, so that the door stood open and waiting when Heather strode into it, her flowered skirt belling out as she turned on the toes of her sensible pumps. Mrs. Gordon, meanwhile, was already on the phone, alerting whoever had inquired about her return that Heather was once again in the building.

As the old-fashioned elevator, sumptuously appointed in dark paneling and gleaming brass, rose laboriously toward the second floor, Heather took a moment to straighten the square oversize collar that all but obliterated the fitted bodice of her dress, which was short-sleeved in deference to the weather.

As the door slid open once more, Heather greeted the secretary to the head of advertising, who shoved a clipboard and pen at her as she stepped out of the elevator.

"The lifestyle column has to be cut," she stated unceremoniously, "and they're holding print until you okay it."

"What's the problem?"

"A larger than normal advertisement."

Heather sighed inwardly. Carl Platt, the author of that particular column, would be screaming.

"Which advertiser?" Heather asked, glancing swiftly over the reedit as she moved past the receptionist's desk and into the warren of cubicles that made up the magazine offices.

A popular Nashville restaurant that was both a regular and valued advertiser was named. Heather didn't like cutting short one of their most popular features, but she knew too well on which side the Hamilton bread was buttered to kick up a fuss, not that she would have anyway. She added her initials to those of her sister Amy's, endorsing the change, and passed the clipboard back to the twentysomething secretary, who promptly disappeared.

True to form, Carl Platt, whom Heather thought of as a rotund prima donna in a bow tie, pounced the moment she turned the corner. She nodded distractedly as he ranted.

"I know, I know," she murmured sympathetically, tsking at the injustices Carl Platt heatedly recounted. "I'll tell Amy as soon as I see her." For all the good that would do.

Amy made decisions based on the overall needs of the publication and its parent company, but Heather didn't bother pointing that out to Platt.

No sooner had she mollified him than another clipboard appeared beneath her nose. This one involved a title font change.

Heather liked the looks of the original, but it appeared to be impossible to center on the page. The proposed substitute was more uniform in the space required for each letter.

She added an exclamation mark for balance and kept the original font. Then she spent several minutes perusing a paragraph in an article that she was going to edit in its entirety at a later date anyway, before finally reaching her assistant's desk.

In her forties, with teenage children and a husband crippled by a rare form of arthritis, Brenda was efficient, reliable, professional and not at all shy about voicing her opinions.

"Ellen's in a panic. Like that's anything new," Brenda announced, handing over half a dozen phone messages. "Honestly, someone ought to give our beauty editor a personality makeover."

Heather smiled without comment. Ellen Manning was something of a character. Physically stunning with long, perfectly styled ash blond hair, meticulous makeup, vibrant blue eyes and fingernails like manicured talons, Ellen approached her job as if beauty and fashion were the be-all and end-all of human existence. Consequently she was very good at it, which was reason enough so far as Heather was concerned to put up with her high-handed, overbearing methods and short fuse.

Holding up three of the messages in one hand, Heather commented in surprise, "These are from Ethan Danes."

Ethan was the staff photographer currently working with Ellen on a photo shoot at the Grand Ole Opry in Nashville. Tall, dark and breathtaking, Ethan was the new office heartthrob—and for good reason. He had a quick, million-watt smile and a smooth, masculine charm that oozed from his pores.

"Yeah, I guess Ellen's meltdown is justified this time," Brenda conceded. "To hear Ethan tell it, we may not have a Makeover Maven feature this month."

Frowning, Heather pushed through the door into her small office. Not much wider than the single window at its end, the room had just enough space for a file cabinet, a desk, a table wedged into one corner, an extra chair and the small potted plant perched on the windowsill. A large dry-erase board took up the whole of the wall behind her desk, leaving the wall opposite it for a series of framed covers and family photos. Only the ceiling fan, circling lazily overhead, kept the tiny room from becoming a stifling closet in the sultry June heat.

Heather reached immediately for her desk phone and dialed Ethan's cell phone number. He answered on the first ring.

"Crisis central, this is the shutterbug speaking."

"Ethan, what on earth is going on down there?"

"Well, let's see. The makeover candidate is a no-show."

"Again?"

"Yeah, this time she's the one with the flu. Guess she got it from her kid. Anyway, the Opry says we can't reschedule. Again."

"Hasn't Ellen explained the circumstances?"

"Let's just say that Ellen is making enemies and influencing no one," Ethan quipped. "Meanwhile, the window is closing. You'd better get down here and

apply some of that patented Heather healing balm
before we're permanently barred from the most
popular venue in town."

Heather healing balm, was it? She tamped down a
spurt of pride and made a quick decision. Well, she'd
wanted to stay busy today.

"I'm on my way."

"Come around to the side. I'll be there to let you
in."

After hanging up, she headed back the way she'd
come.

"If anyone needs me," she said, breezing past
Brenda's desk, "tell them to ring my cell."

"Better turn it on then," Brenda called as Heather
hurried away, mentally smacking herself in the
forehead. Of course she'd turned off the phone while
she was the hospital, and of course she'd forgotten to
turn it back on again.

She dug in her bag on the way to the elevator and
had the thing operational by the time she started her
descent. It was ringing before she reached the street,
and kept ringing for almost the entire next hour as she
drove her deep blue Saab into Nashville and the
Opryland complex.

After parking in the surprisingly crowded back lot,
she made her way toward the side of the performance
hall. To her surprise, Ethan was waiting for her outside
the building, one scuffed brown loafer, worn sans
sock, propping open a heavy metal door.

Tall and lean with that thick, black-brown hair falling rakishly across his brow, he wore not one but two cameras dangling around his neck on nylon straps. A third hung from his belt, a disreputable strip of cracked brown leather slung low around his lean hips.

As was often the case, he needed a shave. Yet even in comfy jeans and a snug black T-shirt worn beneath an open chambray shirt with the cuffs rolled back and the tail hanging out, he looked more like a model than a photographer. Dark almost to the point of black, his eyes sparkled with a hint of mischief as he smiled a stark white welcome at her, displaying killer dimples that cut long grooves in the square-jawed rectangle of his face.

"You'd better get in there," he told her with a jerk of his head. "Ellen's been snarling and howling since we got here. I'm surprised they haven't tossed us out already."

Heather glanced at her simple, utilitarian wristwatch as she moved past him into the shadowed interior of the building. "They can't toss us. We've still got nearly three hours."

"Fat lot of good that's going to do us if we can't find a makeover candidate and get her here ASAP," Ethan said, following swiftly behind her.

"We'll find one. We have to. We've already spent a small fortune on this shoot."

"Not to mention the makeup artist, hairdresser and wardrobe shopper cooling their heels backstage," Ethan added drily. "End of the hall and up the steps."

Heather moved in the direction that he indicated, listening to the quick patter of their footsteps and the gentle clunking of his cameras as they bumped together. The half flight of stairs was surprisingly dark and narrow, which no doubt prompted Ethan to stay close and place a hand on her shoulder.

"Left," he prompted at the top of the steps.

Heather quickly found herself in a back hallway onto which a number of dressing rooms opened. The strident sound of Ellen's voice pulled her forward from there.

"What is it about this situation that you don't understand?"

"Not a thing," came a calm, masculine reply. "What you don't seem to understand is that I need these premises vacated by 2:00 p.m."

"I have a deadline!" Ellen shrieked. "I've got to have those photos!"

Heather walked into the room and straight into the conversation, her right hand extended.

"How do you do? I'm Heather Hamilton, features editor of *Nashville Living.*"

The poor fellow looked so relieved that Heather knew Ellen had seriously overstepped the bounds of civility. Unfortunately, the public relations manager didn't have much to offer her.

"I'm sorry, we just don't have another slot available within your time frame," he said.

Heather laid a hand on his arm and walked him out

into the hall and away from Ellen's agitated mumbling, not to mention the avid interest of the makeup artist, hairdresser and wardrobe girl. As she squeezed past Ethan he grinned, though what he could find to grin about in this situation she couldn't imagine. Then, at the last possible moment, he winked.

Heather felt color rise in her cheeks. As she took her leave of the public relations manager, she kept wondering what that wink meant. Surely Ethan wasn't flirting with her. The instant she was free, Heather zipped back into the dressing room.

"Now what do we do?" Ellen demanded, folding her arms across the silky middle of the lilac-colored twin set that she wore with a short, straight off-white skirt and sharp-toed high-heeled mules.

"We've got to get another makeover candidate in here *right now*," Heather stated emphatically.

Ellen threw up her pale lilac fingertips, speaking so forcefully that tendrils of her long golden hair shook free of its sophisticated up-sweep. "Don't you think I've tried that? I've called every homely female in Nashville!"

"There has to be someone," Heather argued desperately.

"On such short notice?" Ellen began to pace, throwing out her hands in every direction as she spoke. "I don't think so! I've called every name on my list. I've called women we haven't even screened. I've called my neighbors, for pity's sake!" She spun on one heel, and the instant that her gaze dropped onto Heather's face, her blue gaze lit. "Wait a minute. You! You can do it! *You're* our makeover candidate!" As Heather's jaw dropped, Ellen clapped her hands together in a self-congratulatory manner.

"Me?" Heather squeaked, inwardly cringing. Okay, she was no beauty, but she wasn't *homely.* Was she?

"Oh, honey," drawled Sheryl, the makeup artist, one hand flopping out in Ellen's direction. "You are brilliant. She *so* needs a makeover." This from a female with orange spiked hair and multiple piercings.

Ellen turned to the balding, ponytailed hairdresser. "What do you think, Fox?"

He sauntered forward, comb in hand, to slide his stubby fingers through Heather's hair. "Hmm. Well, if we have time for a coloring and Sheryl can pull off her end, I can hold up mine."

"You'll have to work at the same time," Ellen decreed, turning to Gayla, the wardrobe mistress. "Can we make it happen?"

The cadaverous woman tapped a finger against her protruding front teeth speculatively.

"It won't be what we planned. She's smaller than the other one, but I've got a few size sixes we can use."

"Six!" Heather protested. "I wear a ten."

"That doesn't mean you *are* a ten," Gayla told her.

Ellen clapped her hands. "Okay, let's get to work, everyone!"

Heather backed up a step. "Wait a minute! I haven't—"

A pair of large, strong hands closed around her shoulders and literally spun her.

Suddenly she was looking up into the dangerously attractive face of Ethan Danes.

"This can work!" he told her, his dark eyes burning with unusual intensity. "Think about it." He lifted one of his cameras. "I'll take some unflattering photos." He shrugged. "Trick of lighting, you'll see." He waved a hand, setting the scene like a movie director. "The genius squad here will do their thing. I'll do what I do best." He grinned. "The 'after' photos will be smashing. Trust me." He stepped closer. "I know you try to play it down—the boss lady and all that—but you're really very pretty. It can't fail."

Heather could feel her jaw descending again, but all she could think was that he'd called her pretty— and how very tall he was, taller than she had realized, at least a couple inches over six feet. That made him almost a foot taller than her. Well, ten inches anyway, which meant that the top of her head would reach, oh, say that finely sculpted lower lip of his. Realizing that she was staring, she jerked her gaze away—and found herself swept summarily behind a dressing screen.

"Wait!" Ethan exclaimed, snapping on harsh florescent lights overhead. He appeared behind the screen, clicking away with the camera attached to his belt.

Tugging and pushing, he moved her into the position that he wanted, then crouched and aimed the camera at her. "Tuck your chin."

"What? L-like this?" She tilted her head down until it seemed to her that he was looking straight up her nostrils, and that's precisely when he took the photos.

"Okay. That'll do."

Ethan disappeared with another wink. Gayla stepped up again and stripped Heather to her skin with a few swift movements. After hustling her into undergarments, Gayla handed her a simple cotton robe. As Heather shrugged it on and belted it, Gayla shook out the flowered dress that Heather considered her favorite summer outfit for the office. Holding it out at arm's length, Gayla dropped the dress on a chair in the corner.

"Say goodbye to the 1980s and get ready to meet the new century." With that she pulled Heather from behind the screen and pushed her into the tall chair stationed in front of a narrow counter and lighted mirror.

While Sheryl slapped gunk on her face and wiped it off again, muttering that if she wasn't going to wear foundation she ought to at least use sunscreen, Fox began spritzing her hair with water, then sectioning and cutting it. Heather cringed and bit her lip, hoping she'd have hair left when the stylist was done.

Then Sheryl attacked her with a pair of tweezers. When her eyebrows had been shaped to the makeup artist's apparently exacting standards, Heather's hair was tossed forward into her face.

She could only pray that they weren't all teetering on the edge of catastrophe. How mortifying would it be if, after all this, her "after" photos weren't good enough to print?

Ethan captured shot after shot, bobbing and weaving to avoid the hands that plucked, swabbed, rubbed, combed, buffed, squeezed, folded and painted the new Heather over the old.

Watching the transformation through the lenses of his cameras proved to be a supremely satisfying exercise, and he found his enthusiasm mounting with contemplation of the finished product. He'd wanted to see Heather take some pride in her appearance for the past six months, which was just about the length of time he'd been with *Nashville Living*.

Jobs didn't usually last this long for Ethan. He liked to keep moving. That was part of the reason he'd chosen a career in photography. He could take his pick of assignments, moving on whenever the mood struck. He didn't have the foggiest idea why he'd stuck around Davis Landing this long.

Even coupled with the shabbier neighborhood of Hickory Mills by a pair of bridges spanning the Cumberland River, the graceful old community couldn't have comprised more than thirty or forty thousand people. Although Nashville was "just around the bend," as the locals stated it, living was pretty slow and easy in Davis Landing. Many nights Ethan did nothing more than park in front of the tube, but he figured this experience was worth at least six months of cooling his heels in Tennessee.

From day one he'd wondered why this Hamilton daughter had chosen to hide her gentle beauty beneath boring hair and baggy flounced prints, allowing her delicate features to fade into the background. Her sisters had definitely learned to flaunt their looks. Well, okay, the little flirt Melissa flaunted, almost desperately so; Amy, on the other hand, *projected,* wearing her self-confidence like a mantle.

As attractive as each was in her own way, though, Ethan saw that Heather was the real beauty of the family. She just didn't seem to realize it.

He couldn't remember ever seeing her wear so much as a touch of lipstick, and while her medium brown hair was sleek and healthy looking, she never seemed to do anything with it. Letting it hang straight from that excruciatingly precise center part just made her slender face look longer and more narrow than it really was. He was liking the shaggy bangs and long, tapered layers that were taking shape now much better.

While Fox painted highlights into Heather's newly cut hair, Sheryl started trying foundation colors against her skin and Gayla commandeered her impossibly narrow feet, trying shoes on them until she found a size that would work, at least for the purposes of the photo shoot. Next Gayla laid out an array of clothing and accessories, while Sheryl polished Heather's nails and Fox stuffed all those folded strips of tin foil beneath the soft hood of a portable hair dryer in order to speed the processing of the color. All the while, the makeover team discussed makeup, hairstyles and clothes.

Their limited selections—after all, they'd come prepared for a different model—dictated some of their choices. Ellen dictated others—until she received a call on her cell phone and stepped out into the hallway to take it. Knowing what shots they'd tentatively chosen, Ethan felt justified in making a few suggestions in her absence.

"That clingy red job would look great against that midnight blue light on stage."

Sheryl held a cherry red lipstick next to Heather's creamy ivory skin. "Works for me." She looked up at Fox for his verdict.

"We're not going orange, so the red ought to do."

"Oh, I—I don't wear red well," Heather objected. "It just sort of overpowers me."

Sheryl lifted a pierced eyebrow, declaring, "Well, sugar, you're going to overpower it today."

Ethan managed to hide his grin behind the camera, saying, "What about those skinny black jeans and that little turquoise leather jacket with the red boots? We could park her on a bale of hay."

"The boots are too big," Gayla said somberly.

"She doesn't have to dance in them," Ethan pointed

out. "She just has to keep them on long enough to get her picture taken. It'd be a great theme shot."

"Please God, don't let them say the cowboy hat," Heather muttered, which had Ethan chuckling.

"Are we doing exteriors?" Sheryl wanted to know.

Ethan dropped the camera that he held in his hands. "We talked about it, but I'm not sure. I'll go ask Ellen."

He stepped out into the hall, only to find it empty. That wasn't like Ellen. Usually she wanted to personally oversee every stroke of the mascara wand and click of the shutter. Shrugging, he ducked back into the dressing room.

"Guess we play this one by ear."

Sheryl gave him a disgusted look. "Are we doing exterior shots or not?"

Ethan glanced at a pair of white cuffed shorts and a filmy, lace-edged top that Gayla was holding up and figured, *Why not?*

"Yeah. Yeah, we are." He took one more look at that slinky red dress and made another decision. "Normally we'd start with the casual exterior shots, move into the foyer and then finish up on stage with that red number, but with our time running out, we're going to have to reverse that. Can you handle it?"

Sheryl dove into her makeup kit. "I'll use a neutral brown shadow and cream lipstick so it wipes off easy."

"How much longer?" Ethan asked, checking his watch.

Fox glanced at his timer. "Give us twenty-five minutes."

"And not a minute more," Ethan warned. "I'm going to get set up."

He grabbed a pair of tripods, a reflector and a small electric fan before taking off for the auditorium at a dead run. His light meter was in his pocket. Thank goodness the Opry had state-of-the-art lighting.

He was still playing with the set when Sheryl ran onto stage. Flinging out an arm she cried, "Ta-da!"

Ethan looked around in time to see Fox and Gayla hauling Heather out of the wings and into the light. For a long minute all he could do was stare and hope his mouth wasn't hanging open.

The long strapless gown fit as though it had been handmade for her. The organza train of the slender skirt pooled gracefully around stiletto heels that he knew were too big but nevertheless elongated the slim leg revealed by a side slit. Crystals graced her delicate throat and wrist and dangled from her dainty earlobes, working in concert with the gleaming hair piled on top of her head and wisping about her face to call attention to the graceful length of her neck. Rich auburn highlights and sable eye shadow had turned her light-brown eyes into enormous amber orbs, while vivid red lipstick plumped and defined a lush mouth beneath that pert, classical nose.

Right at the base of her neck, almost at her collarbone, was a small pinkish brown mark that she kept covering almost absently with her hand. A rose tattoo? he wondered, but no, Heather was not the sort to have that done. Strolling closer, he saw that it was a birthmark, irregular in shape, completely unique. Utterly fascinating.

He'd known she was pretty, suspected that she could be beautiful in a soft, delicate fashion. He'd had no idea that she could be stunning, breathtaking even.

"Talk about hiding your light under a bushel!"

He didn't realize he'd said it aloud until Heather gusted a nervous laugh.

"That's what my mom always says," she admitted shyly, hunching her shoulders and shifting nervously.

Fox, who was busy trying to tweak the froth on top of her head into perfection, scolded her. "Keep still or I'll be putting this up again!"

Ethan glowered at him. Didn't the jerk realize who he was talking to? This wasn't any plain Jane off the street. This was Heather, a Hamilton and, as it happened, the boss.

"Get out of my shot, Fox," he ordered, turning his attention to the camera fixed to the nearest tripod. "Now listen up, boss lady. I want you to do exactly as I say. When I tell you to walk, I want you to put one foot directly in front of the other. Long, fluid strides. And keep your hands down unless I tell you otherwise. Okay?"

Heather nodded. She'd been around photo shoots

often enough to know the drill, so he wasn't worried. He set the shutter speed and palmed the switch.

"Walk forward. Look up. Way up. Stop. Half turn. Look at me!"

Click after click, he shot two rolls in rapid succession, moving from one camera to the other, directing her actions and catching the poses that took away his breath.

"Ladies and gentlemen," he muttered to himself, "a star is born."

He couldn't have been happier for her. He liked women too much not to relish seeing such a sweet-natured one as Heather Hamilton come into her own in such spectacular fashion. She was never going to be the same after this. She couldn't possibly be.

She could scrub off the makeup and give back the clothes, but once she saw the before and after photos, she could never again believe herself to be the insipid, mousy sister that she'd pretended to be. She'd have to acknowledge what a beauty she truly was.

She still probably wouldn't give him the time of day, though.

It was a depressing thought, but of all the single women in the office, Heather alone had never exhibited so much as a passing interest in Ethan. In fact, despite Melissa's blatantly flirtatious manner, Ethan figured that he was not considered good enough for a Hamilton.

As an army brat whose parents had fought their way from posting to posting and finally to a divorce, he hadn't expected anything else, which was all the more reason to take satisfaction in being part of Heather's transformation, so far as he was concerned. No matter where he went after this, he suspected he'd have a hard time finding more enjoyable work or greater satisfaction in it.

Chapter Three

❦

"It's not like Ellen to take off from a shoot without a word," Heather said, sliding her sunglasses into place and looking out across the parking lot. "I hope she's okay."

"Ellen's the sort who can take care of herself," Ethan observed. "But you're right. She usually micromanages every detail of a shoot. Have you tried her cell?"

"No answer."

He shrugged unconcernedly. "Well, then I guess I have to beg a ride. Hope you've got room for my gear."

"No problem."

"I knew I should have brought my car," he muttered.

It was company policy for employees on the same assignment to share a vehicle. Why compensate two for mileage when one car could take them both where they needed to go? Apparently Ellen had insisted on driving her car for some reason. Fox, Sheryl and Gayla had already departed, but all of them were freelancers and none lived in Davis Landing anyway.

Heather helped Ethan drag his considerable gear to her car, still feeling a little embarrassed by the whole makeover thing. Once she'd finally gotten a look at herself in a mirror, she'd been wearing her own dress again, so only her head looked as if it belonged to somebody else. She wasn't quite certain that it didn't. The effect had been startling, to be sure.

The dress itself suddenly seemed too large, and she wondered why she'd taken to wearing the wrong size. She didn't think she'd lost more than ten pounds since college and that had pretty much been due to a natural change of eating habits as she'd gotten older. Somehow she hadn't adapted as she ought to have.

The hair was the biggest difference, though it had not, as she'd feared, all been chopped off. In fact, the back layer was only three or four inches shorter than before, and oddly enough, the other layers—which graduated from her shoulders to the bottoms of her ears, the tops of her cheekbones and mideye before finally ending with short, feathery bangs—actually made it seem as if she had more hair rather than less. The color was what surprised her most, however.

It had never occurred to her that she might make an attractive redhead. Yet, the auburn tones looked perfectly natural. Fox claimed that was due to the painting technique that he had used, resulting in the "expert integration" of her natural mousy brown with the richer reds.

The makeup seemed heavy-handed to her, and Heather wished she'd had time to remove, or at least lighten, it before they'd had to vacate the premises. She had no intention of re-creating this look on a daily basis, of course. It wasn't as if she was going to have her picture shot every day, after all, let alone published! Nevertheless, it wouldn't hurt to buy a new lipstick and maybe even some eye shadow.

After seeing how she could look with a little—all right, a lot—of effort she was a little embarrassed by how lazy she'd become with her appearance. It had been a long time since she'd bothered with makeup or even plucking her eyebrows.

In some ways, the results of the makeover had shocked her, and yet she couldn't deny the pleasure that she felt at realizing she wasn't quite as hopeless as she'd imagined, especially when those dimples of Ethan's cut grooves in his cheeks every time he looked at her.

They had almost reached her car when Ethan asked, "So, was it as bad as you feared it would be?"

She glanced up at him, her arms full of tripod and folded reflector. "Let's just say it was strange being on the other side of the camera."

"In case you're wondering, Fox isn't usually that rude to models."

Heather sent him a slightly amused look. "I realized that, and in case you're wondering, I didn't see any reason to object. I was a reluctant subject at best, and sometimes as boss it's more important to bring the shoot in under deadline than throw your weight around." When he stopped dead in his tracks, she had to stop, too, and turn to face him. "What? You don't agree?"

He blinked as if seeing something he hadn't seen before. "I guess I just never thought of it that way. I mean, throwing around their weight is what bosses do. Usually. Which is why I've always preferred to be a lowly wiseacre."

She sent him a skeptical look. They both knew he enjoyed a reputation as a first-rate photographer.

"I just prefer to make sure that the job gets done when it's supposed to get done," she told him. "And I don't think of you as a wiseacre."

"No?"

She gave her head a slight shake and hitched the tripod higher in her arms.

"I think of you as an artist with a well-developed sense of humor."

"I like your version best," he told her. Grinning widely, he repositioned his own burdens and started forward again. "Any chance we're getting close to your car?"

"The blue Saab on the right up there." She followed him, feeling the heat rise in steamy waves from the pavement.

"Aero," he said, naming the model of her car. "Sweet. I'd like to tool around town in a racy little Saab, but I have to drive an SUV because I have so much gear to haul. Not all of our sites are as well lit as this one, you know."

She placed her load on the ground and opened the hatch back, saying, "My brothers all voted for the SUV or the wagon, but my sisters thought I ought to get the convertible."

He shook his head and started loading his gear. "Naw, this is you, I think. Quality, high-performance but sensible."

She laughed because those were exactly her own thoughts on the matter. He straightened abruptly, almost as if she'd taken a sudden swing at him.

"What?"

"I'm just still getting used to the new you," he said, grinning again. "This new look is going to cause some waves back at the office. You mark my words."

A hand rose to touch her hair self-consciously. She could only hope that she didn't look as strange as she felt.

Ducking her head, she hurried around to slide behind the driver's wheel, leaving Ethan to carefully stow away his gear. She dug her phone out of her purse, deciding that it might be a good time to check in with her parents, and dialed the hospital.

Nora told her that, owing to the severity of her father's condition, the doctors were urging Wallace to consider transferring to the hospital in Nashville right away, but he wanted to remain close to the family—and the business—as long as possible. Once they started preparing Wallace for the bone marrow transplant, however, he would be in sterile seclusion, his immune system so compromised that the slightest infection could kill him.

Heather ended the call and bowed her head, the phone still clutched in her hands.

Oh, Lord, I just keep coming to You with this, but he's so very ill and You are a God of miraculous power. Please heal my father. Please let us find that perfect bone marrow donor, and please help my mom and all the rest of us through this.

The passenger door opened and Ethan dropped down into the seat. Heather sat up a little straighter, stashing her phone in a convenient recess in the dash.

"Something wrong?"

Surprised that he could so easily read her mood, she let a second or two pass before saying, "I just talked to my mom at the hospital."

"How is your dad doing?"

Heather sighed and started the car to get the air conditioner going. "His condition is serious enough to keep me on my knees, I can tell you."

Ethan cocked his head. "On your knees? Is that a Tennesseeism I'm not familiar with yet?"

She stared at him, thinking that the meaning would surely click in place for him momentarily, but then she realized that his confusion was entirely genuine. Faith was such a part of Heather's life that she sometimes forgot that it held little or no place in the lives of others.

"I just meant that I've been spending a lot of time in prayer over this," she explained gently.

The light finally dawned. "Ah. Well, that makes perfect sense. For you."

"But not for you?"

He shrugged. "I guess I just don't know much about that sort of thing."

"But surely you've been to church."

"Couple times, you know, for weddings and such."

How sad, Heather thought, but she smiled and said, "Maybe you'd like to visit my church sometime? Northside Community. It's across the river in Hickory Mills. I really love it there. Quite a few singles our age attend."

"I don't know about that 'our age' thing," he teased. "I figure I'm a good bit older than you."

She let the church issue drop and backed the car out of the space, saying, "I don't believe that. I'm twenty-seven, by the way. Called your bluff, didn't I?"

Grinning as wide as his face, he nodded. "You sure did, but I win anyway. I'm thirty-two."

"Five years is nothing," she said flippantly. "At least, that's what my baby sister always claims."

He laughed at that, and conversation maintained a lighthearted tone from there on out.

She noted that he seemed at ease with her behind the wheel, which fit with his laid-back attitude. As a result, she didn't feel as uncomfortable as she might have with him in the passenger seat. Tim, Amy and her dad, for instance, always made her nervous when they rode with her, but Chris, Jeremy and her mom never did. Neither did Lissa, but for an entirely different reason. She'd been hauling Melissa around since she'd first received her license, just as her older siblings had done for her.

Heather wondered again what her baby sister had gotten up to and when she was going to put in an appearance. As much as Melissa tried to avoid the unpleasant aspects of life, she would never forgive herself if she was off gallivanting around when something happened to their dad.

It was useless to worry about her, though, or even to be angry with her. Melissa would just bat those big, doelike eyes, flash a cheeky grin and throw her arms around your neck in a hug of such exuberance and affection that you'd forgive her anything.

When they reached the office, Heather dropped off Ethan and his equipment at his midsize SUV in the graveled lot across the street, Mill Road, where Hamilton Media employees parked. Then she drove around and took her assigned space at the front of the building on Main. By the time she'd gotten out of the car and reached the curb, Ethan had jogged up next to her, having stowed everything in his customized

SUV, except for the trio of cameras, which he carried by the straps in one hand.

They walked along the sidewalk to the revolving door at the front of the Hamilton Building. Ethan started it moving, then stepped back to let Heather go first. On the drive up from Nashville, she'd almost forgotten her changed looks, but as she stepped into the lobby, Mr. Gordon rose to his feet and lifted a stalling hand.

"Do you have an appointment, Mi—" The question died on his lips as Heather drew closer. He tilted his head, looking like a quizzical owl behind his overlarge glasses. "Miss Heather?"

She fingered her new hairstyle self-consciously and kept going. "I, um, had to step in as the make-over subject."

Both of the Gordons were staring at her open-mouthed as she punched the elevator button for herself. Fortunately, the door slid open immediately.

Ethan quickly joined her. He waggled an eyebrow at the Gordons as the door slid closed on them, then dropped a knowing look on Heather.

"Waves," he whispered, rolling his free hand in an up-and-down motion. "Huge, crashing waves."

Whether that was good or bad, Heather still couldn't say, but she fortified herself with a deep breath as the elevator drew to a halt. When the door slid open, Ethan stepped out first. Heather, in fact, was seriously considering going right back down and taking herself home to a hot shower, hoping it would be her old self who emerged from the steam.

She never got the chance.

Ethan reached inside the elevator, took her by the arm and insistently tugged her out into the reception area. Then he just stood there, clasping his cameras behind his back while the receptionist smiled in greeting, glanced at Heather, dismissed her, did a quick double take and dropped the pen in her hand.

"Waves," he said again quietly, taking Heather by the arm once more and swinging her around, propelling her in the direction of her office. "Great big rolling waves."

He made a sound like a wave crashing against the seashore. Heather couldn't suppress a smile, even as she cringed at the attention she was bound to receive from everyone she met today.

The receptionist must have gotten on the phone at once, because people began popping up out of their cubicles. As she passed her coworkers, Heather heard various comments, most of them sotto voce.

"Whoa."

"Wow!"

"I've gotta get my hair done."

Even, "That can't be who I think it is."

Ethan grinned as if all the attention was for him.

When they reached Brenda's desk, Heather's usually loquacious assistant slowly rose from her chair. Jaw dropping as she confirmed for herself that it was Heather standing before her, Brenda bobbled the water bottle from which she'd been drinking, splattering her blouse before she got it back under control.

Ethan announced in a ringing tone, "Heather had to substitute for the makeover candidate, and I think it might well be our best one so far." Heather gulped, still uncertain whether to be pleased or embarrassed.

Amy was walking by just then, a clipboard and pen in hand. Hearing Heather's name, she paused. Her eyes went wide as she took in the change that had come over her sister.

"Did I hear you say that Heather was this month's makeover subject?" she asked Ethan.

"See for yourself."

Amy let the clipboard drop, declaring, "Ellen's outdone herself!"

"Uh, actually," Heather muttered, "Ellen wasn't there. I—I thought she might've come back here."

Amy shook her head, eyes still wide, and muttered absently, "I was just looking for her. Nobody's seen her."

"Oh. Well, she'll probably be in later," Heather surmised uncomfortably. "I'd like her to know that we at least got the shoot finished before our time ran out."

"I'd like her to know that the shots are spectacular," Ethan put in, lifting the trio of cameras that he still carried. "And I'll soon have the pictures to prove it."

With that he slanted Heather an I-told-you-so look and sauntered away.

"Will you look at you?" Amy declared. "You're gorgeous!"

Heather glanced at Brenda and then back to her sister. "You really think so?"

They both exclaimed, "Yes!"

"Except for that dress," Amy qualified apologetically.

Heather looked down at herself with a grimace. "It's too big, isn't it?"

Amy nodded. "Too big. Too out of style. Too frumpy. I love your hair!" She started as if an idea had just come to her. "Let's go shopping later. Engel's has their summer stuff on deep discount."

"And it's still out of my league," Brenda complained, dropping back into her chair. "But the new you deserves a shopping spree." To Heather's amazement, she actually teared up. "I can't get over how different you look!"

"Oh, Bren! It's all right. I haven't changed inside, you know."

"I know," Brenda wailed, sniffing. "But now you're as lovely on the outside as you are inside!"

Heather laughed and looked to her elegant, sophisticated, beauty queen sister.

"Okay," she said. "Shopping it is. In for a penny, in for a pound, I guess."

Amy did a little victory dance and went on her way. That pretty much summed up how Heather was feeling at the moment.

It was just too bad that the person who had set this in motion wasn't here to see the results of her handiwork.

Heather straightened the seams of the tiered chiffon skirt before pulling on the white knit top, then slid her feet into thong sandals with tiny heels. As inexplicably nervous as the day before, she slowly turned to face the full-length mirror on her closet door.

Surprisingly, the flowered, coral-hued chiffon that ruffled about her knees looked just as trim and fashionable as it had in the dressing room of Engel's department store. Moreover, the simple scoop-necked top set off the skirt perfectly, and she didn't even mind that it exposed her birthmark.

Tentatively skimming her fingers over the irregularly shaped spot, she remembered how intently Ethan had focused on it yesterday. He'd murmured something about it being shaped like a rose as he'd positioned her to get the best shot of it. Funny, she'd never thought of it like that, but now that he'd mentioned it, she was seeing the mark in a whole new way. She was seeing everything about her appearance in a whole new way, from the top of her newly styled head to the tips of her toes in their flirty coral sandals.

She stepped closer to the mirror. As her image filled up more of the space, the spring green walls, ivory lace and French Provincial furnishings of her roomy bedchamber receded. Heather focused on her face, trying to find fault with the subtle cosmetics that she had applied earlier.

She hadn't forgotten how it was done, after all, and she couldn't deny that she was pleased with the result. Touching her fingertips to the mirror, she half expected to feel them against her cheekbone. It was as if she were really seeing herself for the first time in a long, long while.

Suddenly ashamed, she bowed her head, telling God how sorry she was for thinking that He'd short-changed her in the looks department when all along the problem had been her own laziness and perhaps a misplaced sense of modesty, as well. Not to mention an unwillingness to compete with her sisters. She shook her head at that, marveling that she could have been so silly.

Maybe she wasn't a raving beauty, but the resemblance between herself and her sisters was stronger than she'd realized. Even more surprising was how much she looked like her beautiful mother, especially around the eyes. Their coloring was different, of course. Heather's hair and eyes were a medium brown, or rather a rich chestnut with fiery highlights now, while Nora was blond and hazel-eyed. Nora's mouth was a little wider, her face more classically oval and her frame even more petite, but Heather was suddenly liking her more angular, slightly sharper features now that the subtle cosmetics and the new hairstyle had softened them a bit.

"I'll make the most of what You've given me from now on, Lord, I promise," she whispered. "And please be with Dad and Mom today. I know You can heal him, Father, and I know You will. Amen."

Nodding confidently at her smiling image, she went out to meet the day. Her feet fairly skipped along the landing and down both flights of the sweeping central staircase to the large foyer below, her heels clicking daintily on the polished hardwood floor. She gathered her handbag and briefcase from the antique wardrobe that stood against the parlor wall.

Actually, there were two parlors, the front parlor, which contained her grandmother's grand piano and a very good collection of antiques, and the family room, where the marble fireplace furnished the focal point for comfortable, overstuffed couches and chairs. The interior wall shared by the two rooms contained a pair of wide pocket doors that could be opened to make one enormous room for entertaining, making the library at the back of the house the most private of the public rooms.

The dining areas on the opposite side of the foyer from the living area had once enjoyed a similar arrangement, but with the kitchen—complete with butler's pantry and laundry room—rather than the library, beyond. Now, however, the formal and informal dining spaces had been combined into one large room with an enormous table handmade to accommodate six children and company.

All of the bedrooms, six in total, were on the second and third floors. Two others had been sacrificed to private baths and larger closets, changes her great-grandfather probably could not have even envisioned when he'd bought and renovated the elegant old redbrick Greek Revival–style house on the very outer edge of north Davis Landing.

There were larger, grander houses in the area, frankly, but not a single Hamilton would have traded this grand old place, with its expansive grounds, for any one of them.

Rather than exit via the front door with its heavy leaded glass inset, Heather turned and quickly made her way down the central hall and out the back to the terraced patio, where her mother habitually took her morning tea, weather permitting. Nora sat there now in one of the heavy, wrought-iron chairs, the morning paper spread out over a glass-topped table and fluttering unheeded in the breeze that sang softly in the tops of the trees. Clad in silk pajamas and a matching robe, she stared unseeingly across the property.

Heather dropped a hand upon her mother's shoulder, feeling the frail bones keenly. Nora turned up a distracted smile, then twisted around in her chair as she got a good look at her middle daughter.

"Just look at you! How I wish your father could see you this morning."

Heather bent forward to kiss her mother's cheek.

"I'll go by the hospital later, give him a preview of this month's Makeover Maven feature."

"It would do his heart good, I'm sure," Nora told her. "It has mine. Goodness, you look so young all of a sudden."

"Not so dowdy, you mean," Heather retorted, wrinkling her nose.

"Funny what a haircut and a new wardrobe can do," Nora mused, "or maybe I'm just feeling old this morning." She sighed and made an effort to smile.

Heather put down her bags and wrapped her arms around her mother's slender shoulders. "It's going to be all right, Mom. I just know it."

Nora nodded. "I've been thinking about the hundred-and-third Psalm." It was one of Nora's favorites, and Heather knew it by heart.

"'Bless the Lord, O my soul,'" she quoted softly. "'And all that is within me, bless His holy name.'"

"'Who pardons all your iniquities, Who heals all your diseases,'" Nora whispered, patting Heather's arm. She looked up suddenly. "I don't suppose your sister came in during the night, did she?"

Heather shook her head. "Not that I'm aware of."

"You don't think Melissa's in some kind of trouble this time, do you?"

"I think she just can't bear to see Dad in that hospital bed."

Nora's gaze drifted away again. "I don't blame her for that."

"Neither do I," Heather agreed gently.

"Get on with you, darling. I'll see you later at the hospital."

Sensing that Nora needed solitude at the moment, Heather left her to her contemplation and hurried to her car, parked beneath the sheltered passage that ran between the main house and the old carriage house.

The morning had a golden cast to it that Heather could attribute only to God's goodness.

Chapter Four

Heather smiled at the Gordons, who gave her a thumbs-up and silent applause as she strode toward the elevator. Dropping a silly curtsy as the elevator door rolled closed, she felt ridiculously pleased and oddly happy.

How strange that it should be so now, when her father was so desperately ill.

Yet wasn't that the Lord's way, to bring joy in the midst of woe? Even a small joy was doubly welcome when cares were so heavy.

Suddenly Heather remembered the verse between the ones she and her mother had quoted earlier that morning.

Bless the Lord, O my soul, and forget none of His benefits.

She felt a decided zing pervade her steps as she strolled toward her office. It was early yet, so the receptionist was not at her desk. Heather could hear a few voices in muted conversation but saw no one as she made her way through the warren of cubicles.

To her surprise, Ethan Danes sat perched on one corner of Brenda's desk. Clad in khakis and a dark brown T-shirt, he was studying a print, the top one of a stack that he held in his hands.

"Good morning," she said brightly, aware of a shiver of excitement. Or was it trepidation?

Ethan looked up, a smile at the ready. That smile stilled, then gradually grew as he took in this latest version of the "new" Heather.

"Well," he said, placing the photos on the desk, "I thought I'd picked my final shot."

"Oh?" She craned her neck, trying to look past him to get a peek at the photo he hoped would close the piece.

He folded his arms. "The butterfly has not only broken out of her cocoon, she's spread her wings, I see."

Heather inclined her head, laughing. She couldn't help it. Who wouldn't be pleased with such a statement from the best-looking man around?

"I'll take that as a compliment."

He winked at her. "And so you should." Dropping his hands to the edge of the desk, he shifted around, crossing his ankles. "I think I'm finally seeing the *real* Heather, and that's the 'after' photo I'd most like to see on the printed page."

Heather tried not to let that please her too much.

"And what does Ellen have to say about it?"

"I wouldn't know. Haven't seen her. Haven't heard

from her. Haven't been able to reach her. That's why I brought these straight to you."

Heather frowned at that. "I wonder what's going on with her? Oh, well. I get the final say anyway."

Nodding, Ethan got to his feet and swept up the stack of photos, which he held out to Heather.

"I've marked my picks, for what that's worth. Let me know if you need anything else."

"Will do. And thanks for going the extra mile with this yesterday. If not for you, we'd have had no feature this month."

"That's what you pay me for. Besides, you're the one who saved the day."

Setting aside her bags, she took the photos into her hands, then found that she didn't have quite enough courage to go through them with him standing there.

As if he knew it, he gave his head a little jerk, humming a bit as he moved away. "Mmm-mmm. The guys are going to beat a path to your door now. You know that, don't you?"

Stunned, Heather just stood there stupidly and watched him walk away, the photos clutched in her hands. After he'd disappeared from sight, she absently looked down, staring at the woman in the photo. Chic and feminine with shining amber eyes and a secretive smile, this was not the image of an old maid.

Old maid. When had she decided that she was an old maid?

Heather blinked, trying to see in this woman's face the acceptance that she would never marry. It was not there.

How had she come to believe that God didn't intend for her to marry and know the love of a mate? Was that assumption another product of her own laziness and hesitance?

Shocked at herself, Heather stopped to carefully consider her future. She wasn't even thirty. She had lots of time left to find the love of her life.

Something warm and bright and sharp unfurled inside her, something she hadn't let herself feel in years, something very like longing. Or was it hope? Had the longing always been there, but she'd only now started to hope again?

It had been aeons since she'd had a real boy-friend—since college.

Oh, she'd been on dates, but it would be nice to actually be asked out instead of always being "fixed up" by some well-meaning friend or family member.

Maybe, just maybe, some guy would notice her now. Ethan had.

Of course, it wouldn't be Ethan who would ask her out. That went without saying.

It wouldn't even be anyone like Ethan.

If it happened.

If.

But why not? The possibility was there.

She smiled.

And forget none of His benefits.
Small joys.

Heather ran her gaze down the list of articles on bone marrow transplant displayed on the computer screen. Even the titles were confusing, but she was determined to learn as much about the process as she could, if only to make her prayers more specific.

She opened an article on protocols and preparations for transplant, but before she could read the first paragraph, Brenda strode into her office through the open door.

"Have you checked your e-mail recently, like in the last ten minutes?"

Heather shook her head. "No, I've got something going right now."

"Well, you'd better take a look," Brenda insisted, folding her arms. "I just got copied on a message from Ellen to Amy."

Heather quickly minimized the window and pulled up another, murmuring, "It's about time."

"Actually," Brenda retorted drily, "it's about a lack of time."

"What?"

But Brenda didn't bother to answer. She didn't have to. The message was short and—okay, sweet would have been a stretch.

"Ellen's resigned!" Heather exclaimed.

"Effective immediately. No notice, no explanation,

nada," Brenda confirmed, folding her arms. "Can't say I'm sorry to see her go, but how on earth are we supposed to replace her in time for this issue's deadline?"

"Oh, no," Heather groaned, collapsing back in her chair. "The Makeover Maven feature."

She realized what had to happen, and she really wasn't happy about it.

"I don't suppose you want to try your hand at writing a beauty column?" she asked Brenda hopefully.

"Sure," Brenda said blithely. "You take care of the layout on the entertainment feature, and I'll write this month's makeover story."

Heather made a face. "Right. My lack of expertise—not to mention patience—with the layout software is why you're here."

"So I guess you'll be writing the makeover story, unless you think maybe Ethan…"

"Ethan's a photographer," Heather said, "an excellent photographer, but he's no writer."

"Better use a pseudonym," Brenda counseled wryly, turning to leave, "unless you intend to do this every month."

"No way," Heather declared.

Surely they could find a beauty editor before the next column had to be written.

Brenda sauntered back out to her desk, leaving Heather to deal with this latest catastrophe.

Reluctantly Heather reached for the folder containing the photos that Ethan had brought her that morning. She'd thumbed through them before, cringing at the earliest of them, marveling at the latter ones and critically studying the in-betweens for illustrative interest.

As usual, Ethan's instincts were right on target. His picks were also her picks. Unfortunately, like all photographers did, he'd chosen too many, so it was up to her to narrow the choices down to no more than half a dozen, some of which would be severely cropped or shrunk in order to fit the entire piece on two and a half pages. She'd do that after she'd written the article.

After a couple of false starts, she decided that the smartest way to begin was to simply state that this month's makeover subject was none other than the features editor. She tried to take the same approach that Ellen had used in the past, describing the candidate and her lifestyle, then detailing the changes that were made.

It was tough going. She didn't really like writing about herself, even in the third person, and tended to get bogged down in the details.

At one point she realized that she was spending too much time on the hair. The wardrobe was a problem, too, since none of it had really been chosen for her. Then she got sidetracked describing the venue.

Throughout the exercise, she kept glancing down at that minimized window tag at the bottom of her computer screen, her mind wandering to her father's illness and what had to happen in order to save him. All in all, writing that article was like pulling teeth.

When Ethan stopped by Brenda's desk in order to confirm the office scuttlebutt concerning Ellen and heard that Heather was writing the article, he stuck his head into Heather's office. She heartily welcomed the interruption, turning away from the computer screen with an impulsive smile.

He tilted his head, then pointed a finger at her, declaring, "You need a break."

Sighing, she parked her elbows on her desktop and rested her head in her hands, framing her face.

"I need a beauty editor."

He gave his head a truncated shake. "Fresh out. Would you settle for a cup of coffee?"

Heather pushed back her chair and grabbed her purse.

"Do I have a choice?"

"Sure. You could go for the cheese Danish, too."

"Uh-uh," she quipped, slipping out of the office past him. "This calls for *real* distraction. I'm having Betty's cherry turnover."

"Ooh," Brenda crooned, "bring me one, will you? And some of that apricot iced tea. It's too hot for coffee."

"Deal," Heather said over her shoulder, having fallen into step beside Ethan, who was moving through the cubicles.

"Too hot for coffee?" Ethan scoffed teasingly,

sliding his hands into the pockets of his chinos. "There's no such thing!"

"Yeah, hasn't she ever heard of Frappuccino?" Heather cracked.

Ethan put his head back and laughed, and Heather marveled at how her spirits seemed to lift every time he was around.

Ethan couldn't keep his eyes off her.

Heather shined. Yet beneath that new polish lay the serenity that he'd always sensed in her. It made for a very compelling package: beauty, serenity and a sweetness of personality that had always drawn him. The woman was very nearly impossible to ignore now.

Every time he looked at her—and he couldn't *keep* from looking at her—she made him want to smile. When she smiled back, he wanted to laugh. If he didn't watch himself, he was going to get downright giddy.

"What are you chuckling about?" she asked, just as the elevator set down.

He shook his head, but then he said, "Ellen has her best idea yet, and she's not even smart enough to stick around and take the credit."

"Tell me about it."

The door slid open, and they stepped off in tandem.

"You figure she just got a better offer or what?" Ethan asked, waving at the Gordons.

Heather shrugged.

"Are you out for the day, Miss Heather?" Herman Gordon wanted to know.

"No such luck. Just heading over to Betty's."

Mr. Gordon dug into his pocket.

"Oh, hey, don't suppose I could get you to bring me back a cup of coffee, could I?"

"Sure," Ethan said, waving away the old guy's money.

It was always this way whenever Ethan went to Betty's Bakeshoppe. He habitually came back laden with extra orders.

"He doesn't need any of those streusel muffins, though," Mrs. Gordon called after him.

"Aw, Louise, his waistline can take it."

Ethan tossed a smile at her as he stepped into the revolving door behind Heather.

"I take it you're in the habit of bringing coffee to the Gordons," she said once they'd reached the sidewalk.

"Just like you're in the habit of bringing tea back for Brenda."

"At least a couple times a week," she confirmed, squinting against the bright sunlight.

"So we're a couple of soft touches," he concluded, nodding a greeting at Murphy, who stood behind the street-side counter of his newsstand, right next door to the Hamilton Building.

"I guess that's a good thing," she mused.

Taking her arm as they stepped down onto the crosswalk, Ethan checked the traffic in both directions.

"Are you saying that being generous might not be a good thing?"

"Not at all."

They hurried across the street. He noticed that she needed two steps for every one of his and purposefully slowed.

"It's just that sometimes," she said, "I think I do things because they're expected of me, you know?"

"And that's bad?"

"No. But it's not *intentional*."

He followed her up onto the opposite curb, reluctantly letting go of her arm.

"Habitual generosity is a good trait."

"I suppose."

"Sounds to me as if you don't give yourself enough credit," he said, taking the last few steps to the front of the Bakeshoppe. "Now me, I give myself all the credit I can steal."

She cut her gaze at him skeptically.

"That's not what I've heard."

"No?" He grinned because she was so easy to tease. "Must be working."

He reached around her to pull open the painted glass door to Betty's Bakeshoppe and Bookstore.

The delightful aromas of fresh coffee, old leather and the best baked goods this side of the Atlantic Ocean nearly lifted him off his feet. He inhaled appreciatively as he followed Heather inside.

The unusual establishment owned and operated by

Betty Owens and her two daughters, Justine and Wendy, was a Davis Landing staple. A plaque on the wall stated that it had been founded as a bakery in 1941 by Marten and Agnes Nylund, Betty's parents. Over the years the bakery had morphed into a combination coffeehouse, restaurant and used bookstore that took up three storefronts along Main Street.

The decor bordered on kitsch but was just clever enough to be unique. The permanently pulled back "drapes," for instance, were painted directly onto the glass. Likewise, the ornate "area rugs" had been painted onto the hardwood floors.

The original bakery counter with its glass display case remained in place, buffering the dining area from the busy kitchen. All of the furnishings had been painted a flat black, lending continuity to what was in reality a hodgepodge of mismatched bits and pieces.

The walls were covered with bookcases from ceiling to floor, the upper shelves occupied by a collection of interesting objects, everything from old manual typewriters to butter churns. The remaining shelves contained an amazing array of books, the majority of which moved in and out very quickly. For that reason, Ethan usually took a few minutes to look over the new arrivals; he'd learned not to dither when something he wanted came in.

Today, however, he escorted Heather straight to one of the chairs arranged about a small, round table. Since the lunch hour was past, only a few other tables were occupied, their patrons absorbed with various combinations of books, coffee and food. The place could be counted on to be intermittently busy later during the afternoon, as it was a favorite place for Hamilton Media employees to meet for their breaks. Just now, however, Ethan didn't recognize anyone else there.

He pulled out Heather's chair for her and saw her comfortably seated before dropping down beside her.

Betty bustled out of the kitchen, drying her hands on the front of her flowered apron. As usual, her gray-streaked brown hair was coiled into a tight bun at the nape of her neck. The lines around her light brown eyes deepened as she smiled a greeting.

"Be right with you," she called, moving to the beverage counter in the corner to pour two glasses of ice water.

Sturdy and pleasant, Betty seemed to toil tirelessly. At times, she seemed burdened, yet her friendly nature and quick smile made her easy to talk to.

"Why, Heather," she said, placing the glasses on the table, "how pretty you look today."

"Thanks."

"I hardly knew it was you."

Betty's face turned red as she realized how that sounded, but Heather just laughed and said, "I hardly knew me, either, this morning."

Betty quickly took their orders and beat a hasty retreat.

Heather shared a smile with Ethan, who thought she must be one of the most gracious individuals he'd ever met. She drank some water, then placed the glass on the table and ran the tip of one finger around the rim of the glass while he shopped his mind for a suitable topic of conversation other than her appearance. He didn't have to look too far.

"So how is your dad doing?"

"As well as can be expected, I guess."

"Must be tough for you and your family."

She nodded. "Yeah, it is. We're all so used to Dad being at the helm, you know. I mean, my brother Jeremy's doing a good job running the company, but it's just not the same. Everyone's tense and little things seem to get blown all out of proportion."

"Life doesn't stop for a crisis, does it?"

"Unfortunately, no. Then again, maybe that's for the best." She shrugged. "I don't know. I just want my father to get better and everything to go back to normal."

"And what's normal?" he asked. "I've always wondered if such a thing really exists."

She chuckled and inclined her head. "Probably not. And the truth is, I know that nothing will ever again be the same as it was."

Before he could stop himself, he reached out and smoothed a lock of hair that curved against her cheekbone. He, for one, wouldn't want everything to go back to the way it had been. She hadn't even looked him in the eye before the makeover. As if reading his thoughts, she ducked her head, and he tucked his hands beneath his thighs before he could embarrass either one of them again.

Betty brought the coffee and plates of warm cheese Danish and hot cherry turnover. She left a little pot of cream on the table. Once Heather had determined that he was not going to use it for his coffee, she poured some over the top of her tart, explaining, "Fewer calories than ice cream."

"Like you have to be concerned with that."

Her gaze darted up in surprise, then quickly skittered away again.

"I mean, all the Hamilton women are on the slender side," he added quickly.

She nodded at that and took a bite of her turnover, then daintily dabbed at her mouth with a paper napkin before asking, "What about your family? Any brothers and sisters?"

"Nope. Just me."

"An only child," she said. "You must be very close to your parents."

"Not especially. They, uh, don't live around here."

"Where do they live?"

Ethan sipped his coffee and set the cup back into the saucer. "Well, Mom's in Dallas. She's a graphic artist, works with an ad agency there. Dad's a helicopter pilot in Las Vegas."

"So which place is home?" Heather asked.

"Neither."

"Oh. Well, where were you born then?"

"Georgia."

"A Southern boy."

He shook his head. "Not really. Dad was in the military, and Mom's none too stable herself. We moved around a lot. Still do. Guess we're just a family of gypsies."

"That must have been difficult," Heather surmised.

He shrugged. "Just how it was. Even after they divorced, I was constantly shuttling back and forth between them. I'd fly off to spend the summer with Dad in, say, Germany, and Mom would move while I was gone. Got to the point where we only booked one-way tickets until we knew for sure where I'd be flying back to."

Heather stared at him for several long moments, and he could tell that she was shocked.

"Wow. I—I can't even imagine…"

"That's pretty much how I feel about sticking in one place forever."

Betty reappeared with a carafe of hot coffee and refilled their cups, not that they really needed refilling. Obviously she had another agenda.

"Heather, what I said earlier, I only meant—" She broke off, looking miserable.

"That before she was simply pretty and now she's a knockout?" Ethan supplied helpfully, and Betty breathed a silent sigh of relief.

"Exactly."

Heather beamed and confided, "I had a makeover yesterday. You know that column we do, the Makeover Maven? Well, the candidate didn't show up, and I had to step in, and Ethan took the pictures…." She spread her hands. "Anyway, here I am."

"Wait until you see the photos," Ethan put in. "She looks like a fashion model or a movie star." He looked at Heather. "Actually, I think I like this version best."

Heather's cheeks pinkened as she looked down at her lap, but she was still smiling.

"You be sure to let me know when that issue comes out," Betty said.

Heather nodded. "I will."

"Oh, and I've been meaning to ask about your father," Betty continued. "Is it true he's in the hospital?"

"I'm afraid it is."

"Nothing serious, I hope."

"Very serious, unfortunately."

Betty seemed genuinely distressed. "That's…that's too bad. If there's anything I can do…"

"Not unless you're a registered bone marrow donor," Heather said kindly.

Betty's forehead furrowed. "You mean, like for a transplant?"

"That's right."

"I don't understand. I thought it had to come from family."

"Ideally, but none of us is a match."

Betty seemed disturbed by that. "Bone marrow transplant," she muttered. "So it's some sort of cancer?"

"Leukemia."

Betty blew out a breath of air. "Wh-what are you going to do?"

Ethan watched as determination firmed Heather's features. For an instant, he glimpsed a kind of inner strength that surprised him.

Interesting. She was not as fragile as she seemed, apparently.

"We're going to trust God," Heather stated evenly, "and we're going to find a donor."

"I'll say a prayer for him," Betty promised.

Ethan gave her their "to go" orders, and Betty hurried away to get that together while he and Heather finished their coffee and pastries.

They chatted about Ellen's leaving and the mess that had created.

"Well, if I can help, you know you just have to ask," Ethan told her.

Betty returned just then with two stapled brown paper bags and a single ticket, both of which she left on the table.

Ethan immediately picked up the check, but Heather reached for her purse, saying, "How much do I owe?"

"Aw, don't worry about it. I've got it."

"No, no, I'll pay for mine."

"That's not necessary."

"But you shouldn't have to pay for all of it," she protested.

For some reason that irritated him.

"Look, I may not be in the same league as the Hamiltons financially, but I can afford to pay for a cup of coffee and a cherry tart."

Heather stared at him with those enormous amber eyes of hers, looking perplexed.

"But there's Brenda's order, and Mr. Gordon's, too."

He knew that she was just trying to be thoughtful and fair, but still it rankled.

"Would you just say thank-you and let it go?"

Heather blinked, and just that tiny movement was so elegant, so graceful and so baffled that he felt like an undeserving worm.

"Thank you," she said softly, and suddenly his chest felt tight.

"We'd better get back," he muttered.

Rising swiftly, he crossed to the old-fashioned cash register and paid the bill, leaving Heather to gather up her purse and the sacks full of tea and cherry turnover, coffee and, yes, streusel muffins. She was standing at his elbow when he stuffed his change into his pocket.

Lifting a hand, he escorted her to the door and out onto the sidewalk again. This time, he kept his hands to himself when they crossed the street. Once they reached the other side, he paused at Murphy's Newsstand and bought a copy of the *Davis Landing Observer,* saying, "I like to keep an eye on the competition."

Strictly speaking, the *Observer* was no competition for the magazine, but the *Observer* and the *Dispatch* went head-to-head on a daily basis.

It wasn't merely loyalty to his employer that fueled Ethan's opinion that Hamilton Media's *Davis Landing Dispatch* was the better paper. For one thing, the *Observer* regularly dealt in what Ethan could only think of as gossip masquerading as news. For another, the writing was, in general, simply better in the *Dispatch,* at least in his opinion. Considering that he'd worked for papers and magazines the world over, he felt entitled to make the judgment.

They delivered coffee and muffins to the Gordons and made the elevator ride upstairs in silence.

The instant that they stepped off onto the second floor, Heather was accosted by two clipboard-wielding assistants wanting her to make decisions that should have been Ellen's. With an apologetic glance, Heather parted company with him.

Reminding himself that he had work waiting in the darkroom, he strode away, but he couldn't help feeling dismissed like the lowly employee that he was.

Chapter Five

Betty took a last swipe at the final table and straightened, a hand going to the small of her back. Aches and pains of one sort or another seemed to constantly plague her these days, but she supposed that was what came of getting older. That thought provoked another.

Wallace Hamilton was two years older than herself, and quite likely dying.

She pulled out a chair and sagged down into it, bracing her elbows on the tabletop and letting her head fall forward.

It didn't seem possible that Wallace could die. Of all the people in the world, he was the one she'd have thought was immune to something as common as disease. Then again, she'd always been hopelessly enamored of Wallace Hamilton.

Closing her eyes, she remembered bumping into him in the high school hallway as if it were yesterday.

He hadn't even known who she was back then, a sophomore from the wrong side of the river. He'd been a senior and the big shot on campus, everybody's favorite person. She'd never dreamed that he would turn his eye on her. Then one night he had.

Just one night.

She wondered if he'd realized that she was in love with him or if he'd just considered her foolish and easy. God knew that she had been both. It was only by His grace that she'd met Harold Owens so soon after that night.

A soft smile curled her lips. Harold had been her salvation and, eventually, the love of her life. She missed him still, after all these years, and she didn't envy Nora Hamilton the heartache if Wallace did die, knowing too well what awaited a woman who lost a beloved husband. The children would suffer, too, no matter that they were all grown now.

Her own daughters, just seventeen and twelve at the time, had been devastated when a heart attack had felled Harry. It had come out of the blue, completely unexpected. At least he hadn't suffered weeks or months or years of illness. That was what the girls had always said, anyway.

As if her memory made her appear, her eldest daughter, Justine, walked in off the street, a smile on her lips. Tall and slender with short, dark brown hair that curled around her pretty face, Justine had just turned thirty-five. Ever a dutiful daughter, like her younger sister, Wendy, she'd worked at Betty's side since high school, only marrying a few months ago.

"What are you doing here, hon?" Betty asked.

It wasn't Justine's afternoon at the Bakeshoppe, but Wendy was out running errands and Justine might have felt that she needed to help Betty close up. Business had been slow, though, so she could manage on her own. It was five-thirty. She wouldn't lock the door for another half hour, and she'd had at least that long already to clean the dining room uninterrupted.

To Betty's surprise, Justine pulled out a chair and sat down opposite her. She reached for Betty's hands and just sat there, holding them for some time.

"What's got into you?" Betty asked uncertainly.

"Do you remember yesterday when you were asking me if I was ever going to make you a grandmother?"

"Yeah," Betty murmured cautiously. "And?"

"Last night, Otis and I prayed about it, and this morning he told me he's ready if I am."

Betty grinned. "I knew I liked that boy!"

Justine laughed.

"Anyway, I went to the doctor today, you know, just to be sure everything's in proper working order, and she said there's no reason not to think we won't have a healthy baby. Just think, this time next year, I could be a mommy!"

She hunched her shoulders, giggling like the girl

she'd been before her daddy had died. The man she thought was her daddy, anyway.

Betty bit her lip, and instantly Justine squeezed her hands.

"Mom, what's wrong?"

Blinking back sudden tears, Betty got to her feet.

"Not a thing, sweetie. I'm thrilled for you and Otis, but I've got work to do in the kitchen yet." With that she made a beeline for the back of the building.

It was only to be expected that Justine would follow, but Betty hoped that she wouldn't. She didn't want to say the words that had crowded into her mouth when Justine had giggled.

Betty was busy scrubbing baking pans when she felt Justine's hand fall gently upon her shoulder some minutes later.

"I know what you're thinking," Justine whispered, sliding her arms around Betty's shoulders. "You're thinking that Daddy should be here to enjoy his grandchild."

A sob took Betty by surprise.

Whirling around, she wailed, "That's just it, Justine! Your father might be here still."

Justine pulled back, clearly shocked.

"What?"

Tears ran down Betty's face. For so long she'd kept the secret; she hadn't wanted to think it, let alone say it, but what if Wallace died? Justine would never have the chance to get to know him then. And what if she should somehow learn later that he might be her father? Betty gulped and lifted her chin, praying that Justine wouldn't judge her too harshly.

"It's p-possible that W-Wallace H-Hamilton is your father."

Justine took another step back, her eyes going wide with confusion.

"You can't mean that. It's crazy!"

"Oh, Justine, I'm so sorry!" Betty cried. "I should've told you before. O-or maybe I shouldn't ever have told you, I don't know!"

"Mom, I don't understand. How could this be?"

Betty put her trembling hands to her head. "I-it happened so long ago. I was only twenty-two, and I'd always had a crush on Wallace, but he was just so far above me. Then one night, he…we…"

She turned away, unable to get the words out that would describe what had happened that night.

After a moment Justine asked, "Did Dad… Did *Harry* know?"

Justine nodded, wiping her eyes with her apron. "Yes. He knew it was a possibility." She spun around then. "And he didn't care, Justine. You have to know that. We met and married just after Wallace and I were together. I found out a few weeks later that I was pregnant, but it didn't make any difference to Harry. As far as he was concerned, you were his from the moment he knew you existed."

Justine took a deep breath, looking a little lost and wild-eyed. Then she nodded decisively.

"Well, that's that as far as I'm concerned, then. Harry Owens was, and will always be, my father."

Betty nodded, fresh tears flooding her eyes. There could be no denying that she'd prefer it that way.

"He was such a good man," she whispered. "I'm so blessed to have found him."

Justine tilted her head, a groove appearing between her eyebrows.

"Why now? What made you tell me now?"

"Wallace has leukemia."

Justine blinked. "You mean, he might be dying?"

"He needs a bone marrow transplant."

Justine stared at her for a long moment.

Finally Betty said, "None of the…family were a match."

Justine just stood there as if carved in stone, but Betty knew, *knew*, what she was thinking, because she was thinking it herself.

Justine might be a match.

She didn't want to know whether Wallace Hamilton was her natural father. She didn't want to feel that she ought to get tested as a bone marrow donor because surely that would tell them if she and Wallace were connected biologically.

She wanted to get pregnant, not donate bone marrow to a man who shouldn't be any part of her life.

"Maybe they'll find a donor soon," she whispered.

Betty closed her eyes and prayed that they would.

Curtis Resnick slipped out onto the sidewalk and quietly closed the door to Betty's Bakeshoppe behind him.

Rocking back on his heels, he looked at the Hamilton Building across the street and silently congratulated himself. What had begun as an effort to wring a little gossip out of Betty over a cup of coffee had turned into a personal mother lode.

He'd always considered Betty to be an excellent source of information. That old biddy must know the business of everybody in town, not that she was easy to get information out of.

Curtis was careful to drop in at the end of the day when business was slowest, and even then he usually had to ratchet up the charm to get her to talk. He was good at that, though. He just had to bat his big baby blues at the old girl, flash her that thousand-watt smile of his and murmur a few trite phrases of concern to get the old gal jabbering. Even at forty-three, Curtis thought smugly, the ladies still liked his California surfer boy looks.

Of course, if the Hamiltons hadn't been stupid enough to keep his little embezzlement scheme quiet, charming Betty might have been a problem. Goody Two-shoes Jeremy had seen to that for him—and then had actually expected him to be grateful!

Curtis shook his head.

All that money, power and prestige, and Jeremy expected him, Curtis Resnick, to be happy with *not* being prosecuted. But only after he'd made restitution, of course. As if that twenty grand meant anything at all to the Hamiltons. Good thing they didn't know about the other thirty, which allowed him to hang around this one-horse, two-newspaper town.

Thanks to the stupid Hamiltons, he was living a life of leisure at the moment, pumping a little iron to keep the ol' bod well defined and scheming to repay the Hamiltons. He was going to get back a little of his own if it was the last thing he ever did.

Curtis slipped a hand into the pocket of his pale, pleated slacks as he crossed the street to the newsstand, the breeze toying with the sandy blond lock that fell forward across his bronzed brow. He paid for a copy of the *Dispatch,* folded it and tucked it beneath one arm, striding quickly down the sidewalk toward his car.

It never hurt to keep tabs on the competition, not that he'd gotten himself hired at the *Observer.* No, indeed. That would have been much too obvious. It was better by far for Ellen to go to work there.

He chuckled to himself.

Wouldn't the Hamiltons just choke if—*when*—they discovered that Ellen had jumped ship to go to work for their only real competition? But it wasn't better pay or position that had enticed Ellen away from a successful regional magazine to a local daily paper.

It was the opportunity to make a little trouble for the mighty Hamiltons.

She hadn't wanted to do it, of course.

To her it was a step backward in her career. But to Curtis it was a leap forward in getting back at the Hamiltons. And Ellen would do anything for him. Anything at all.

Once he'd learned of the job opening at the *Observer,* he really hadn't given her any choice. Besides placing her in a position to do the Hamiltons harm, it had removed the possibility that her own quick temper and growing resentment would result in the sort of blunder that would put the Hamiltons on their guard.

Yes, it had all worked out very satisfactorily, indeed.

He was perfectly poised now to deal the Hamiltons a little of what they so blithely gave out with their cavalier behavior.

Now all he had to do was decide how to use this interesting little tidbit he'd just overheard.

He chuckled aloud. Who'd have thought that Justine Grimes would be the illegitimate daughter of the high-and-mighty Wallace Hamilton, not to mention half sister to the holier-than-thou Jeremy? The very thought of Wallace with stout ol' Betty made Curtis want to howl with laughter. It was almost too delicious to keep to himself, which of course he had no intention of doing.

Curtis was nothing if not thoughtful, however. Growing up on the mean streets of L.A. had taught him that smart was better than strong. He'd wait for the right moment to blow the lid off Wallace's one-night stand with Betty Nylund Owens.

He could hardly wait to find out what the good folks down at the country club and over at the church would think of *that.*

After letting himself into the luxury sedan that he'd paid for with Hamilton funds, he tossed the newspaper onto the passenger seat. He'd dissect it later with Ellen, and together they'd laugh at the pathetic attempt at real journalism. It was small satisfaction for the resentment, envy and humiliation that the Hamiltons had made him feel. Soon, he vowed, that shoe would be on the other foot.

He could hardly wait.

But he would.

He'd wait for exactly the right moment.

And then he would savor it.

Amy lightly tossed the printout onto Heather's desk blotter and folded herself down onto the edge of the only available chair, crossing her long, elegant legs at the knee.

"You didn't like it," Heather surmised, deflated.

"Let's just say, given the results, I find the makeover story…bland."

Heather sighed, tucking the hair that curved against

her left cheek behind her ear. It promptly fell forward again. "It's not easy trying to capture Ellen's style."

"Then don't."

"So what do you suggest?"

Amy leaned forward. "Write it in first person. Give us the story from the subject's point of view."

Heather grimaced, recalling how uncomfortable and nervous she'd felt. "I'm not sure that's a good idea. In some ways, it wasn't a pleasant experience. In fact, it was downright embarrassing, if you really want to know."

"Then write that." Amy leaned back again. "Just be sure to say that it was worth it, because we both know it was."

Biting her lip, Heather considered.

So much of the time during the makeover she'd been wondering what Ethan was seeing through the lens of his camera as he'd snapped away. Were her plucked eyebrows red and splotchy? Were a few highlights worth looking like an alien in a bad sci-fi movie in front of the most attractive man she knew?

Would the outcome be enough to change the way he saw her, or would she appear as though she was wearing a costume?

"Look," Amy explained patiently, resting a forearm along the edge of Heather's cluttered desk, "being made over is all about being jolted out of your comfort zone and into a new way of looking at yourself. That's bound to be a little nerve-racking, but isn't it also, well, liberating?"

Heather considered that and quickly found that her big sis was all too correct. Until the makeover, Heather hadn't really felt free to be herself. It was as if she'd needed permission somehow to look her best, as if looking her best was a bad thing.

Now she understood that she'd just been hiding her envy and fear behind a veil of false modesty, telling herself that being the plain sister was God's design for her when the truth was that she'd been afraid to compete, afraid to be compared in any meaningful way to those whom others found attractive. In some ways, changing her appearance had become a spiritual experience for Heather, and that was something she could convey only in the telling of a very personal story.

Heather reached forward and picked up the few pages of written text.

"All right." Leaning back, she dropped the papers into the wastebasket at the end of her desk. "I'll try it your way."

Grinning triumphantly, Amy rose to her feet and turned toward the door in one smooth, fluid motion, the slender tailored skirt of her designer suit displaying just enough of her graceful legs to leave no doubt as to the tone of her muscles.

Just as Amy reached the door, Heather's cell phone

rang. As it lay atop her desk within easy reach, a quick glance at the tiny screen was all that was needed to tell her who was calling.

"That's Mom," she announced, picking up the little phone and flipping it open.

Amy halted and waited as Heather greeted her caller. "Hi. What's up?"

A sob had Heather sitting bolt upright in her chair. "Mom? What's wrong?"

Alerted to trouble, Amy strode back toward the desk.

"Oh, Heather! What are we going to do?" Nora wailed.

Heather was on her feet in a heartbeat.

"What's happened?"

Her distress must have shown clearly on her face, for Amy's suddenly mirrored it.

"I have to tell you in person. Where's your sister?"

"Amy's here, Mom," Heather answered in a trembling voice, dreading the worst.

"You have to come to the hospital. Quickly."

Tears filling her eyes, Heather looked at her sister.

"Mom needs to talk to us in person at the hospital. Right now."

Amy swung around and made for the door. "Tell her we're on our way."

Heather was right behind her. "We're coming, Mom. Hold on. We're coming."

"Hurry," Nora sobbed. "I'm so sorry. I'm so very sorry." With that she hung up.

Heather broke into a run, spurring her sister to do the same. Neither of them were in any state of mind to answer Brenda's startled, "What's wrong?"

Just as they came to the end of the corridor, Amy lurched to a stop.

"Car keys!"

Heather looked down at the vacant spot where her handbag would normally hang against her hip, her cell phone gripped in one hand. It was then that Ethan turned the corner and nearly bowled them over. He threw his arms out, steadying both women.

"Oops. Sorry."

Heather seized a handful of the black T-shirt that he wore with black jeans and boots.

"Can I have your car keys?"

"We've got to go!" Amy exclaimed, as if that explained everything.

His alarmed gaze zipped from Heather to Amy and back. "No," he said. Reaching up to pluck Heather's hand off his chest and grip it in his own, he turned back the way he'd come. "But I'll take you wherever you need to go."

Relief swept through Heather, only to be instantly replaced by urgency. "To the hospital!"

"Hurry!" Amy ordered, bolting toward the elevator, which they quickly discovered was on its way back down to the ground floor.

They took the stairs, then tore across the lobby, ignoring the Gordons, and shoved their way through the revolving door. Heather and Ethan crowded into the same space and spilled out onto the sidewalk beyond. Even then he did not release her hand.

As they sprinted to the corner and across the street, Amy in the lead, Heather hung on with all her might. That heated palm seemed to ground her in the moment, locking out worrisome speculation.

Ethan dug his keys from his pocket before they reached the parking lot and called out directions to Amy as they ran. Aiming the remote device, he unlocked the doors on the dark gray SUV just as they got to it. Amy headed for the back driver's side, and Heather followed, piling in behind her. Ethan finally let go of her hand in order to slide behind the wheel.

Feeling bereft and adrift without that anchoring contact, Heather reached for her sister. The two clasped hands, and as the sturdy vehicle sped through the streets, Heather began to pray aloud, not even thinking the words before they fell out of her mouth.

"Oh, Lord, please don't let him be dead. Please don't let it be that. We still need him. You know we still need Daddy in so many ways, and You take care of our every need, Father, so we're trusting You in this. Be with Mom. Give her strength, and get us there safely. Thank You for Ethan. Thank You that he came along just at the right moment."

She went on and on. The next thing she knew, the SUV was swinging into a space, and she heard Ethan say, "That's your brothers."

Amy exclaimed, "What on earth?" as she yanked open the door.

Heather's gaze found Jeremy and Tim right in the middle of the traffic lane that ran in front of the hospital, and before she could think, before she could even process what she was seeing, Jeremy shoved Tim. Gasping, Heather watched in disbelief as they yelled and gestured wildly, right in each other's faces.

"Uh-oh," Ethan muttered, yanking open his door. Suddenly galvanized, Heather did the same. By the time she got her brothers in her sights again, Amy was already running toward them.

Heather started after her, only to feel Ethan's grasp on her elbow, steering her away.

"Hold on. That's enough of a circus as it is."

Irritation and disappointment overwhelmed whatever shock or curiosity had impelled her. She lifted her chin, thinking of her parents and what might await them upstairs, and directed her steps toward the entrance. "You're right. Whatever that's about, Amy can handle it."

They were shouting something about Tim getting what he wanted and it always being all about Jeremy, whatever "it" was. Heather blocked out their words, angrily chalking up the unfortunate scene to the stress of their father's illness and the incessant rivalry between her two eldest brothers. She said as much to Ethan on their way up to Wallace's room, though

Ethan didn't ask about or comment on what he'd seen, just clasped her shoulder with his big, warm hand.

"I can't thank you enough for getting us here," she told him, stepping off the elevator and hurrying toward her father's suite.

Ethan sent her an odd look and shook his head, mumbling, "Not that big of a deal."

Heather drew up and took just a second to steel herself before pushing into the sitting room. Her mother sat on the sofa, leaning forward with her elbows on her knees and her face in her hands. Gulping, Heather noted that the door to her father's room was closed. Nora looked up as Heather crossed the floor, her face ravaged by tears. She stood as Heather drew near and fell into Heather's arms, sobbing.

Feeling Ethan behind her, Heather closed her eyes as she folded her mother close, whispering, "What happened?"

Strong hands settled atop her shoulders, as if bracing her against the strong tide of emotion.

"He told him," Nora wailed, which made not the least sense to Heather.

"I don't understand. Who told who what, Mom?"

Nora lifted her head from Heather's shoulder and made a swipe at her cheeks. "Your father told Jeremy..." She looked away, her enormous hazel eyes taking on a haunted glaze. "Wallace told Jeremy that he's not his father."

The world tilted crazily, seeming to drop from

beneath Heather's feet as she fought to make sense of that. "Dad told Jeremy," she began uncertainly, "that he's not…" She shook her head, unable to think, let alone say the next words. They simply didn't compute.

Then Nora turned a doleful gaze on her daughter and said sadly, resignedly, "I was pregnant when I met Wallace."

Chapter Six

It was a simple but incredible story.

At twenty, Nora had been in love with and engaged to a man named Paul Anderson. She hadn't even known she was pregnant when Paul had been killed in a motorcycle accident. Four months later, terrified and in a state of grief, she'd met Wallace, who had pursued her shamelessly.

"I tried to discourage him," Nora said tearfully, grasping both of Heather's hands as they sat together on the sofa, almost as if she feared that Heather would pull away. "You have to understand, I'd just found the Lord, and I wanted desperately to do the right thing, but Wallace wouldn't take no for an answer. So finally I told him the truth."

Heather's mind was reeling, but she could easily believe what her mother was saying. More than once she'd heard her father proudly tell how he'd made up his mind to marry the beautiful, delicate Nora

McCarthy the moment he'd laid eyes on her, and anyone who knew anything about Wallace Hamilton knew that he went after whatever he wanted relentlessly.

"How could I not love a man who was so willing to give another man's child his name?" Nora asked. "He's never said a word of reproach to me about Paul, not one. We named Jeremy after Wallace's grandfather, Jeremiah, and Wallace made me promise never to tell anyone that Jeremy wasn't his. Much of the time, I simply forgot that Wallace wasn't his father!"

Nora shook her head, amazed at how easy it had been. She told Heather that she'd realized suddenly that her memory of Paul had faded and with it the knowledge that he had fathered her son.

"Then Wallace would look at me with love in his eyes, and I couldn't seem to recall that there had ever been another man in my life."

As the years had gone by, Jeremy grew to be more and more like Paul in personality, Nora said, though she'd never mentioned it to Wallace.

"I would never have guessed," Heather murmured. "Dad groomed Jeremy from the beginning to step into his shoes one day."

"That day just came sooner than any of us imagined it would," Nora said. "Long before Wallace was ready to let go."

"Is that why Dad told him?" Heather asked.

"I don't know," Nora told her, "but this is not your

father's fault. He's done the very best that he could, for me, for Jeremy, for all of us. It's this illness, the helplessness. If they hadn't been arguing over that stupid accounting contract…"

The door swung open and Tim staggered into the room, pushed by a resolute Amy, who followed at his heels.

Tim's hair was mussed, and his tie was askew, his expensive Italian suit rumpled. Heather saw that he was still very angry. Obviously he or Jeremy or both had told Amy the astounding news, for she looked as shocked as Heather felt.

Nora slumped forward, covering her mouth with her hand. After a moment, she straightened.

"Where is your brother?" she asked, pressing her fingertips together.

"He's no brother of mine!" Tim retorted angrily.

"Timothy!" Amy scolded. "You know that's not so."

At the same time, Heather gently reproved him. "Jeremy will always be our brother. He's a Hamilton in every way that counts."

Tim rounded on her, flinging an arm out wildly. "A Hamilton doesn't quit! And that's just what he's done, quit the business, quit the family! You should have heard him!" He mimicked Jeremy's voice. "'No wonder I was never good enough!' And he's had everything, been first at everything!"

"Hey. That's enough of that."

They all gaped at Ethan, who stepped forward with his arms akimbo. Heather had forgotten he was even there!

"This is a hospital," he went on calmly, sternly, "and whatever you think of Jeremy, that's your sister you're talking to. And I imagine your mother's had about all she can take at the moment."

Tim tossed him a surly look, but it was laced with more than a little remorse and a great deal of pain. Pushing back the sides of his coat, he copied Ethan's stance. Then he bowed his head.

"Fine. I apologize. This isn't accomplishing anything anyway." He sighed and pinched the bridge of his nose before straightening his tie and the hang of his coat. "I've just been handed an enormous responsibility so, Mom, if you'll forgive me, I'm going where I can do the most good."

Nora sniffed, swallowed and said, "Do what you need to, son."

Nodding, Timothy turned and moved past Amy to the door, saying grimly, "If anyone needs me, I'll be trying to keep the family business out of the red."

After the door closed behind Tim, Amy raised an eyebrow at Ethan, a speculative gleam in her blue eyes. Ethan held her gaze for a moment, then stepped back and resumed holding up the wall.

Amy switched her attention to Nora, who looked so dejected that the sisters traded concerned glances. As Amy crossed the room to take a seat on the sofa next to Nora, effectively bracketing her with the support of her daughters—the two who were present anyway—the older woman once more dissolved in tears.

Though her own eyes were brimming, Heather crooned, "Don't cry, Mom. Don't cry."

"It's going to be okay," Amy offered. Then, with a pointed look at Heather, she asked, "How's Dad?"

That made Nora sit up a little straighter and sniff.

"The doctor sedated him. He was angry when he said it, and then when he realized what he'd done..." She bit her lip and shook her head. "I think he and Tim are as hurt as Jeremy." Suddenly she looked around. "Where is Jeremy? Where did he go?"

Amy telegraphed her concern to Heather over the top of Nora's head.

"He didn't say."

Nora gripped each of them, her hands like iron talons as they curved around their thighs.

"You've got to find him! He can't be alone at a time like this. There's no telling what he might do. You don't know how upset he was."

"I'm sure he'll calm down," Amy said.

But she wasn't sure. Heather could see it in her eyes.

"Maybe I should call Chris again," Nora mused in a lost voice. "They said he couldn't be reached before, but if I tell them it's an emergency..." She let that thought dwindle away.

An emergency of some sort was likely the reason

he couldn't be reached. Emergencies were the stock-in-trade of a police officer, after all.

"I'll go," Ethan said.

Nora looked up as if seeing him for the very first time.

"It's Mr. Danes, isn't it?"

"Ethan's...Ethan's a friend," Heather said, holding his gaze. "He drove us to the hospital."

A smile tugged at one corner of his mouth before he looked down.

"I think it's a good idea," Amy stated suddenly. "Ethan and Heather can look for Jeremy. I'll stay here with you, Mom."

Nora patted Heather's knee, closing her eyes in relief. "Thank you. Thank you all."

For the second—make that the third—time since he'd bumped into her in the corridor, Heather felt a profound gratitude toward Ethan Danes.

Giving her mother a final squeeze, Heather rose to her feet. Ethan stepped forward as if to steady her. It was what he'd been doing all along, Heather realized.

After promising to call the moment they located Jeremy, Heather let Ethan escort her out into the hall. No sooner had the door closed behind them than it opened again, and Amy slipped through it, looking quickly in both directions.

"Listen," she said, stepping close, "after that public spectacle down there in the street, it may be too little too late, but if it's at all possible I think we ought to keep this just between us." She glanced at Ethan. "Us and the rest of the family, I mean."

"No problem," he replied tersely.

Heather nodded, hoping it wasn't already too late. But, no. Despite that scene downstairs, neither Tim nor Jeremy was likely to go around airing the family's dirty laundry once their tempers cooled. Just the opposite, in fact.

Both had probably closed themselves away somewhere to sulk by now. In their shoes, Heather might have done the same. If she hadn't had Ethan by her side, that was.

She didn't know quite how that had happened, but as they walked away together, Heather silently thanked God that it had.

"He's not at the office," Heather said, closing her cell phone. "Guess the next logical place to look is his apartment."

"Just give me an address," Ethan told her, guiding the SUV smoothly through the streets.

She did so. Ethan recognized it as belonging to the Enclave, a self-proclaimed "community" of upscale condominiums within walking distance of the Hamilton Building.

Ethan liked to live close to the office himself, but the Enclave was a little rich for his pocketbook. He'd sublet his studio apartment on the other end of downtown, then let the lease revert to month-to-month. The rent was a little higher month-to-month, but it was easier to pick up and go that way.

He sat in the truck at the curb outside the gated entrance to the Enclave and waited for Heather to go in and check, since as a family member she would have no problem getting into the building. She returned a few minutes later with the news that Jeremy hadn't answered his door and the security guard hadn't seen him since he'd left that morning.

"So where to next?" Ethan asked, guiding the vehicle back onto the street.

Heather bit her lip and tried to tuck a strand of hair behind her ear.

"Okay, um, the Bakeshoppe, maybe, since it's nearly lunch time. After that... All of his friends work during the day, but I guess it wouldn't hurt to drive by a few of the addresses I know. Then there's the church."

Ethan tried not to appear surprised by that.

"The church? On a weekday?"

Heather nodded. "It's in Hickory Mills. There's a little prayer chapel just off the sanctuary. He's been going there pretty regularly since Dad's diagnosis."

These Hamiltons did a lot of praying, or at least it seemed so to Ethan, but he kept that thought to himself.

"Okay. So where to first?"

"The Bakeshoppe, I guess. It's closest."

This time he did the checking. Heather still looked pretty shaky, and he wanted her away from prying eyes as much as possible. Anyone who knew her would see at once that she was upset. Besides, it was the work of a moment for him to jog across the street from the parked SUV and scan the dining room through the window.

"Not there," he told her, dropping behind the steering wheel once more.

Heather sighed. "Take Mill Road then, and I'll tell you when to turn."

While Ethan drove, Heather sat quietly, her head leaning against the window, arms folded in a tense pose that told him she was still trying to process her mother's shocking revelation. They checked one address after another, and finally she sent him across the river to Hickory Mills.

The church was on the far north side of that blue-collar neighborhood, set in the midst of a forested acreage. Situated on a gentle rise, it rose in humble majesty above a sweep of shady green lawn that rolled from the edge of a neat, tree-studded parking lot right down to the tree-lined edge of the Cumberland River.

A dignified, steepled building of white-painted brick with tall stained-glass windows and a number of broad steps leading up to a columned portico, the church projected a feeling of serenity and solid permanence. The rectangular, flat-topped, two-story addition at the back of the original structure was obviously of more recent construction but in no way detracted from the quiet dignity of the whole. All in all, a very pretty picture, especially, Ethan mused, if photographed from the right spot across the river.

Unfortunately, Jeremy's vehicle was not among those few in the side parking lot.

"I don't know where else to look," Heather said helplessly.

After a moment of consideration, she decided to try to reach Chris. She didn't get through, but before they made their way back across the river, Chris returned her call.

Her relief was palpable.

Openly eavesdropping, Ethan gathered that Chris had not seen or heard from Jeremy, but he seemed to pick up at once on Heather's distress. With a quick glance in Ethan's direction, Heather said only that Jeremy and Wallace had argued again and that Chris really should get by the hospital and speak to Nora as soon as he could manage it. Then she hung up.

"You didn't tell him," Ethan pointed out needlessly.

She grimaced.

"I couldn't tell him that our mother...that our father isn't our brother's father. At least not while Chris is on the job. He knows me well enough to realize that something's going on, though." She smiled wanly. "It's that twin thing."

Ethan hadn't realized that the tall, muscular police officer whom he'd glimpsed from time to time around the Hamilton Building and petite, gentle Heather were twins. He couldn't begin to imagine what it must have been like growing up as part of that, but he'd always liked the idea of having a twin, a mirror image of himself, someone who'd sense his moods and share his thoughts. Funny, he'd never thought about having a twin so completely dissimilar from one's self.

Chris had made a suggestion where to look next, and as Ethan drove back toward the center of town and a place he knew well, he thought it might be a good spot to end their search, whether Jeremy was there or not. Heather had received a great shock, and despite what she'd said about her connection with her twin, it seemed to Ethan that none of her family appeared very sensitive to her distress. Perhaps their own shock blinded them to her needs.

And maybe he was just more attuned to Heather Hamilton than he wanted to think he was. Regardless, she needed some time to come to terms with what she'd heard this morning.

Sugar Tree Park, where Jeremy, like Ethan, was apparently in the habit of running, lay in the heart of Davis Landing.

The small lake around which the park was built fed into a small stream, which, in turn, fed into the river. A grove of trees provided shade for picnic tables and charcoal grills, while pea gravel cushioned a large playground for the children. In one area a couple of sand pits for volleyball nets partnered a pair of concrete slabs and basketball goals.

The running track, complete with a footbridge and flanked by the occasional bench, circumvented the lake, which featured a water spout at its center. A Victorian-style gazebo could be seen in the distance beyond the small amphitheater that had been carved out of a slope in the green lawn. Adjacent to it, near one of several parking areas, was a large circular pavilion paved with cobblestones. It was there that various vendors gathered, weather permitting.

Ethan parked, and they both got out of the vehicle, deciding to walk the mile-long track in search of Jeremy. That would be faster than driving around to check the various parking areas and side streets. They set off at a fast clip, but after a while, with no sight of Jeremy, their steps slowed.

Conversation along the way was desultory at best, with Ethan commenting that he ran here three or four times a week and occasionally picked up a basketball game at the court and Heather humming nonverbal acknowledgments. By the time they neared the pavilion again, she had ceased to do even that.

Concerned, Ethan picked out a bench and led her toward it. Before they got there, her cell phone rang. It was Chris again, and she became instantly engrossed in what her twin was saying. From her expression of relief, Ethan assumed that Jeremy had at least contacted their brother, but then the tears started again.

Ethan positioned her and pushed her down to sit on

the bench. She complied without ever making eye
contact. He parked himself beside her and spread his
arms out along the edge of the seat back to wait.

She finally hung up.

"Thank God."

"Someone's located Jeremy?"

"He was waiting for Chris when he got back to
the station."

"Should we call your mom?"

"Jeremy already has." She turned tear-filled eyes on
Ethan, adding, "And he told Chris."

"About having a different father than the rest of
you," Ethan clarified.

She nodded, whispering, "I don't know what this
is going to do to my family."

Nothing good, Ethan imagined, but wasn't about to
say so.

"Jeremy has resigned his position at Hamilton
Media," she went on, "which has infuriated Tim—
even though Dad's appointed him in Jeremy's place—
because he thinks Jeremy has abandoned the family.
Chris says that Jeremy's shocked, angry, unsure who
he really is now. It's all so confusing." She put a hand
to her head. "I thought I knew everything there was
to know about my parents."

"No one knows everything there is to know about
their parents," Ethan said. "But, hey, everything will
sort itself out eventually."

It sounded lame even to his own ears. Wishing that

he could give her something more, he dropped his arm around her in a comforting gesture, but the moment he did so, she bowed her head. Several seconds ticked by before he realized that she was again praying, silently this time. Sensing her deep communing, he felt as if he were an intruder.

His stomach rumbled, and it was no wonder, since they'd skipped lunch. A glance in the direction of the pavilion revealed a choice between stale bread for feeding the ducks that inhabited the shoreline of the lake, popcorn, ice cream and soft drinks.

Slipping away as quietly as possible, he bought an ice-cream sandwich and a packaged cone topped with nuts and chocolate, along with two bottles of water. When he resumed his seat beside Heather, she smiled wanly and reached for the cone.

"Thank you."

He shrugged. "Couldn't very well eat in front of you, now, could I?"

She bumped her shoulder against his in a wanly playful scold. "I meant, for more than the ice cream."

He contemplated the slab of vanilla ice cream sandwiched between two soft chocolate cookies in his hand.

"You're welcome, for more than the ice cream."

She shook her head. "I'm sorry you got dragged into this."

"I'm sorry you're going through this, but I seem to remember volunteering." He copied her movement from earlier, bumping her shoulder with his. "I'm not the sort who allows myself to be dragged anywhere I don't want to go, Heather."

She nodded, then bluntly admitted, "I am."

"You're nicer than me," he said.

"I don't think so."

"Oh, yeah, you are," he argued lightly. "You have to be, with all those brothers and sisters. Me, I can be as selfish and self-indulgent as I like."

She turned those big, doleful eyes on him. "Then you must like being a nice man, Ethan Danes, because that's what you are."

Suddenly he found himself wondering what she'd do if he kissed her.

Quickly turning off that ill-timed thought, he resorted to teasing.

"Maybe I just like hanging out with the boss."

She rolled her eyes. "It's not as if I'm your supervisor, Ethan."

"Okay," he amended with a smile, "maybe I just like hanging out with good-looking women."

For a moment she looked stunned. Then a pink blush tinged her cheeks.

Her tone was partly teasing and partly disbelieving when she said, "There are plenty of better-looking women than me."

"Good-looking *Hamilton* women, then."

"I'm not even the best-looking Hamilton."

It irritated him that she would put herself down, but he kept his tone light.

"I'm not much into blondes, if you really want to know."

"So you've been running me all over the area because I'm a Hamilton and I'm not blond?" she asked, the twinkle in her eye belying her indignant tone.

Ethan grinned unrepentantly. "You left out the good-looking part."

"What good-looking part?" she asked innocently.

He chuckled and watched her bite into her ice cream.

"I notice you're not sitting over there waiting for me to deny it."

"Not hardly," she admitted with a grin.

Laughing, he shook his head.

"I've never seen you out here on the track," he mused, "so what do you do?"

She seemed to have to consider that.

"Actually, I write poetry."

He gave her a droll look.

"Oh, yeah, I can see that." He pantomimed scribbling, then wadding up a piece of paper and tossing it before flexing his biceps. "I meant, what do you do to stay in shape?"

Heather shook her head. "I don't. My pastimes tend to be more…"

"Cerebral?" he suggested.

She wrinkled her nose. "Inactive."

Leaning forward, he braced his elbows on his knees and slid his gaze over her petite, slender form.

"I wouldn't spread that around, if I were you."

She lifted both of her gently arched eyebrows, making her eyes as big as saucers.

"You don't think my poetry can be any good?"

"I think the rest of the female populace will turn green with envy if they find out that you keep that slim figure by writing poetry," he stated drily.

She stared at him for several heartbeats, then she licked her ice cream where it was starting to melt.

"Do you have to work at being that charming?"

Very seriously, he shook his head and said, "Nope, it's a gift."

When he cracked a grin, she sputtered laughter. He did his best to keep her laughing until the ice cream was gone.

Finally, she sat back with a satisfied sigh, and a companionable silence enveloped them. A sense of peace settled over Ethan, peace and a little pride because he had successfully distracted her from her problems. All too soon, however, Heather made as if to rise.

"Bad as I hate to, I need to get back to the office."

"You should take the rest of the day off," he said, feeling unusually protective, but she shook her head.

"I have to work on the makeover column."

"Ah." He got up. He really had no right to dictate to her, even if it was for her own good. "I thought the feature was done."

She made a face. "Amy wants me to rewrite it. In first person."

That struck him as a very good idea. He might even read the column himself if it was written from her personal point of view.

"Sounds interesting."

"Might be, if I could actually remember everything. That day is pretty much a blur."

"Well, maybe I can help," he offered lightly. "I was there, after all, and I have the photos to prove it."

She smiled. "You know, that might be a very good idea."

"Let's get to it, then."

Playfully, he offered his arm. She slipped her own through it, and for some reason he found himself holding that arm tight against his side as he walked her to the car.

He told himself that it was just simple consideration for a friend who'd been dealt a great shock, but the truth was that nothing had ever felt less like simple friendship than this did. And that was reason enough to worry.

Of all the women he'd ever known, Heather Hamilton was the very last one with whom he should be starting a relationship. Heather was a permanent kind of woman, and he was a temporary kind of guy. It would undoubtedly be best for both of them if he did not forget that.

Chapter Seven

Heather stared at a hideous photo of herself sprouting a head full of tinfoil strips.

"How about this for a caption? 'Come in, Planet Earth!'"

Ethan laughed.

"Why not? It goes with the playful tone of the article."

She wrinkled her nose. That day had not been nearly as much fun as the article implied, at least not from her point of view. Ethan had made it sound like such fun, though, that she'd naturally adopted that tone, and Amy had wholeheartedly approved. In truth, writing the article had turned out to be much more fun than the makeover experience itself.

After yesterday's shocking revelations, Heather was only too glad to end the week on an up note.

"Oh, why not?" she muttered, turning to the computer keyboard.

Just as she hit the enter button, Brenda waltzed through the door.

"Thought I'd better check something out."

Heather spun around in her chair.

"What's that, Bren?"

"The Tennessee Media Awards Gala tomorrow night."

Heather groaned.

"Oh, no! I completely forgot!"

"Well, that answers one question," Brenda drawled. "The next one is…" Brenda dropped the wisecracking attitude, her gaze openly curious. "Will Jeremy still be your escort?"

The news that Jeremy had resigned as the president of Hamilton Media had swept through the building like wildfire yesterday. Today the gossip was all about *why*. No one had come right out and asked, but the whole family knew that was the question on everyone's mind. As a result, Tim and Amy had collaborated on a formal announcement for both the paper and the magazine. It had been published in this morning's *Dispatch*, and said simply that, deeply affected by Wallace's illness, Jeremy had resigned in order to pursue personal goals.

That, of course, did not explain why Jeremy would not be escorting her to the regional media awards banquet tomorrow evening.

Heather doubted that he'd even remembered. She hadn't, and she was receiving an award for feature editing.

She cringed at the thought of attending the gala now that Jeremy's resignation was public knowledge, especially alone, but Jeremy had made it clear that he needed some time to himself. Apparently he was trying to decide what he was going to do with the astonishing information that he was not, after all, the son of the man whom he'd strived his whole life to please.

Heather couldn't blame him. Had she been standing in Jeremy's shoes, she'd have needed some time apart to reconcile this new reality, too.

She'd let him know that she loved him unconditionally and would be keeping him in her prayers. He had looked so lost and forlorn that she didn't have the heart to ask him about escorting her to the ceremony. So it looked as if she'd be attending the gala alone.

For a moment, Heather toyed with the notion of not going at all, but now was not the time for that sort of self-indulgence. The family and the business needed her to be there, putting as normal a face as possible on things. Besides, she was receiving an award.

Heather shook her head at Brenda.

"Jeremy's not available, I'm afraid."

"Shall I turn in the extra meal ticket then?" Brenda wanted to know.

Heather sighed. She'd rather take a beating than go to that banquet alone, but it was too late to ask Chris to take her. He was the only Hamilton man who did not own a tuxedo, and it was too late to arrange for a rental. She supposed that she could appeal to Tim, but the weight of his new responsibilities, when added to those he'd already been carrying, were onerous enough.

"I guess," she said in answer to Brenda's question. "There are never enough meal tickets for those things."

"No kidding," Ethan put in. "I couldn't believe it when they told me that mere photographers assigned to cover the event would not get dinner."

Heather blinked at him. "That's right! You're covering the awards ceremony for both the paper and the magazine."

"Which makes me the perfect escort," Ethan said, sitting up straight in his chair and spreading his hands.

Heather laughed delightedly—but briefly.

"Oh, but…the dinner's black-tie."

"Well, I wasn't planning to go in my jeans," Ethan told her wryly.

"You've already rented a tux," she surmised on a sigh of pure relief.

Cocking an eyebrow, he folded his arms.

"I prefer my own clothing, thank you very much. It's not the first black-tie event I've attended, you know, even without the camera."

Heather bit her lip, embarrassed at her presumption, but then he cracked a wide grin and she knew that she was forgiven.

"Ethan, I don't know how to thank you."

"Dinner ought to do it," he told her, eyes twinkling. "I'm told they actually put out a pretty good spread."

"They do. That's one reason the meal tickets are so dear."

"Well, then, we're both benefiting."

Heather beat back a swell of delight, forcing herself to address the particulars of the arrangement.

"Let's see. The dinner starts at seven, with the awards ceremony around eight-thirty or so, so I suppose we ought to pick you up in the limo about six. Will that work for you?"

Ethan stroked his shadowed chin pensively.

"Limo. Hmm. I don't know." He smiled. "I guess that'll do."

"I guess!" Heather exclaimed teasingly.

"And I guess that's that," Brenda quipped, wiping her hands together in the time-honored expression of accomplishment. Grinning ear to ear, she left them.

Ethan placed his palms on the top of Heather's desk and rose.

"If that was the last caption, then we're through here."

Heather shoved a pen and notepad at him.

"Not until you've given me your address."

She could always check the personnel records for it, but this way would be easier.

Bending over the desk, he jotted down the address and suggested the easiest route for the limo.

"See you then," he told her, tossing down the pen and strolling for the door.

"See you then."

He paused, turning a glance over his shoulder, to say,

"You know, the timing of this is perfect. Knock 'em dead, kiddo. Give them a great big dose of the new you, and no one will even remember you were supposed to be on your big brother's arm. I guarantee it."

He gave her a wink and went on his way.

Heather sat back in her chair, dismayed afresh.

Picturing the dress that she'd intended to wear, she inwardly cringed and made a sudden, impulsive decision. Looked like she was going to be doing some last-minute shopping. And that wasn't all.

Reaching for the telephone, she punched in her sister's extension. "Tell me the name of your hairdresser again."

"Turquoise is one color flattering to every complexion," the prim clerk insisted, just as Heather emerged from the dressing room in rich cherry red.

Heather bit her lip as the clerk walked around her, eyeing the fit of the dress as if taking Heather's measurements with her eyes. Abruptly, she turned and rehung the turquoise gown on the wheeled rack.

"Well," she said, folding her arms. "It appears we've found your color."

Heather tucked her hair back behind her ears and turned this way and that. She'd tried on every possible gown in the Engel's department store evening wear section, and it was just possible that her "personal shopper" effused over this one from sheer desperation.

"I don't know. It's awfully...bold."

"But, Miss Hamilton, you can pull it off," the trim woman assured her, reaching down to twitch the full, frothy skirt into place. "Just look how your hair and eyes glow."

Next to hers, the clerk's image in the mirror appeared wan and colorless. Heather suspected that the woman twisted her own pale hair up and wore such nondescript clothing on purpose, so as not to outshine the clientele. It worked, at least in this instance.

The cut of the gown was simple and elegant. Fitted to below the waist, the strapless bodice hugged Heather's slender curves with loving precision before the skirt flared to soft, winsome fullness. Still, despite the yards of shimmering fabric, Heather felt strangely bare. Tentatively, she touched the birthmark on the curve of her collarbone, remembering that Ethan had chosen a strapless bright red dress for her at the photo shoot.

"Ooh," the saleswoman said, snapping her fingers, "do you know what would set that off?"

Without waiting for an answer, she bustled away, returning just moments later.

She had in her hands what looked like a tube constructed of fine red tulle sewn to either end of a length of stretchy, skin-toned fabric. She helped Heather slide it up over her arms from the back and settle it over her shoulders. The effect was that of short, detached sleeves and a stand-up portrait collar all in one. It softened the whole effect of the bodice and added a touch of glamour, while easing her fears of being overexposed.

"I'll take it," she announced decisively, and was at once beset by fresh doubts. She wasn't the haute couture type, after all.

Fortunately, the sales clerk didn't give her a chance to change her mind, hustling her quickly through the shoe and jewelry departments and out the door with her purchases.

Heather sucked in a deep breath and mused that at this rate in a few short weeks she would make up for years of imbalance between her sisters' clothing expenditures and her own. She rationalized that in this case it was for the company's benefit, but she was too honest to let it go at that.

The truth was, she wanted to look her best for Ethan. She didn't want him to be embarrassed by the woman on his arm, even if it was a business function. She wanted, in fact, to "knock 'em dead," as he'd put it.

With that in mind, she drove over to the beauty salon and put herself in the hands of Amy's hairdresser, praying that she wouldn't regret any part of what would come of this day.

The afternoon passed in a whirlwind of busy preparations for the banquet. Heather barely had time to think, let alone stop and take careful stock of her appearance. When she did glimpse herself in the mirrors in her room and private bath, she scarcely recognized the woman who looked back at her. The elaborate twist of her hair and the tendrils that framed her face made her eyes seem enormous, her cheekbones pronounced and her mouth oddly luscious, especially after she'd gotten out her cosmetics bag and did her best to recreate the look that Sheryl, the makeup artist, had produced for the photo shoot.

After she'd lightly lined and shadowed her eyes, a touch of blush, pale pink lipstick and dark mascara completed her attempt. She didn't know what to think about the effect, and she really didn't have time to worry about it, especially since she'd promised her mother that she'd stop by the hospital on her way to the banquet.

Heather hadn't seen her father since before he'd blurted the truth of Jeremy's paternity. Whatever his reasons for doing such a thing, it was important to Heather that both of her parents, as well as her brother, know that it changed nothing so far as she was concerned. No matter what had happened thirtysomething years ago, her parents were her parents and her brother was her brother. Period.

After struggling into the necessary foundation garments, the dress and stole—or caparison, as the clerk had called it—Heather pushed her feet into daintily strapped heels with embroidered toes and clipped on her jewelry. Faux rubies dripped from her earlobes and neck in long, slender chains and wrapped four or five inches of one wrist.

She did look in the full-length mirror, but somehow she couldn't seem to take in the whole picture, concentrating instead on myriad details: the gleam of her lips, the enormity of her eyes, the birthmark at the place where her neck curved into her collarbone, tendrils of rich auburn hair, the sparkle of red tulle framing her neck and shoulders, the gleam of gold against the skin of her upper chest. She saw the nip of her waist and the swirl of chiffon about her ankles and feet, the expanse of rubies banding her wrist. She saw everything and nothing.

Confident that she'd done her best, she went out to meet the limo that already waited in front of the house.

As the driver, a familiar, portly, fiftysomething gentleman named John, opened the door for her, he murmured that she was looking fine. Heather thanked him as she ducked into the backseat and spread out her skirts.

At the hospital, she left the limo humming at the curb while she ran upstairs to her father's suite.

The sitting room was empty, so Heather tapped at the interior door and pushed it inward. Her father was watching a news program on the television encased in a large armoire at the foot of his bed. He turned his head as she entered the room. A look of wonder came over his thin face, and he switched off the television with the remote at his side.

"Now that is a sight for a sick, bored old man," he said warmly.

Heather held out her cherry red skirts and twirled on one toe.

"Think I'll do for the regional awards banquet?"

"You'll do for an audience with the queen of England," he said, reaching out a hand to her.

She laid her freshly manicured hand in his thin one and allowed him to pull her closer to the bed. The effort seemed to exhaust him, because he fell back against the pillows with a gasp.

"Where's Mom?" she asked, concerned.

"I sent her home. She hoped to get there before you left. Obviously you've missed one another. She'll be sorry about that."

"I don't have time to go back," Heather said regretfully.

"I'll let her know that you'll check in with her when you get back home. And you do that, no matter how late it is. She won't want to miss seeing you like this."

Heather smiled. "All right."

Wallace sighed, a deep melancholy settling over him. "I suppose you'll soon be leaving home, too."

"Now why would you say that?"

"Why wouldn't I? Melissa's gone off with Dean Orton to only God knows where."

"How do you know that?"

"Christopher did some checking at your mother's request."

Heather lifted an eyebrow.

"Seems that having a policeman in the family comes in handy after all."

Wallace made a face and chose to concentrate on Melissa rather than Chris.

"What does she see in that long-haired, cowboy-booted scallywag?"

Heather could only shake her head.

"Escape, I imagine."

"Escape." Wallace snorted. "Defection, pure and simple. Just like Jeremy," he muttered.

Heather made an exasperated sound. "What did you expect, Dad? Did you think he'd thank you for telling him that you're not his father after thirty-five years of living as your son?"

Wallace's face appeared wooden, but that only accentuated the pain in his eyes.

"It seemed like the right thing at the time. I love Jeremy, I really do. He's my son in every way that counts, but Tim... The rightful heir should be acknowledged somehow, don't you think?"

"What makes Tim any more your heir than the rest of us?" Heather wanted to know. "The fact that he agrees with you?"

A frown pulled at Wallace's face.

"I'll admit that's a part of it. I'm concerned about the direction that the company's been taking, but I regret how I said it. It shouldn't have come out in anger, but the truth is, Heather, keeping that secret has done a great deal of harm. In an odd way it may have done as much damage to Tim as Jeremy. My dilemma's always been how to be fair to both of them."

"I'll agree that the truth is always best," Heather said carefully, "and I do trust that Jeremy's faith will help him weather this shock, but as I see it, there's only one way to be fair to both Tim and Jeremy, and that's to love them equally. You have to make each of them understand how much you love them."

Wallace smiled sadly.

"You're right, honey. You usually are."

He moved sideways in the bed, giving her his full attention once more in an attempt to change the subject, as she knew very well.

"You're certainly right about that dress. I never realized how truly stunning you are until tonight."

Pleased with the sincerity of the compliment, Heather bent and pressed a kiss to his temple.

"Thank you, Daddy."

He waved her toward the door, saying, "Enjoy yourself tonight. You've earned it." Then he lifted his head, looking her right in the eye. "But don't let any young scoundrel charm you out of your good sense."

Heather laughed. He'd been saying that to her and her sisters since their teen years.

"Have I ever?"

He smiled and said, "No, thank the good Lord, you

have not. Which makes you not only beautiful but brilliant."

Beaming, Heather went out with new confidence. Nevertheless, when she knocked on Ethan's apartment door some ten minutes later, her stomach was tumbling nervously.

"Coming!" Ethan called, stepping over a box of books in his stocking feet on his way to the door.

He clipped the black cummerbund and twisted it around with one hand as he reached for the doorknob with the other.

"Tell Miss Hamilton that I'm running a little late but I'll be right down," he said, turning away even as he pulled the door inward.

"Miss Hamilton says to take your time," answered a familiar feminine voice.

Ethan whirled around, nearly falling over the box that he'd never gotten around to unpacking. He nearly fell again when he got a look at the vision standing in his doorway.

"Sweet, merciful—" He broke off, gulping back what he belatedly realized might be an offensive remark. "I—I mean… Wow."

Heather pressed a neatly manicured hand to her slender middle, laughing breathlessly.

"Thanks. I was afraid it might be, you know, too much."

"No! No, it's... You're gorgeous. **Perfect.**"

She looked every inch like the wealthy, prominent social princess that she was, actually, and suddenly, despite the tuxedo, he'd never felt more like the penniless, rootless army brat.

He glanced uneasily around his small, bland efficiency apartment with its rented furniture, battered boxes and bare counters. A motel room would have been more personal and less cluttered. Heather stood uncomfortably on the edge of the chaos, as out of place as a priceless ruby in a bird's nest.

"Just, uh, give me one moment," he mumbled, backing toward the bathroom where he'd left his jacket and freshly buffed shoes.

As he stomped into the shoes, he gave his chin and jaw a quick perusal even though he'd shaved not fifteen minutes earlier. After smoothing his hair back from his face with his comb, he reached for the jacket that hung on the back of the door.

He tossed on the jacket, quickly tugged at the French cuffs of his blazingly white shirt and checked the simple gold links at his wrists. Pushing out a rushed breath, he stared at himself in the mirror, wondering what on earth he was doing, escorting a Hamilton daughter to a formal affair.

"Work," he muttered. "Just another assignment."

Right. And Heather Hamilton was *just* another woman.

"Danes, you dummy," he said, grinning because

he couldn't be unhappy that the most beautiful woman in the room was going to be on his arm.

Even if the occasion was nothing more than a glorified photo shoot.

Chapter Eight

"Can I get you anything else, Miss Hamilton?"

Heather smiled as she took the water glass from the features editor of a large and prominent state-wide publication.

"No, thank you, but it's very kind of you to ask."

She'd known the gentleman in question for six years, and he'd never before given her more than a distracted smile and a nod. Perhaps it was the award that she was receiving tonight. More likely it was the alteration in her appearance.

Another gentleman touched her elbow, asking, "How is your father, Miss Hamilton?"

"As well as can be expected, thank you."

"And your mother?" asked another.

"She has her hands full with Dad, as you might expect," Heather answered drolly.

That brought a ripple of polite laughter.

"Somehow I think she's up to the challenge," said

a fourth fellow. "You may tell your father for me that he's a lucky old dog. Nora is a woman of rare quality, a true Southern belle."

"Which explains how old Wallace could produce such beautiful daughters," said the features editor.

Heather inclined her head in acknowledgment of the compliment and smiled behind her glass. Cool water slid down her throat, and Ethan Danes swam into her field of vision. She lowered the glass to find him offering his arm, a smile lurking in those dark, dark eyes.

"If you gentlemen will excuse us, Miss Hamilton's presence has been requested at the head table."

As he led her away, she looked a question at him.

"No," he said, grinning, "it was not a ploy to separate you from your admirers. How does it feel, by the way, to be the belle of the ball?"

"Oh, I'm not—" She broke off when he sent her an admonishing look.

"Admit it," he teased. "I was right. Every eye in this room has been on you since we walked through the door. I have to beat my way through guys stacked six deep just to get near you."

She laughed. "I'll confess that I've drawn more attention than I expected to."

"And you've enjoyed it."

"And I've enjoyed it," she conceded. "As you well know, since you've garnered your fair share of attention from the ladies present."

"But of course," he said with mock sincerity, drawing

a small camera from his pocket. "Women decked out in all their finery love having their pictures taken."

"Oh, please."

He grinned, and she gave his forearm a playful swat.

"Now what is this about the head table?"

He sobered. Drawing her to a stop, he brought his hands up to clasp her upper arms.

"Now, don't panic," he told her softly, bending his head near hers. "You can do this."

Her heart sped up to triple speed.

"Do what?"

His hands squeezed gently, offering encouragement.

"I overheard the master of ceremonies and the president of the guild talking before they asked me to locate you. It seems that your brother had agreed to say a few words tonight, and since he's not here, they mean to ask you to fill in."

Heather blinked. Then she sent a horrified glance around the enormous room.

At its far end, the dais, dead center in a line of rectangular tables that measured at least thirty feet in length, stood in front of a huge video screen that would project her image ten times larger than life. Round tables covered in crisp white cloths dotted the expanse of deep red carpet in front of the dais. People in evening wear wandered among the chairs and elaborate flower arrangements, chatting and sipping beverages. Soon they would be sitting down to dine, and then the official ceremonies would begin. And they wanted *her* to speak with less than an hour's notice in front of all these people?

She started to shake her head, but Ethan gently shook her, capturing her gaze with his.

"You. Can. Do. This," he said again. "Just collect your thoughts, figure out what you want to say…"

He stopped and stared at her, tilting his head, and suddenly everything about him softened, relaxed. Confidence gleamed in his eyes. Confidence in her.

"Say a prayer," he instructed. "Right now. Just close those big brown eyes and say a prayer. Then think about what you want to say to these people."

Staring up into his dark gaze, Heather found the strength to beat back the panic and think logically. Someone—Ethan and apparently the master of ceremonies and the president of a professional guild—believed that she could address all these people, that she had something of value to say to her professional peers. A smile took hold inside of her. It spread and it spread until it broke out on her face. Obediently, she bowed her head.

"Thank You, Father," she whispered, "for sending Ethan to show me what I can be. It's so much more than I assumed! I can do this if You want me to, so if You want me to, give me the words to say and the ability to say them. Amen."

She opened her eyes and smiled up at Ethan.

"That's my girl," he said, returning her smile with

such warmth that for a moment she actually believed that she was something special to him.

He began once more to steer her toward the head table at the other end of the room. As he did so, words began to float through her mind.

We at Hamilton Media have always considered ourselves richly blessed, and being recognized here by you tonight is just another reason to be grateful.

Heather posed with the statuette in her hands.

Made of heavy crystal with letters of gold, it depicted a curled page with the words "Knowledge, Joy, Power and Privilege" written upon it. Heather's name was engraved on its base, along with that of the magazine, her job title and the date. This year's winners in all categories clustered around her for this final, formal portrait. Heather focused on Ethan and smiled.

As soon as the flashes ceased, her neighbors began to congratulate one another. Nearly every one of them took the time to mention her speech.

"That's exactly the way I see it."

"Responsibility and privilege with a lot of fun thrown in, that's this gig in a nutshell, isn't it?"

"Never heard it said better."

"Much better than that long-winded keynote speaker."

Since it was the "long-winded keynote speaker" himself who said the last, Heather had to laugh.

She goggled when the guild president said, "I know

one young lady's name who should be on the short list for next year's keynote speaker."

"Dream team," someone else suggested. "Wallace and Heather Hamilton."

Standing off to one side, Ethan grinned and gave that idea two thumbs up.

Heather thanked everyone and extricated herself as quickly as possible, joining Ethan. Her cheeks ached from so much smiling, but she couldn't seem to stop.

He slipped an arm about her shoulders, teasing in a singsong voice, "I told you so."

"And you do enjoy it," she accused playfully, drilling a finger into his chest.

"Hey, might as well, since it's not that often I'm actually right."

He trapped that hand against his shirt front, then spun on one heel, keeping her hand in his and throwing his free arm around her waist.

"Couldn't prove it by me," she said, skipping along as he swept her out of the Tennessee Ballroom.

Moving rapidly, they twisted and turned their way through the Opryland Hotel convention center to the South Plaza, where the limo waited. Ethan waved back the driver and opened the rear passenger door for Heather, then dropped down beside her as she scooted across the seat.

She quickly slipped off her shoes. Sitting, standing for short periods and strolling around the room in

heels was one thing, rushing through crowded corridors was another. Putting her head back, she sighed
in relief and wiggled her toes.

"I cannot believe I pulled it off."

"I wish you could've seen yourself on that giant
screen," he told her. "I ordered the video, by the way.
Thought your parents might like to see the new star
of the family at work."

She lifted her head, surprised and pleased. "That
was sweet of you. Be sure to expense it."

"No way. Then I don't get to keep it."

She tilted her head, asking, "Why would you want
to keep it?"

His expression seemed to say, for a moment, that
the answer should be obvious, but then a shutter of
sorts seemed to come down. The next thing she knew,
that cheeky grin was back.

"It's proof that I am, on occasion, right."

Heather laughed. "You do intend to savor that I-
told-you-so, don't you?"

He narrowed his eyes, murmuring, "I seem to
remember at least a couple of those tonight. I think
it's a new record, actually."

Laughing together, they verbally relived the whole
affair, from the first shocked recognition of the Hamiltons' middle daughter to the last congratulations, with
a few interesting personal notes contributed by Ethan.
By the time they arrived at Ethan's apartment building,
Heather felt relaxed and happy but also exhausted.

She wondered if she should put her shoes back on and walk him to his door, but that hardly seemed appropriate. He wasn't likely to get lost or accosted on his way to his apartment, after all. On the other hand sending him off with a wave and a "See ya!" didn't seem right, either, not after everything that he'd done for her.

He seemed oddly reticent about their parting, too, sitting for a moment with one hand on the door handle and the other splayed against his thigh. Finally, he smiled and leaned forward as if preparing to exit the car.

"Well, you probably want to soak your feet and get some rest, so I'll—"

She laid a hand on his forearm, freezing him in place.

"Ethan, I just want to say…well, thank you doesn't adequately cover it, but what else do you say to someone who's done as much for another person as you have for me?"

He settled back, frowning a bit.

"I guess I don't quite get what you mean by that."

"How could you not?" she asked, genuinely perplexed. "First, convincing me to have the makeover."

"That was Ellen's idea. I just—"

"Then," she interrupted firmly, "driving Amy and me to the hospital."

"Anyone would have—"

"And taking me to look for Jeremy."

"—done the same thing under the circumstances."

"And helping with the article. And coffee." She chuckled. "Not to mention the ice cream. Then tonight—"

He shook his head, protesting, "I was going anyway, okay? Why not go with the best-looking gal in the office? And I got a meal out of the deal, filet mignon, no less."

She sat back, her hands folded in her lap. "Do you know what I'd have done when they asked me to speak if you hadn't been there tonight?"

"You'd have managed."

"I'd have lost that delicious filet mignon all over the dais, that's what I'd have done," she insisted.

"You'd have managed," he repeated. "Because that's what you always do. Whatever it takes, whatever is expected by your family, your peers, the magazine. No matter how uncomfortable it makes you, no matter how uncertain you are of success, you give it your all. That's just who you are."

"Maybe," she said, giving her head a doubtful little shake, "but you've given me confidence and comfort and…whatever it is I needed at the time, and I want you to know how much I appreciate that."

"I've just been in the right place at the right time lately, and I've seen that faith of yours pull you through more difficult circumstances in the past week than most folks face in a lifetime." He looked down then, and a muscle flexed in the hollow of his jaw. "I'm not sure how that works, frankly, but for you it does."

"Not just for me," she told him softly. "For anyone who believes that God cares enough to concern Himself about our lives, for anyone who trusts Him."

Ethan shook his head.

"You have something special going on there, something I don't even understand."

"It's nothing you can't have, Ethan."

One corner of his mouth hitched up at that.

"Aw, I'm not like you, Heather." He shifted uncomfortably, and suddenly that cocky grin was back in place. "Listen, if I've been of help, then I'm glad, okay? But don't make it into anything it isn't. And give yourself some credit, will you? I may have played escort this evening—not much effort since I was going anyway—and I may have reminded you how to find your strength, but that was all you up there tonight." He sat forward and tapped her on the end of the nose with a forefinger for emphasis. "All you."

Heather laughed, feeling a swell of confident delight.

"All you," he said again, leaning toward her.

His fingers brushed at a wisp of hair floating about her face, and for some reason she caught her breath, his gaze holding hers.

"I'd better let you go," he whispered.

She nodded without ever taking her eyes from his. "Good night, Ethan."

"Good night," he said, and then his eyelids dropped. Her own snapped shut just as his lips brushed across hers, coming back to settle gently for one heart-stopping moment. His fingertips stroked her cheek, and then he was sliding out of the open door and onto his feet. Bending, he gave her a wink, and then he straightened and swung the door closed on what had been, all in all, the most incredible night of her life.

She waited until Ethan had disappeared into the building before she pressed the intercom button.

"We can go now, John."

Sighing with an intense feeling of satisfaction, Heather curled her bare feet beneath her and got comfortable for the short ride home, settling deep into the corner of the limo seat. It was a comfort, she realized dreamily, that emanated from inside out. Leaning her head against the night-blackened window, she watched the softly glowing lights of Davis Landing sweep by amidst the subtly limned shapes of buildings and trees and other vehicles.

The thought came that inside this skin of hers was a good place to be, a very good place, indeed. Even if Ethan hadn't meant that kiss in any romantic sense, she had no regrets. He'd helped her see who she could be, who God surely meant her to be, and it was so much more than she'd ever dared to imagine.

She realized now that her own insecurities had placed limits on God. His will was much broader and richer than she'd once assumed, and knowing that somehow made it even easier to trust Him.

Surely God had a reason for allowing her father to

fall ill, for letting secrets be spilled after so many years, for putting Ethan in Jeremy's place tonight. She wasn't self-centered enough to think that it was all about her, of course, but if she'd learned anything lately, it was that God could use anyone and anything—even illness and old regrets, as well as new beginnings—for His ends.

It would be foolish and ungrateful to read more into Ethan's good-night kiss than he'd meant. She wouldn't ruin this sense of peace and contentment by yearning for what she obviously was not meant to have.

Those unpacked boxes in Ethan's apartment made it clear that he was not the guy for her. She hadn't been able to imagine leaving Davis Landing all those years ago when her college love had made it a condition of his marriage proposal, and she still couldn't.

Ethan, on the other hand, was not the sort to put down roots anywhere.

No, he was not the man with whom she could build a future, but she was grateful that he might well have made a future love possible for her. That was enough reason to close her eyes and thank God.

Brenda stood up behind her desk and applauded as Heather strode closer.

Pausing to look down at herself, Heather took note of her sleeveless shirtwaist dress with its soft, bias-cut skirt. A crisp, airy black and white print splashed with dabs of yellow, red and green, it was tied at the waist with a flirty yellow grosgrain ribbon. Green sandals and a red bangle bracelet completed the ensemble. She thought it feminine, stylish and summery, perfect for a Monday morning in late June, but not her most praiseworthy new garment. Parking a hand on her hip, she looked to Brenda.

"Okay, I give up. Why the applause?"

"Honey," Brenda said, copying Heather's stance, "I have seen the video and the photos."

The hand slid off Heather's hip.

"Of Saturday night?"

"That cutie of yours has shown them all over the office already. Honestly, you'd think *he* was the one who made the speech and took home the prize."

Heather got stuck way back at "that cutie of yours." It was that last word that had her shaking her head.

"Oh, Ethan's not…that is, I assume you're talking about Ethan?"

"Who else?"

"Right. He, um, was the photographer, after all."

"Not to mention your date."

Heather lifted a finger.

"No. Not my 'date.' Ethan's my, er, coworker. We, that is, *he* was on assignment."

"Ri-i-ight. Assignment."

"That's all it was, Brenda, business."

"Mmm-hmm, so you and the shutterbug are not an item?" her assistant asked skeptically.

"Of course not! We're *coworkers*." Heather thought of that kiss—in truth, she couldn't seem to stop thinking about it—and with heated cheeks quickly amended, "Friendly coworkers. But *just* coworkers."

Obviously deflated, Brenda pulled out her desk chair and plopped down into it.

"Maybe someone ought to tell Ethan that."

"Ethan doesn't have to be told," Heather insisted. "He's not interested in me like that. I'm not his type. For one thing, I'm planted here in Davis Landing, and he's footloose and fancy-free, ready to pick up and leave at the drop of a hat. The man's been here six months and he still hasn't unpacked!"

"He took you to the awards banquet," Brenda argued.

"We were both going so we went together. That's all."

"Hmmph." Brenda folded her arms, obviously disappointed in having her theories about a flowering romance nipped in the bud. "And how do you know he hasn't unpacked?"

Heather rolled her eyes.

"I saw the boxes when I picked him up for the banquet, and actually I'm not sure if he hasn't unpacked or if he's packing to go and just hasn't mentioned it yet. Either way, I'd have to be out of touch with reality to think Ethan Danes was going to stick around permanently."

"That's too bad," Brenda grumbled. "You make such a cute couple."

"Cute does not a couple make," Heather told her primly. "Now if you'll excuse me, I have work to do."

"I'll say you do," Brenda drawled, shoving an assignment sheet at her. "They want stories for both the magazine and the paper. According to Amy, your brother thinks that the awards ceremony is good publicity for Hamilton Media. They're already going over the pictures with Ethan, deciding who gets what, but as you've pointed out, he's a photographer, not a writer, so guess who gets to compose both pieces?"

Heather grabbed the assignment sheet and glared at it. Why was it that lately she couldn't get her own work done for writing about herself?

Setting aside the obvious workplace speculation about her and Ethan's relationship, she went into her office and shut the door.

It was an extraordinarily busy day.

Heather rushed from meeting to meeting, and everyone she met had something to say about the photos or video from Saturday evening and the way that Ethan was showing them around. Obviously he didn't realize the kind of speculation that his behavior was causing. She knew that it had more to do with professional accomplishment and his enjoyment of having predicted Saturday night's success than any romantic attachment, but no one else seemed to understand that.

They clearly needed to discuss the situation, but she didn't want to add grist to the rumor mill by seeking out Ethan. She was pleased, then, to meet him in the stairwell on her way back upstairs from the newspaper offices after having personally delivered her story on the awards banquet to Ed Bradshaw, managing editor of the *Dispatch*.

"Hi!" Ethan greeted her with a broad smile.

He was coming down as she was going up and slipped past her to pause on the step below, bringing their gazes level.

"Got time to grab a cup of coffee?"

Heather knew that being seen at Betty's with him just now would not be wise, so she shook her head.

"Sorry. Crazy day."

"Yeah, I hear that. Did you get the copy of the video that I left with Brenda earlier?"

"Yes. Thanks."

"The photos turned out great. Half my day's been spent trying to choose the best shots for the magazine and the paper. We're going with the head shot in the paper, by the way, and two full-length photos in the magazine. The group photo of the award recipients will be used in both, but downsized in the magazine."

"So I've heard."

Ethan's smile dimmed. He tilted his head and leaned a hip against the stair rail. "What's wrong?"

She drew a deep breath, choosing her words carefully. "There's been some speculation going around."

"Oh? What about?"

"Us."

He bowed his head, looking up at her from beneath the crag of his brow. "Ah. And this is a problem because…?"

For a moment she was confounded.

"B-because it's wrong!"

His gaze moved past her and then dropped. "Yeah, well, you know how offices are. Gossip is as inevitable as payday. Right and wrong doesn't seem to be much of a factor."

"That's not what I mean."

He settled back and folded his arms, his gaze blank, expression bland. "What do you mean then?"

She heard an odd note in his voice. Was it challenge or offence? No, that didn't make any sense. He had no reason to be hurt or angry.

"I've tried explaining to a couple of people that we aren't dating," she said.

A muscle flexed in the hollow of his jaw.

"Saturday night obviously was not a date," he agreed, "strictly speaking."

She nodded and went on. "I've pointed out that we have nothing in common. Well, besides the magazine, of course. But everyone still assumes…" She shrugged. "Maybe if we stop, you know, talking about the awards banquet or whatever, and if we aren't seen in each other's company too much, maybe then the gossip will die down."

Ethan lifted his head and looked at her with shuttered eyes.

"Is that so important?"

"Well, yes," she said hesitantly, confused because she couldn't quite peg his attitude. "I mean, right now, given everything that's going on in my family, gossip is the last thing we need, really, especially if it isn't even true."

He swallowed, but when he spoke his tone was light, droll, casual, much as always, in fact.

"I'm sure you're right. Okay, then. I'll see you around." With a quick smile, he turned and headed on down the stairs.

A confusing mix of disappointment, regret and, oddly enough, guilt swamped her. Worse was a sudden feeling of abandonment.

She frowned as she watched him descend the remainder of the stairs and push through the door into the hallway that led to the lobby. She didn't understand any of what she was feeling. Where was the relief that she ought to be experiencing, the gratitude for his understanding and support? And why did she feel that she'd just lost her best friend?

The remainder of the day passed at the same furious pace with which it had begun, but Heather couldn't seem to concentrate, making everything a struggle.

When she finally got home, she practically fell into a tub of hot water and bubbles in an effort to soak away the day's tensions. Afterward, she threw on a pair of sweats and went downstairs, somewhat surprised to find herself at loose ends. With her mother practically camping at the hospital, Melissa gone, Jeremy holed up in his apartment and Chris, Tim and Amy off doing their own things, she considered calling a friend.

Just the day before one of her girlfriends at church had remarked that they hadn't spent any time together in weeks. Yet Heather was reluctant to go out in her comfy sweats or take the effort to trade them for presentable clothing. So after an early dinner with only Vera Mae for company, Heather carried a favorite book of poetry up to her room, switched on some classical music and held her disquiet at bay by actively contemplating the future.

For the first time in a very long while, she wondered if she might not find someone with whom to share her life, after all. Ethan had shown her that she was not as resigned to a single life as she'd once believed. She thought about that kiss and finally admitted to herself that she truly did want to marry and have children. Not with Ethan, of course. What she'd said to Brenda was all true, every word, and after their discussion in the stairwell she was more painfully aware of that fact than ever.

No matter how special it had felt to her, that little kiss had obviously meant nothing to Ethan; his easy acceptance of her suggestion that they not be seen together or talk about the awards banquet anymore had reinforced that quite firmly. The kiss may have been just one more friendly gesture on his part, but it had shown her as nothing else could have that she deeply yearned for a real love, a life mate and a family of her own.

She thanked God that He hadn't let her drift along in that state until it was too late. Even if the discovery felt a bit like a hand or a foot coming back to tingling life after having had the circulation cut off for too long, it was better to know herself and face her own needs and desires prayerfully than to live in denial of them. She could only wonder what else she had been in denial about.

If Ethan had been the tool whom God had used to wake her up to her own feelings, she was grateful. She would not be so selfish as to expect more from the relationship or so foolish as to spin fairy tales in her mind about a possible future for them when they were so clearly mismatched. He was the office hunk, smart and brave and adventurous enough to move in and out of jobs, cities and lives as impulse dictated. She was a hometown girl for whom faith and family were more important than adventure.

It made her sad to realize that Ethan might never be comfortable with family ties, but faith was portable, and she earnestly prayed that one day Ethan would understand that. He had helped her to be the woman that she had once secretly been afraid to be— more the woman, she now believed, whom God meant her to be. She asked only that she be allowed to help him understand that God loved him, too, and could be trusted anywhere and at any time.

Chapter Nine

Heather didn't so much as lay eyes on Ethan Danes for the next two days, and then on Thursday she arrived early at the office to find Ethan pacing in the foyer, a rolled newspaper in one hand. At once she knew that something was wrong. The Gordons reinforced her judgment with wary nods.

"Morning, Miss Heather," Herman said.

"How is Mr. Jeremy?" Louise asked.

Not Mr. Wallace, but Mr. Jeremy. Heather's intuition screamed *catastrophe,* and she turned instinctively to Ethan for answers.

"Come with me," he said grimly.

One hand on her upper arm, he literally walked her to the elevator, stood her in the corner and hit the button that closed the door. He did not, however, send them up to the next floor.

"What is it?" she finally asked.

"This morning's *Observer*," he answered ominously, unrolling the newspaper and showing it to her.

Jeremy's photo covered two columns beneath the headline, "Hamilton Media President Out!" The subtitle read, "Out of a Job and Out of the Family."

Heather's heart dropped.

"Oh, no!"

She quickly scanned the story, which began with a reported sighting of Jeremy and Timothy engaged in a shouting match at the local hospital where Wallace Hamilton was known to be awaiting a bone marrow transplant. It went on to say that Jeremy had left or "been ousted from" his position after it had been revealed that he was "in all probability" not Wallace's biological child. According to the story, records proved that Jeremy was born only three months after Wallace Hamilton wed the former Nora McCarthy and eight months after the death of her former fiancé, Paul Anderson.

Mention was made of the Hamilton family's standing in the community, including the fact that they were prominent members of a number of civic and professional organizations at both the local and state levels, as well as the Davis Landing Country Club and Northside Community Church in Hickory Mills. The article then devolved into speculation about the state of Wallace's health and whether he was settling "personal matters" in preparation for his own demise.

All in all, it painted a rather sordid picture of the Hamilton family in general, but especially of Wallace, Nora, Jeremy—whose ability to lead the business was questioned—and Tim. Poor Tim was described as hard-nosed and shrewd, a "throwback" to the founder of the *Davis Landing Dispatch,* Jeremiah Hamilton, whose "ruthless competitiveness" was, according to the *Observer,* "well-known."

As the possible ramifications of having family scandal reported by a competitor began to sink in, Heather could only moan and collapse back against the wall of the elevator. Thinking quickly, she hit upon what seemed to be the most logical question to ask.

"Where did they get this?"

"It wasn't from me."

Momentarily confused, she looked up into Ethan's worried eyes.

"I promise you," he vowed, "I never said a word to anyone about this."

She blinked. The very idea of Ethan giving this story to the *Observer* was too ridiculous to even contemplate, and she dismissed it out of hand, murmuring, "Of course you didn't."

But it had to have come from someone outside of the family, someone they trusted enough to give the truth, someone like…Vera Mae?

The talkative cook and housekeeper would never intentionally hurt the family, but she might have confided in someone else, her niece or a friend.

Or Chris might have mentioned it to his roommate and best friend, Jason Welsh. Heather shook her head. Jason was practically one of the family. Besides, he would never spread rumors.

Maybe someone had simply overheard, a nurse or orderly at the hospital, perhaps.

Or maybe it had happened at the Bakeshoppe. She and Amy had discussed the situation over a cup of coffee only last Friday.

Heather closed her eyes. The possibilities were varied and numerous. It was impossible to know at this point how the information had leaked, and what really mattered now was what this would do to her family.

Wallace was already eaten up with guilt over having revealed Jeremy's parentage in anger, and in his weakened physical state, he might well lose even more ground when he found out about this.

And Nora! Her dignified, gracious mother would be appalled to have her personal history splattered all over the front page of the *Observer.*

Not to mention what this would do to Jeremy!

And Tim. Perhaps he was competitive, but ruthless? Never.

None of the Hamiltons would escape this fiasco un-scathed, Heather realized.

"I have to speak to my mother," she said, reaching forward to punch the elevator button that would send the car to the second floor. "I can't believe this is happening," she whispered, crushing the paper in her hands.

Ethan slid an arm around her shoulders. "I'm so sorry."

She nodded, eyes misting. It felt perfectly natural to turn into him, to lean against his strength.

"Thank you for bringing this to me."

"I wish I could fix it." He looped both arms about her and hugged her close. "Just know that I'm here if you need me. I mean that. If I can do anything…"

She yielded to the temptation to turn her face into the fold of his neck and return his embrace. In that moment she had no doubt that he would be there for her, that he would do all in his power to be of aid.

It only seemed right that it should be so, despite what she had said to Brenda about them being nothing more than coworkers. Somehow, without her quite knowing even how it had happened, they had become more than that.

Ethan Danes was her friend, and God knew how badly she needed one just then.

Ethan picked up his sandwich and opened his mouth to take another bite when one of his table-mates said, "Food for the vultures."

Ethan looked down at the sandwich in his hands. "What was that?"

"Not that," said one of the guys, a reporter with the *Dispatch*. "He's talking about her."

With a jerk of his chin he drew Ethan's attention to the window of the Bakeshoppe and the tableau unfolding beyond it.

"Oh, no," Ethan muttered, dropping the sandwich to the plate and rising. "Take care of that, will you?" he asked the three other men at the table, waving at the mostly uneaten sandwich. "I'll settle up with you later."

"Sure," one of them said, "we'll take care of your lunch."

"While you take care of her," added another.

Ethan shot a quelling glance over one shoulder, but then he was at the door and yanking it open. He hit the sidewalk at a run, sprinting across the street.

A pickup threw on its brakes and honked at him, but he ignored it, his attention fixed on Heather as she tried to fight her way through the mob of reporters and photographers who had been holding vigil on the sidewalk in front of the Hamilton Building since midmorning.

"That's it. That's it!" he shouted, elbowing and sliding his way through the crowd. Heather's pleading glance was all the permission he needed to slip his arms around her protectively.

A reporter from one of the local Nashville television stations stuck a microphone in Heather's face. "Miss Hamilton, is it true that your father's dying?"

"Has your mother said whether or not Paul Anderson fathered her son?" another reporter shouted.

Ethan could feel her trembling. Anger flashed through him, especially at the photographers who were snapping away at Heather's huddled, distraught figure as if they couldn't see how upset she was. It was an entirely new perspective for him, one he would never forget.

"Miss Hamilton has nothing to say," he announced loudly. "This is a private family matter that no self-respecting news organization would pursue."

"Does that mean the family won't be making a statement?" someone asked.

"That means, Miss Hamilton has nothing to say," Ethan reiterated, holding his palm in front of the shutter of one camera as he hustled her toward her car. Since she had her keys in her hand, he assumed that was where she was headed. "I'll drive," he told her, plucking the keys from her trembling fingers.

She didn't argue, but stepped down off the curb and let him hand her into the car. Closing her inside, he skirted the front end of the vehicle, heading for the driver's seat. As he did, he caught the eye of a photographer whom he knew.

"I'll lodge a complaint against anyone who follows," he warned loudly. Then he leaned in close enough to ask, "Can't you keep her out of it? She doesn't have anything to do with anything."

The fellow nodded and turned toward the building once more, his camera raised as if he'd caught sight of fresh prey. Ethan quickly let himself into the car and dropped down behind the wheel. By the time he was backing the little Saab out of its assigned space, most of the reporters had turned away.

"You okay?" he asked, glancing at her worriedly.

She nodded and sighed.

"I should have known they'd be waiting."

"I'd hoped you'd stay in today," he admitted.

She sat up a little straighter. It reminded him of her mother.

"I have to get to the hospital," she said.

"What's going on there?" he asked, half expecting to hear that her father had taken a turn for the worse.

"Everyone's upset," she muttered, looking out her window.

Obviously she didn't want to talk about it, and given what had happened, he couldn't blame her. Someone was carrying tales about the Hamilton family to their competition, and he figured the less he knew the better at this point.

"You know there's going to be press at the hospital, too, don't you?"

Sighing again, she nodded and confessed, "This is why I work features at the magazine. News reporting by ambush is just not my thing. Plus, the line between news and gossip wears awfully thin sometimes, and I'm just not cut out to walk it."

"I don't think anyone at the *Observer* worries about crossing that line, frankly," Ethan told her.

"How do they justify printing that kind of stuff?"

He didn't answer that because they both knew the answer already.

Certain elements of the press had been using the public's right to know important information to justify printing whatever would nab the attention of consumers since the first broadsheet had been disseminated. Gossip and salacious stories of all sorts were often the price that print media paid to stay in business, though Ethan had to admit that Hamilton Media held itself to a pretty lofty standard when it came to what was deemed fit to print. It was one of the reasons he'd taken a job with them in the first place.

He'd heard a few complaints from some of the more ambitious staffers about Hamilton's high standards. Ellen had been one who'd considered gossip and personal exposé a legitimate way to promote her byline, so he wasn't surprised that she'd left.

When they reached the hospital, they found a phalanx of media people milling around in front of the hospital's main entrance.

"What do you say we go in through the emergency entrance?" he asked Heather.

She shrugged. "Whatever you think is best."

He drove around to the emergency area at the side of the hospital. There were a couple of guys with cameras hanging out on the sidewalk some distance away from the doors, which the hospital would, no doubt, have insisted upon. He parked the car in the first available space.

"Okay, I'm coming around to get you. I'll have you upstairs as quick as I can. Now stay close. If you walk behind me and keep your head down, they won't be able to get a printable shot. You can hang on to me if you want, all right?"

She bit her lip and pushed her hair behind her ears, staring worriedly at the hospital.

"Maybe you should just drop me off at the door."

"Okay. We can do that, so long as no emergency vehicles show up. Hospitals frown on private cars blocking access to emergency lanes. Unless you mean the front door, which I wouldn't advise."

She mulled that over.

"No, you're right. We'll do it your way. I wouldn't want to see a photo of my car blocking an emergency lane on the front page of the *Observer.* Why give them more *news?*"

"Good point," he said, getting out of the car.

He walked casually around to her side, hoping to draw less attention that way.

"Remember," he told her as she got out of the car, "right behind me, and when we get close, grab on because we'll be moving fast."

Nodding, she backed up so he could swing the door closed. Then he turned and led the way, feeling her fall in right behind him. He kept his pace as close to normal as possible, but as they drew near, one of the photographers recognized him. Theirs was a fairly small fraternity, after all. The fellow would naturally assume that Ethan was still working for the Hamiltons.

"Hang on," he said, reaching back for her hands. She clamped them at his waist. He fixed his own hands on her elbows, keeping her close, and picked up his pace.

She did a good job of staying with him, so much so that neither of the photographers could have gotten a decent shot. Once they were inside the building, he stepped aside and pushed her in front of him until they were out of sight, blocking shots from the back.

Moving quickly, they traversed the emergency room waiting area and a long corridor to the nearest elevator. It was there that Heather put out a hand. "Maybe you shouldn't come up," she suggested, and he knew from the expression on her face why she was saying it.

He considered before asking, "Is your father ill or angry?"

"Both," she stated flatly, a hint of apology in her tone.

Ethan hit the elevator button. "I'm going with you."

"You!" Wallace accused, pointing a finger at Ethan. "You're the only one outside of the family who was here that day."

"Maybe so," Ethan replied smoothly, "but it didn't come from me." He kept his shoulders back and his arms straight at his side in a pose that would have done a military man proud.

Come to think of it, Wallace seemed to remember

from one of Ethan's references that Ethan's father had been a sergeant major in the army. In fact, if he wasn't mistaken, the reference had come from a general, no less.

Wallace studied the younger man's face for a moment and found himself inclined to believe him, which probably meant that someone else was the leak, perhaps without even realizing it. Tired but determined, he turned his attention to Heather and Nora, who stood at the foot of the bed, arm in arm. Nora looked weary and distressed, Heather only marginally less so.

"Who else did you tell?" Wallace asked, mentally wincing at the tone of his own voice.

Old habits and poor health seemed to have combined to rob him of his usual sensitivity and tact. His mind was constantly going in a dozen directions at once these days. He just couldn't escape the feeling that time was running out with so much left to be done.

"No one," Nora replied, sounding puzzled and resigned at the same time, "except Vera Mae, but she wouldn't mention it to anyone."

Vera Mae, the cook and housekeeper, had been with the family since before Melissa was born. Wallace felt confident that she would not talk out of turn. He settled his gaze on Heather, who had not yet answered him.

"Well?" he prodded, and to his surprise, Ethan Danes spoke up, figuratively leaping into the breach.

"Heather would never intentionally—"

Wallace stopped him dead with a pointed glare. He knew his own daughter well enough to know that she would never intentionally do anything to harm the family. What he hadn't realized was that Danes knew her so well, too.

"No, of course she wouldn't," Wallace said, attempting to soften his tone, "but *un*intentionally, any one of us could have leaked this information."

"Not Heather," Ethan insisted. "Amy warned us both about keeping it quiet, and Heather would never do anything to hurt her family."

The protectiveness that Danes demonstrated by defending Heather's integrity surprised Wallace, but it was an emotion that he recognized and understood. He'd felt it himself from the moment he'd first laid eyes on Nora, and it put an entirely new light on Ethan Danes. Wallace wondered if the man even realized where that fierce protectiveness originated. If not, he soon would. Remembering the moment when he'd realized how deeply he loved Nora and to what lengths he was willing to go in order to protect her, Wallace felt a certain sudden kinship with the photographer and a certain bittersweet delight for Heather's sake.

"I haven't discussed this with anyone," Heather said softly, "other than the family."

Wallace nodded, accepting that at face value.

She went on somewhat hesitantly, "I did have a

late lunch with Amy at the Bakeshoppe last week, but we were the only ones there. Other than Betty, of course."

Wallace traded a look with Nora, who said, "Betty might gossip a little, but she'd never carry tales to our competition."

"And I couldn't even say that she overheard," Heather put in. "We were talking quietly."

"Well, someone's carried tales to the *Observer*," Wallace groused, collapsing back on his pillows as if suddenly exhausted, "and I, for one, don't like the idea that someone we would take into our confidence has betrayed us."

"My concern is what this is doing to Jeremy," Nora said. "He was already upset. Imagine how he must feel, seeing himself on the front page like that."

Wallace carefully made his face a blank, but pain and guilt cut deep. Even as he murmured words of caring and comfort to his wife and said goodbye to his daughter and Ethan Danes a few minutes later, he relived the moment when he'd blurted the truth.

Emotions had been running high over the accounting issues. Tim resented the fact that Jeremy would not prosecute his one-time friend, Curtis Resnick, for the embezzlement. Jeremy had argued that losing his job was enough punishment in light of the fact that Curtis had expressed remorse, begged for forgiveness and promised to make full restitution.

The real issue, however, had been whether or not

to close the accounting department and contract for accounting services outside of the company. Jeremy's and Tim's positions were diametrically opposed. Wallace had agreed with Tim; he still did. Eventually Jeremy had gotten fed up.

"It's my job and my decision!" Jeremy had shouted.

"Then maybe it shouldn't be!" Wallace had shouted back.

"What?" Jeremy had retorted. "You're going to fire me just because I don't agree with you?"

"Of course you don't agree with me," Wallace had snapped. "You're not even a real Hamilton!"

Wallace closed his eyes. He would never forgive himself for blurting it out that way. He'd tried to go back, but words could not be unsaid. It wasn't long before Jeremy had pulled the whole story out of Nora.

The shock, the horror, of learning the truth had been stamped on Jeremy's face.

"All this time," he'd said, "I told myself that you didn't really love Tim more than me, that it was just that the two of you are so much alike and that I'm more like Mom. And all along you wished I'd never been born!"

That was not true. It had never been true, and Wallace had tried to tell Jeremy so, but lately Wallace had come to realize that he had some unresolved issues about Jeremy and, more to the point, Paul Anderson.

Yes, he was concerned with the direction in which

Jeremy had taken the company, and he had been thinking a lot about whether it was fair to Tim, who was as passionate about Hamilton Media as Wallace himself, to let Jeremy stay in charge. Now he knew that it had been more than that.

Wallace did not—and never had—blamed Nora for loving Paul first. How could he, when he hadn't even met her until after Paul's death? He'd known almost instantly that Nora was the woman for him, and it hadn't mattered what had come before. Yet he couldn't forget that she had loved Paul. Losing her fiancé had affected Nora deeply. It was that grief which had driven Nora to her knees and into a personal relationship with God.

Nora had always told Wallace that she considered meeting him so soon after she'd discovered she was pregnant by Paul to be an answer to her prayers. But what if Paul had lived?

Would she have chosen him, Wallace, then?

If she could have gone back and changed it all, would she have chosen Paul and Jeremy over what she had now as Mrs. Wallace Hamilton?

Wallace truly did not doubt that she loved him and their children, but deep down he'd always wanted her to believe that he was the better man, the better husband, the better father. Now he could only pray that he'd have the opportunity to truly be the husband, father and man that God meant him to be.

In one terrible moment of weakness, he had let

long-buried fears cause harm to Jeremy when the truth
was that he had always loved that boy, always considered him his son. If anyone else had blurted the truth
to Jeremy in such a fashion, Wallace would have been
enraged. The question now was how to undo the
damage he had done…before time ran out.

Chapter Ten

Ethan had recognized the pain, guilt and desperation in Wallace's eyes, but it was the sadness in Heather's that cut through him like a knife. That was why he put his arm around her as soon as they had left her parents and were alone in the sitting room of Wallace's suite.

"I'm sorry," she whispered. "They don't know you like I do, and everyone's so upset just now."

"Including you," he said.

"Can you blame me?"

"No more than I can blame them," he answered honestly.

He wasn't so sure, really, that Wallace Hamilton did not suspect him of leaking the scandal to the competition, but in his place, Ethan thought he might feel the same way.

"They do believe you," she assured him. "I can tell."

He smiled, less concerned with their opinion than with hers.

"As long as you believe me, that's all that counts."

"I do. You know I do."

He did know, and the knowledge warmed him in a way that nothing else had ever done. Maybe that explained this growing need of his to take care of her. So much for keeping their distance from one another.

"I want you to sit down and relax a minute before we have to run the press gauntlet again, all right?"

Nodding, she let him lead her over to the sofa, where she sank down. He sat next to her.

"They'll be ready for us this time," he warned, "but it'll be okay."

She shoved her hair back, saying, "Sometimes I wonder if it'll ever be okay again."

"You can't think like that," he admonished gently, taking her hand in his. "This'll be yesterday's news before you even know it."

That won a small smile from her. "You're right."

"Hey, my record's improving," he quipped.

Instead of laughing, as he'd hoped, she suddenly gripped his hand very tightly. "Will you pray with me?" she asked.

Taken aback, Ethan could only stare at her for a moment. She looked so sad, so wounded, and he knew suddenly that he'd do just about anything to make her happy.

"Sure," he muttered, bowing his head and hoping desperately that she didn't expect him to actually say the words himself.

Heather scooted closer, and he instinctively wrapped his free arm around her.

"Father," she began in a soft voice, "first of all, thank You for Ethan. Somehow You see to it that he's always here when I need him."

That was the second time that she'd thanked God for him in his hearing, and a poignant warmth spread through him. At least God ought to know his name now, not that he'd ever given the matter much thought before.

"You always know what we need, Lord," she went on, "even before we do, better than we do. So, Father, You know that my family is hurting, especially my parents and my brother Jeremy. I don't know how to help them, Lord, and I don't understand why anyone would want to hurt them. But I know that You love them, Father, even more than I do, and I know that You have allowed these things to happen for a reason, maybe many reasons. Just please be a comfort to my brother now, and to my mom and dad, to all the family. And thank You again for Ethan and the way his friendship is such a comfort to me."

She added a plea for improvement in her father's health and mentioned her sister Melissa before closing her prayer and lifting her head.

Ethan saw a certain peace reflected in those beautiful amber eyes of hers, and to his surprise, he even felt it himself. He felt that peace and something else, something he'd never expected to feel, something more than simple friendship.

He knew how foolish that was. Her parents and family would expect Heather to choose a man from their own social group, not one of their employees, and understandably so. She was a Hamilton, and everything he owned could be packed into his truck—and often was.

But if his friendship was what Heather wanted, needed, then he would be the best friend she'd ever had for as long as she needed him to be.

The call came on Monday afternoon, not long after Heather and Amy had returned from having lunch together at the Bakeshoppe again.

When the phone rang, Heather was standing in front of her desk, wondering if she had imagined Betty's interest in her conversation with her sister or if it was a product of paranoia. Granted, having her family's secrets revealed in print had made her a bit suspicious, but she certainly had not imagined Betty's concern for Wallace's health. The woman had asked flatly how he was faring and if a bone marrow donor had been located.

The phone rang again, and Heather reached for the telephone receiver.

A few minutes later she found herself standing not in front of her own desk, but Ethan's.

"My father may be dying," she heard herself saying.

One moment Ethan was sitting there, a pencil

clamped between his teeth, photos spread out across the work table behind him, the next she was in his arms.

"I'm here," he said, turning her toward the doorway of his cubicle. "Do your siblings know?"

Somehow she couldn't think.

"I—I'm not sure. M-Mom didn't say."

As he walked her out into the corridor, one arm slanted across her back, he handed her his cell phone. Only then did she realize that she didn't have her own. It rested inside her handbag back in her office. She would not return for either. Instead, she began punching numbers into Ethan's phone as he steered her toward the exit.

Both Amy's and Tim's numbers were busy. Chris, mercifully, answered on the first ring and was already on his way to the hospital. Like her, he had been alerted by Nora, but he didn't know how far the word had spread.

Heather called Jeremy's apartment next, but he did not pick up. She hated doing it, but she left a message on his answering machine. She was dialing Melissa's cell number when the elevator doors opened. Tim and Amy were inside. Both were on their phones, and it quickly became obvious that Amy was on the line with Jeremy while Tim was leaving a grim message on Melissa's voice mail.

Heather ended her call before it could ring through and stepped onto the elevator. While quietly urging Jeremy to join them at the hospital, Amy lifted an arm, and Heather slid beneath it, handing Ethan's phone back to him.

Tim hung up, and for a long, tense moment, he and Ethan stared at each other, an undercurrent of suspicion and defensiveness flowing between them. Heather brushed a hand against Tim's arm. He broke the stare. She reached then for Ethan, offering him her hand. He slipped the small phone into a pocket and wrapped his hand around hers, stepping forward.

No one said a word while the elevator made its descent.

Out on the sidewalk, it was tersely decided that everyone would go together in Tim's BMW. Heather and Ethan piled into the backseat while Amy got into the front with Tim. Ethan slipped his arm around Heather, and she gratefully leaned into him, almost too numb with fear even to pray as Tim got them moving.

After several moments Tim suddenly said, "I saw the spots and bruises on Dad's skin a couple days ago, but it didn't even occur to me that it was from bleeding."

"Mom said he had a nosebleed yesterday," Amy added, her voice choked with concern.

Now, according to Nora, the leukemia had reached a crisis point. Wallace was bleeding internally and, if it could not be stopped, he would soon die. Heather laid her head on Ethan's shoulder and closed her eyes, beseeching God with deep yearning. Ethan folded her closer, letting her tears soak the front of his cotton sport shirt.

As the BMW pulled up at the hospital, Heather was relieved to see Christopher's motorcycle parked near the curb. She did not, unfortunately, see Jeremy's car.

It was bad enough that Melissa would not be here at such a time, but to have Jeremy missing, too, would crush Nora, not to mention how it would affect Wallace and Jeremy himself. Heather knew without any doubt that God was in control of the situation, but as she slid from the car, her hand in Ethan's, she understood that she was about to face the most difficult moment of her life and that God had sent Ethan to help her through it.

Ethan placed the sandwich in its cellophane wrapper on the table next to the chair where Heather sat, waiting for word from the doctors.

"Sorry," he said, crouching in front of her, "but the cafeteria's already stopped serving dinner, and that's the best the vending machine has to offer."

Heather picked up the sandwich and plucked at the wrapper with her fingernail then laid it aside again.

"I'm not hungry anyway."

"Sis, you need to eat," Christopher urged gently from the chair next to her.

Heather sighed and split a wan smile between her brother and Ethan.

"I know. I just…" She glanced at Nora, who sat across the ICU waiting room between Tim and Amy, gripping one hand of each of them. "I wish Melissa and Jeremy were here."

Christopher shifted and murmured, "I'm pretty sure Melissa's with her boyfriend, Dean Orton. They went missing about the same time." He leaned forward and addressed Ethan directly. "Orton thinks of himself as some kind of musician, and I hear he may be traveling around with a band." Chris sat back in obvious disgust. "What I don't understand is why Melissa won't answer her cell phone. She knows Dad's in bad shape."

"Which is exactly why she won't answer. She just can't seem to face this," Heather said softly. "I doubt she even has her phone with her."

"I wouldn't know about Melissa," Ethan said, glancing over his shoulder at Nora and Tim. He kept his voice low, as much to spare Nora as to avoid setting off Tim, who seemed to be walking the knife edge of anger just now. "But as for Jeremy," he went on, "I'm pretty sure he's outside. I think I saw him when I went for the sandwich."

Christopher's eyebrows rose, and then so did he.

"I think I'll go get some…air."

"Good idea," Heather murmured, glancing at their mother again.

Ethan eased into the chair that Christopher had just vacated. He didn't know any of them well, but of Heather's three brothers, Ethan liked Chris the best. He guessed it was that uniformed service thing. He'd never felt inclined to join up himself, but he admired military and police personnel. Besides, it seemed to him that Chris was the most supportive of Heather, perhaps understandably so, given that they were twins.

"I hope Jeremy will come in," she said softly, leaning toward him. "It would help Mom to see him."

Understanding that she didn't want Nora to overhear in case Jeremy chose to keep his distance, Ethan lifted his arm to drape it around her shoulders and moved a little closer.

"Always worrying about everyone else," he whispered.

"I can't help it," she admitted quietly. "If Dad doesn't come through this, the family's going to be devastated."

"You Hamiltons do seem unusually close," Ethan commented. "Everyone keeps missing Melissa and Jeremy. I mean, I get that Tim is furious with Jeremy, but I sense that it's mostly disappointment, not real animosity."

Heather nodded. "You're right about that. As far as Tim's concerned, who Jeremy's biological father was shouldn't matter. Jeremy's one of us, and you just don't abandon your family. That's why, for everyone's sake, it's so important for Jeremy to come in and be with the rest of us. But even if he doesn't, at least he showed up." She looked past him then, staring unseeingly out the fourth floor window. "If the worst happens," she whispered, "Melissa will never forgive herself for not being here."

Ethan was more concerned about Heather than either of her siblings or anyone else.

"You're the one with the soft heart," he told her, "and I've seen you with your dad. I know how badly losing him would hurt you."

"Just thinking about it hurts," she admitted, "but at least I know that, whatever happens, he'll live on in heaven, and one day, I'll join him there. We all will."

Ethan wasn't so sure about that. He couldn't imagine heaven. Well, maybe he could. For her. And he was glad if the belief gave her comfort.

The door to the waiting room opened, and Chris walked through, looking back over his shoulder. He stood there for several heartbeats, holding the door open, then finally he let it swing slowly closed. Facing Heather, he shook his head, his carefully schooled expression telling them both that he had spoken to Jeremy but had not convinced their brother to join them.

Ethan felt Heather sink into herself and tightened his arm around her shoulders.

"I'm sorry. But look, if he didn't care, he wouldn't have come around at all, would he?"

She lifted sad eyes to him.

"Surely," she whispered, "if Dad doesn't make it, Jeremy will come to Mom."

"Oh, yeah, sure he will."

"It's just, you know, he has so much to work through."

Ethan nodded, anything to help her reconcile these things that hurt her.

"Christopher, come and sit down," Nora called, waving him over. "It can't be much longer."

Chris walked over and took a seat next to Amy. Reaching around her, he gave his mother's hand a squeeze.

"It's going to be all right," Nora announced, squaring her shoulders. "I just know it. Pastor Abernathy was by earlier to let us know that the church is holding a special prayer service for your father tonight. I expect he'll come by again later."

At that very moment the doctor strode into the room. "Nora," he said, instantly commanding the attention of everyone in the place.

Ethan clamped his arm a little tighter around Heather's shoulders, just in case, although the doctor didn't look as if he had bad news.

"Wallace is stabilized. The bleeding has stopped, and we've transfused him with platelets and whole blood."

A collective breath of relief gusted through the room.

Heather sagged against Ethan, whispering, "Thank You. Oh, thank You, God!"

"It gets better," the doctor said, pausing for effect. "We have a donor."

Heather gave a small cry of joy. Nora clapped her hands together, rocking forward in an attitude of prayer, while Chris grinned broadly.

Amy hugged their mother, whispering words of

thanks to God, while Tim rose to brush back the sides of his suit jacket and park his hands at his waist, breathing out a long, audible sigh of relief.

Heather turned a beaming face up to Ethan.

"My father's going to be all right. He's really going to be all right!"

Ethan laughed because he was so glad for her sake.

The doctor cautioned them. Wallace still had to get through the transplant and his weakened state would make him even more susceptible to infection. Even if he survived the week or more required to destroy his own diseased bone marrow and prepare him to receive the donated tissue, he could die before it did its work. Meanwhile, he would be transported to a larger hospital in Nashville and sequestered in sterile isolation, which would continue for several weeks after the transplant. All visits would be severely restricted and monitored, with careful attention given to infection control.

Still, they had hope, and that was enough to put a smile on Heather's face, enough to make Ethan so grateful that he found himself doing something he couldn't remember doing ever before. He thanked God.

It was a simple, silent prayer, and he didn't even know if God heard him.

He didn't know if this latest reprieve would even last, if Wallace would ultimately survive or if grief would eventually claim the whole Hamilton family.

He only knew that somehow Heather's happiness had become very important to his own.

"How you doing?"

Heather put down her pen and smiled, rocking back in her desk chair. Ethan smiled in response, thinking how pretty she was.

"Okay. You?"

"Good," he said.

"How'd the shoot go?"

"Well. I think." He held up a number of small plastic film canisters clumped together with rubber bands. "We'll soon find out. You should have been out there with us. It's a glorious day for the park."

"Little too muggy for me," she said, wrinkling her nose. She looked relaxed and polished in a pale turquoise suit and a soft multicolored blouse of patterned silk.

"Yeah," he agreed, "with all the rain the last couple of days. Still, it was your idea to shoot the fashion layout for the end-of-summer issue in our own Sugar Tree Park."

"I'd forgotten just how lovely it is out there until we went looking for Jeremy that day."

Ethan stepped fully into her office, leaning against the door frame. "Speaking of Jeremy, have you talked to him lately?"

She shook her head. "He talks to Chris once in a while, and he's promised to see Mom soon."

"What about your sister?"

"Melissa?" She sighed. "Not a word."

Ethan nodded. "So how's your dad?"

"It's rough," Heather told him, "but the transplant is scheduled for Monday, so I guess the doctors are confident enough."

"That's good news."

"I think so. Mom's been with him every day, of course, and staying close by at night in case he needs her. Amy and I are going in to Nashville tomorrow to see him, and we're going to try to convince Mom to come home with us. I think she will. The last Sunday of the month is reserved for family dinners, and Chris is trying to talk Jeremy into coming."

"So you've got your weekend all planned, then," Ethan said lightly, struggling to subdue a sense of disappointment.

He would have liked to have spent some time with her away from the office and the hospital, maybe provide some distraction. He said nothing, though. She didn't need any sort of added pressure just now, however well-meaning.

"What time is the transplant on Monday?" he asked.

"They say between one and two in the afternoon."

"So you'll be leaving about lunchtime, I guess."

She breathed in deeply through her nostrils before letting the air out again. "I don't know. The doctors say it's not much different from a blood transfusion.

Takes about four hours or so, barring complications. Mom says we shouldn't worry about it, but I still think I ought to be there."

"I understand."

"Amy said something about having a lunch meeting with Tim and some of the distributors, so I might go on my own. They'll probably come later."

"I'd be glad to go with you," he offered immediately.

"Really?" She sat up straight.

"I'm assuming I'll have no problem getting off work." She beamed at him. "I'd say that's a safe guess."

"So what time do you want to leave?"

"Can you go early?"

"As early as you want."

"Eleven, then. We'll get an early lunch before we go. I'll buy."

He laughed at that. "Deal."

She relaxed back in her chair as if the weight of the world had just been lifted from her shoulders, and he knew he'd do a lot more than take off a half day of work and drive into Nashville to make her feel that way again.

Chapter Eleven

Nora placed the low multicolored flower arrangement in the center of the white cloth covering the long rectangular table and stepped back, viewing it with satisfaction.

Vera Mae was off on Sundays, so the family usually did for themselves during these monthly dinners. Vera Mae would put up dinner for them on Saturday, and they would work together to reheat and get everything on the table. Since Wallace had fallen ill, however, the beloved cook and housekeeper had insisted on coming in to help out.

Heather came in through the butler's pantry from the kitchen, carrying a heavy casserole dish. Nora positioned a wrought-iron trivet on the ornately carved buffet, inhaling appreciatively. As Heather lowered the dish onto it, Vera Mae's chicken pot pie sent delicious aromas wafting around the dining room. Steam rose in curly tendrils from the slits in the golden brown crust.

Amy came in behind her sister and deposited a layered fruit salad in a footed crystal bowl next to the pot pie. Opening a drawer, she extracted a stack of neatly pressed and folded white linen napkins. Just because they were dining with less formality than usual was no reason not to observe the niceties, so far as Nora was concerned. Then again, in her opinion, white linen could add a touch of elegance to a picnic.

Amy began counting out the napkins. She hesitated when she got to five.

Last month all eight of them had sat around that long, gleaming table. Now, with their father in the hospital, Melissa in the wind and Jeremy somewhat estranged, there could well be only five this month, six at the most.

Nora beat back the grief that so often threatened to consume her these days and willfully reminded herself of all for which she should be thankful. Pushing her long hair off her shoulders, she folded her slender hands. Her pantsuit bagged in places, she knew, but the rich azure silk picked out the blue bits in her vibrant hazel eyes, and she counted on that to distract from the fact that she'd recently lost weight. Stiffening her spine, she looked at her eldest daughter.

"The correct number is still eight," she decreed softly. "Some of us may only be here in spirit, but the table will be properly set."

"Of course, Mom," Amy murmured, counting out three more napkins.

Heather went to the china cabinet and carefully extracted eight plates, one after the other, while Nora began gathering the heavy silver flatware from a velvet-lined drawer. Heather carried the plates to the table and set them down. Amy began placing them while Heather went back for the glassware. Nora laid the first place setting of silver and reached for the crystal tumbler that Heather offered. Just then, Christopher walked into the room.

"Mom, Sis, twin," Chris said with a smile.

"Christopher." Nora went immediately to hug him and kiss his cheek. He bent down to receive her kiss, his strong arms looping about her, but then he straightened and stepped to one side.

Jeremy stood uncertainly in the doorway to the hall.

Nora briefly closed her eyes. *Thank You, God.* As she rushed forward, Jeremy came to meet her, his arms opening. She hugged him tightly.

"Jeremy!"

"Mom."

"I've missed you so much!" She pulled back, holding on to his arms just above the elbows, and willed away the tears gathering in her eyes. "Are you all right?"

Jeremy swallowed. "As all right as I can be, I guess."

It broke her heart to see the sadness in his eyes. "Jeremy, I'm so sorry."

"You didn't do anything wrong."

"I should have told you the truth when you were younger."

"Why didn't you?" he asked, sounding truly puzzled.

"Your father—" She broke off and inhaled deeply. Somehow, she just couldn't think of Wallace as Jeremy's stepfather. In every way that counted, he was Jeremy's true father, but she understood that Jeremy was not yet ready to accept that. "Wallace didn't want anyone to know," she said carefully.

"I expect he was trying to protect you," Jeremy surmised, sounding reluctant to assign even that much good to the deception.

"Maybe. But that was only part of it," she told him. "He wanted to be your father. He wanted there to be no question about you being his son."

"Until I disagreed with him," Jeremy shot back. "Then he was perfectly willing to shove me aside for his *real* son!"

"It wasn't like that."

"Wasn't it?"

Nora shook her head. "Jeremy, he regrets blurting it out like that. He regrets losing his temper."

"He regrets ever putting me in control of Hamilton Media. He regrets not being able to mold me in his own image," Jeremy said bitterly.

"He never meant to make you feel unloved," Nora insisted.

"And he did raise you as his own," Tim said

loudly, entering the room through the same door as his brothers.

Nora frowned at his scathing tone of voice, though she understood that Timothy, too, had been wounded in this. They all had, including Wallace. And yet, she couldn't help holding onto the hope that it was all somehow for the best.

Jeremy whirled around as Timothy strolled farther into the room.

"He treated you as the oldest son, put his faith in you, but have you even asked how he is?"

The acid tone of Tim's voice made it clear that he still blamed Jeremy for the argument which had prompted Wallace's revelation, and Nora sighed inwardly.

A muscle worked in the hollow of Jeremy's jaw.

"Stay out of it, Tim."

"He nearly died less than a week ago, Jeremy!" Tim pointed out hotly. "Not that you care."

"Timothy," Nora admonished quietly, hurting for both sons, one whose world had been turned upside down, one who did not yet possess the spiritual maturity to understand that God gives different gifts to different people.

Jeremy shook his head, turning back to her.

"I'm sorry. Coming here now was obviously not a good idea."

"Jeremy," Nora pleaded. If only they could talk out their differences, these two sons of hers, they could look past them to the love they shared.

"I'll call you," Jeremy promised. He looked past her to his sisters. "Heather, Amy." He smiled wanly, such pain in his eyes. "I'll be in touch."

In other words, thought Nora sadly, *don't call me.*

"Take care, sweetheart," she said softly.

He turned to go, and she reached out to him without really meaning to, but he merely squeezed her hand, glanced pointedly at Chris and walked out of the room.

It took every ounce of her self-discipline not to go after him, and still she took a step forward before she could stop herself.

"Let him go," Tim said, lifting a hand as if to stop her. "If he doesn't want to be a part of this family, then just let him go!"

"He doesn't know what he wants right now." Nora sighed.

"Could've fooled me. Nobody made him quit and walk out."

"That's not fair, Tim, and you know it," Chris said calmly.

"How would you feel if it was you?" Amy put in.

"I'd be shocked. I'd be hurt," Tim answered, "but I'd live up to my responsibilities, and I'd try to remember that the sick old man who raised me deserves my consideration. Dad was at death's door a few days ago, but did Jeremy even bother to call and ask about him? And what about Mom? Doesn't she—"

"Jeremy was there," Heather said, glancing at Chris.

Nora split a shocked look between her twins.

"He was at the hospital?"

Chris nodded. "Yes, he was at the hospital, but he didn't want what just happened here to happen there, so he stayed out of sight until he knew Dad was going to make it."

Nora clasped her hands together in the center of her chest, silently thanking God once more. Jeremy did care about Wallace. Of course he cared about Wallace. And Wallace cared about him. One day soon they'd both get past the pain and the confusion to realize that fundamental truth.

Tim's gaze skittered around the room and finally hit the floor.

"He could've let Mom know," he muttered.

"And you could ask yourself why you can't cut him a break," Chris said.

"Enough," Nora ordered. She wasn't going to lose any more of her children, even temporarily, to misunderstanding and strife. "We're not going to solve anything tonight. We're going to sit down and have a pleasant dinner together. Understood?"

Chris nodded, and so did Tim.

Vera Mae entered the room carrying a basket full of steaming biscuits in one hand and a butter dish in the other.

"Get 'em while they're hot," she said with a nod of her head, which was wreathed in its usual gray braids. Her cheeks bunched, framing her endearing smile and narrowing her twinkling eyes to mere slits. That did not prevent her from noticing that the table had not yet been properly set. Plunking down the breadbasket and butter plate, she brought her plump hands to her ample hips and clucked her tongue.

"Now if this don't beat all. Déjà vu all over again, that's what it is." She shook a finger at them, just as she had when the children had been small and she'd struggled ruthlessly to teach them each to set a perfect table. "I'm just going back in there for the tea," she announced sternly, "and I expect that table to be laid before I get back."

Nora bit back a smile and lifted her eyebrows as Vera Mae huffed out of the room.

"Well, I guess she told us," Chris quipped.

"When does she not?" Amy asked with a grin.

Even Tim seemed properly chastised.

"Pass me that silver."

"I'll get the glasses," Heather said with a chortle. She sent Amy a look that had Amy scooping up the napkins.

Nora watched her now grown children scurrying to get the table laid, her heart seeming to expand in her chest. How often had this scene played out over the years? The cast had aged, and yet the continuity held, weaving them together with common experience and purpose. That was what these monthly family dinners were all about.

Her eyes fell on her middle daughter, and a sense of satisfaction, of well-being, rose up in her, welcome despite a niggling concern. More had changed there than could be seen on the outside, and Nora strongly suspected that Ethan Danes had something to do with it. That didn't mean that anything would come of that relationship, of course. Only time would tell, and they did seem to have several marks against them.

Ethan was something of a rolling stone, for one thing, and Heather would never be happy with someone who didn't share her deep faith, for another. It was also possible that Ethan had divulged information harmful to the family to the *Observer,* but somehow Nora didn't think so. And, unless she missed her guess, neither did Wallace, though he hadn't specifically said as much. Besides, she had noticed the way Ethan looked at Heather when he thought no one was watching, the way she turned to him for support and comfort.

Yes, this could be a very good thing for her daughter. Or a very bad one. Nora prayed for the former, but either way she trusted that Heather's faith would see her through.

Faith would see them all through whatever crisis God allowed to come their way. Nora believed it with her whole heart.

It was faith that renewed her strength, faith that let her look at the empty chairs around the table and trust that they would each be filled again soon.

Heather marveled at the difference in the atmosphere of this waiting room as compared to the last one in which the family had gathered. It had nothing to do with the room itself, of course. This one was small and intimate, a private lounge with brightly upholstered armchairs, low tables, a TV mounted high in one corner, a coffeemaker and a sink. The last time, everyone had feared the worst. Today it felt as if they were turning a corner, and everyone had hope that it would lead them onto the pathway to restored health for Wallace. Heather prayed that it would also lead to healing for the family.

Jeremy had stayed away, and after his last clash with Timothy, she couldn't say that she blamed him. There had still been no word from Melissa, and Chris had been called in to work, but Amy and Tim had come in an hour or so after Heather and Ethan, and Chris called frequently to be sure that all was going according to plan. In fact, between him, the pastor and others, Nora had spent more time on the phone than off, but that was good, in Heather's opinion. The calls and the hourly visits to the treatment area were keeping Nora too busy to worry about the outcome of the transplant.

Heather turned the page in the national news magazine that she was perusing. Ethan glanced away from his novel to take a look.

"Oh, wow. That's a great shot." Closing the paperback on his thumb, he shifted closer as she tilted the magazine so he could get a look at the credit written in tiny letters below the caption. "Figures."

"Do you know this photographer?" Heather asked.

"Yep. She's good, and even more ambitious."

"Did you ever work together?"

"Briefly. Like I said, she's real ambitious, ambitious enough to take assignments in war zones."

"Have you ever considered doing that?" Heather asked, her heart suddenly in her throat.

It occurred to her that he could leave the magazine for more challenging assignments at any time. What if something should happen to him?

Ethan shrugged. "Yeah, I considered it, but my old man pitched a wall-eyed fit. Being military, he knows too well the dangers involved in that kind of thing. He never interferes in my life, so I figured he meant business and let it go."

Heather breathed a silent sigh of relief as Ethan went back to his book. It was, she noticed, a techno thriller. Her own taste ran toward romance novels and poetry, but she also read a great deal of nonfiction in the course of her job and would read almost anything in a pinch. She would read the cereal box at the breakfast table if no other alternative presented itself.

All the Hamiltons were voracious readers. Tim was at this moment sitting across the way with a stack of newspapers from around the country. He'd always been able to digest several a day. Their mother, on the other hand, had been working on a history of the Christian church in Asia for a week or more now. Amy took Nora's approach, devouring popular novels piecemeal, an hour or two of an evening. Chris, meanwhile, was always studying some training manual or Bible commentary. Wallace read very eclectically, keeping several books going at the same time, while Melissa routinely shut herself away to devour her interest of the moment from cover to cover in one sitting. Jeremy loved historical novels, especially Civil War-era material.

Heather got to the end of her magazine and went in search of another, digging through the rack attached to the wall next to the door. She had just chosen a travel publication when Luke Strickland walked into the room. He went over and sat down next to Nora.

"He's done," the doctor announced. "Everything went smoothly."

Luke explained again that it would be several weeks before they knew whether the procedure could be termed a success. During that time Wallace would remain in sterile isolation. He would be allowed short visits only by family members, who would be required to observe strict infection-control protocols. If all went well, he could be transferred back to Davis Landing Community General in two to three weeks and from there, home.

Once home, Wallace would have to continue to take great care as the danger of contracting a serious infection would remain quite high, but at least life would resume with some measure of normalcy. Even if the transplant was technically successful, however, it could take as much as a year, the doctor warned, for

Wallace's body to begin generating healthy bone marrow on its own.

"In other words," Luke said, getting to his feet again, "so far, so good. And now we wait." He looked at Nora and added, "You can see him again in a couple of hours. He's sleeping now. Meanwhile, if there's a problem, I'm on call."

Nora thanked and hugged him before he departed. Heather was glad to note that her mother seemed strong and together today, very much the Nora upon whom they had all depended throughout their lives. She looked every one of them in the eye and announced, "You all should go home."

"Not without you," Tim said flatly. "We promised Dad that we'd see to it you get a good night's sleep tonight. I'll stay until you can see him, then I'm driving you home."

"And Chris will drive you back here tomorrow morning," Amy put in, "unless you allow us to hire a driver to ferry you back and forth."

"Actually, I've already taken care of it," Tim said. "No arguments, Mom. We've all discussed this and decided it's the best way. Besides, it's what Dad wants. Got it?"

Nora smiled at her children, her long silver-high-lighted ponytail hanging sleekly against the back of her head.

"Got it," she said, "and I love you all for wanting to take care of me and for understanding that I need to be here for your father. Just don't think you're going to get away with this high-handed behavior forever."

Tim groaned, and Amy shook her head, but Heather laughed, glad to see Nora's indefatigable spirit returning. She'd been through so much these past weeks; it was good to know that, though her strength may have temporarily waned, her energy, resolve and faith remained powerful.

Some time later as Heather and Ethan made their way through the confusing maze of corridors, elevators and lobbies that made up the large Nashville hospital, Heather realized that she was famished.

"Well, I'm not surprised," Ethan commented in a slightly scolding tone. "You've been eating like a bird."

"How do you know?" she retorted with lighthearted defensiveness.

"I know," he said, "because I know you." He slid a look over her. "Besides, you're thin as a rail."

Dressed in sandals, capris and a gauzy top with bell sleeves and a gathered waist, her hair caught up in a soft, wispy twist, she felt light as air. Grimacing, she had to admit he was right.

"I can't help it. I take after my mother. Stress diminishes my appetite."

"All the more reason to feed you now while I have the chance," he said, taking her by the arm. "I know a great steak place down on the river away from all the neon madness. What do you say?"

"Yum," she answered quickly. Ethan laughed and threw his arm across her shoulders.

Dinner was excellent: steamed asparagus, baked potatoes and filets about two inches thick. Heather had worried that she would be underdressed, but since Ethan was wearing jeans, boots and a pale yellow T-shirt, she figured they would be underdressed together. When she'd seen that the restaurant was little more than an atmospheric hole in the wall with a great second-story view of the Cumberland River as it wound its way through town, she'd relaxed.

Situated above a convenience store in an old building that had the word "Mercantile" chiseled into the stone front, the place could seat maybe fifty people in circular booths scattered around a creaking wood floor. Limited lighting provided ambiance and softened the rough brick walls, exposed plumbing and rafters overhead. A lack of background music— a rarity in the acclaimed Music City—combined with unobtrusive service and unpretentious comfort to produce a cozy, almost serene atmosphere.

After the very hearty meal, Heather sipped some of the best iced tea she'd ever tasted and watched Ethan demolish an enormous hunk of something called "Brown sugar cake," which was doused with caramel and chocolate. She didn't know how he could keep eating. She was seriously concerned about splitting a seam herself. She'd only managed about half her steak, and his had been even larger than hers, yet here he was gobbling up dessert.

"How can you eat so much?"

He waved a spoon in reply to her question. "Got it from my dad. He's a world-champion eater, always had to take along extra rations on maneuvers. Otherwise he'd come back looking like a walking cadaver."

"Sort of like my dad right now," she said softly.

"Your dad's going to be okay," he reassured her.

"I hope so. What makes you think it?"

He shrugged, took another big bite, chewed and swallowed. "I guess because that's what you deserve."

Heather popped her eyebrows at that. "What *I* deserve?"

"What I mean is, I just can't see God punishing you with a tragedy like that, not when you believe so strongly."

Heather was flabbergasted.

"Ethan, is that how you see God, as someone waiting around to punish us?"

He stopped eating long enough to stare at her. "I don't know. Why?"

She shook her head. "Because that's not how I see Him."

Ethan put down his spoon. "So how do you see God?"

"As a loving, caring, all-powerful Father Who knows and does what's best for us whether we like it or not."

Ethan seemed to think that over.

Finally he asked, "If that's so, then how do you explain your father's illness? I mean, what good can possibly come from something like that?"

"I don't know," she answered truthfully. "But I don't have to know. It's enough to know that God has our best interests at heart."

"How can you be so sure of that?"

"Because, for our benefit, He didn't spare even His own Son."

"You'll have to explain that to me," Ethan said doubtfully. So she did.

They talked for hours, exploring her beliefs and how she had come to them, as well as his lack of the same. Heather quickly realized that he simply had no frame of reference. Both of his parents appeared to be agnostic, and the fact that they had each been on the move practically his whole life meant that Ethan simply hadn't had opportunities to be exposed to issues of faith until now.

That was difficult for Heather to understand, having been raised in church, and she was all but speechless when she realized that Ethan had very rarely wandered through the doors of a church building, except for the odd wedding. Nevertheless, he seemed open and curious. Heather began to think that what Ethan needed more than anything else was exposure to what she had taken for granted most of her life, so she invited him to church the next day.

"With tomorrow being the Fourth of July, it won't be like a Sunday service, but it will be interesting," Heather told him. "There'll be some short speeches and lots of singing. Then afterward we'll have dinner on the grounds, followed by games and socializing until it's time for the fireworks."

"Sounds good."

"Why don't you come with me then? We'll make a whole day of it, really do the Fourth up right."

He sat back, holding her gaze, and smoothed his hands down his thighs. Finally he shrugged. "Why not?"

Heather smiled. "Exactly."

"So what do I wear?"

"Red, white and blue?" she suggested playfully, only half teasing.

His brows drew together. "My suit's black."

Heather laughed. "It's Independence Day. No one's going to be wearing a suit."

"Ah."

"What you're wearing now is fine." He smoothed a hand over his chest in a rather self-conscious gesture, as Heather leaned forward and added, "But red, white and blue."

"You're serious."

"The redder, whiter and bluer the better," she confirmed, grinning. "Think you can handle it?"

"Sweetheart, I can out-patriotic you any day of the week."

"Yeah?"

"Yeah."

"We'll see."

She folded her arms in challenge and began planning the most outrageous costume she'd ever dreamed of wearing, and all the while one word kept circulating around the back of her mind. *Sweetheart.*

He'd called her sweetheart.

Chapter Twelve

Following a long, eloquent prayer from the pulpit by the associate pastor, Ethan leaned to one side and said out of the corner of his mouth, "I thought this wasn't a regular church service."

"It isn't," Heather whispered back, her warm, dark amber eyes showing some amusement.

Couldn't prove it by me, Ethan thought, but then what did he know about it? He was starting to realize that he'd missed something important in his vagabond life. In many ways, he didn't even have enough information to form a personal opinion about matters of faith.

Straightening, he turned his attention back to the front of the building, allowing his gaze to take a meandering path along the way.

The vaulted ceiling, spanned by heavy polished oak beams, gave the impression of soaring space. White walls added a clean brightness, while extensive natural oak appointments glowed golden in the light of brass chandeliers. Vibrant colors spilled into the space from tall, arched stained-glass windows on either side of the building.

A choir of perhaps four dozen, attired in alternating red and blue robes with white collars, launched into a stirring rendition of the national anthem, bringing the filled-to-capacity crowd to its feet in an undulating wave of patriotic colors. Salutes to the flag followed. After the pledge, a patriotic film played on a screen hidden behind motorized oak panels, showing snapshots of local scenes interspersed with professional photographs of flags, fireworks and national monuments.

Finally, a large redheaded man of perhaps forty stepped up to the pulpit and beamed at the assembly. His broad, freckled face and wide smile inspired instant liking, while his tall, blocky form gave the impression of leashed power. Dressed informally in a red and white vertically striped shirt and dark blue jeans, he put Ethan in mind of a jolly giant. Barely a sentence into his remarks, however, it became obvious that—Ethan glanced at the printed program to get the name—Charles David Abernathy was a born preacher. He quickly enthralled his audience, speaking about the blessing of religious freedom, the intent of the founding fathers and God's good graces.

At the close of the pastor's brief message, Ethan rose with everyone else to sing a patriotic hymn, his own limited baritone blending seamlessly with Heather's breathy alto. Holding one side of the hymnal with his left hand, he glanced at his wristwatch and was surprised to find that twenty or more minutes had passed in what had seemed like mere seconds. Abernathy was obviously made for the pulpit, Ethan would give him that.

After the service, Ethan was surprised to find that, rather than making a mad dash for the exit at the rear of the building, people were in no hurry to leave. Indeed, they seemed intent on sticking around to shake hands and visit. Many of them seemed to make a beeline straight for him. Certainly he shook more hands and received more introductions in the next few minutes than he had in the past several months, too many to keep the names and faces straight in his head.

He had to grab hold of Heather in order to keep from getting separated from her, Nora and Amy. Chris, like most of the local police force, was working, though Heather had mentioned she expected him to put in an appearance at some point. Tim would almost certainly come later, according to her, though Jeremy, who apparently was usually very reliable in his church attendance, almost certainly would not.

When their group finally stepped out onto the broad portico, Ethan could see the warm late-afternoon sunshine sparkling on the broad surface of the river in the distance. The lush sweep of the lawn leading down to it resembled something straight off an old postcard commemorating past Independence Day celebrations.

A band box had been set up on a level piece of ground, and the musicians were already assembling. Booths had been erected and games organized. A track had even been mapped out for races. Long tables were set in a grove of trees, and an amazing array of food was appearing.

Ethan went with Heather to retrieve blankets and folding lawn chairs from the back of his SUV, while Amy and Nora hurried to stake out a prime picnic spot for their group. Heather had also brought a big soft bag with her, but he hadn't given it much thought at the time. He'd been too knocked out by her outfit, a skirt-and-shorts combination in royal blue, and a simple top that seemed constructed entirely of red, white and blue scarves, red for the front, blue for the back and white for the wide, airy sleeves. Her sandals were also white, but she'd tied tiny red and blue ribbons to the toe pieces, forming little pom-poms. His mundane red T-shirt, jeans and white sneakers paled by comparison. Then she pulled a big, floppy stovepipe hat in an American flag pattern from her bag and plopped it onto her head, and he could only laugh.

"No, no," he protested, grabbing for a camera with one hand and her with the other when she reached upward as if to remove the hat. "It's adorable." He couldn't resist the impulse to snap a few shots of her. "Just like you."

She wrinkled her nose. "Adorable is for puppies and babies."

"Well, there's adorable and there's uniquely, wildly, stunningly adorable." He grinned over the top of his camera. "And, of course, there's always slightly corny adorable."

She hit him playfully with her hat. "Yeah, well, who's the most patriotic, though, hmm?"

"Oh, that would definitely be you. Most patriotic, most adorable and most beautiful."

She beamed at him, and that was one picture he had to have. What was it about her that made him so... happy?

That was exactly what it was. For some reason, Heather Hamilton made him ridiculously happy.

She made him ridiculously happy throughout the afternoon, which included lots of eating.

Ethan sampled everything: fried chicken, hot dogs, potato salad, zucchini, watermelon, oranges, blueberry muffins, apple pie and too many flavors of ice cream to mention. The menu was endless, and all of it was washed down with iced tea and lemonade. The three Hamilton women joked about the amount of food that he could put away, and eventually he found himself eating just to entertain them.

All of that food conspired to make him sleepy, though, so with the sun sinking below the bend in the river, he stretched out on the blanket and found himself nodding off during the recitation of the Gettysburg Address, one of a number of significant speeches from the nation's past recited by a group of particularly precocious children. He told himself to sit up, and the next thing he knew, Heather was gently shaking him awake again to the sound of a strangely familiar voice saying, "Oh, no, don't wake him. I'll stop by again later."

Ethan sat up, as he'd meant to all along, sucked in a head-clearing breath and said, "No need. I'm not asleep." When his gaze finally focused he found himself face-to-grinning-face with Pastor Abernathy, who crouched in front of him.

"Hard to stay awake on these sleepy July afternoons," said Abernathy, lowering himself into a sitting position. "I had to get up and go for a walk to keep myself awake."

Since the man seemed to be getting comfortable, Ethan did likewise, folding his legs and bracing his elbows atop his knees as he glanced around. He noticed that Tim had shown up and now occupied the chair that Ethan had vacated before his unplanned nap. Seeming preoccupied, Tim followed his mother's direction as she quietly pointed out various activities going on around them.

Amy stood at some distance, talking to a trio of women who looked vaguely familiar to Ethan. He was sure that he'd seen one of them around the office;

the other two he couldn't quite place. Then he realized that he'd seen at least one of them at the hospital. She waved at Heather, who was kneeling on the blanket next to Ethan, and Heather waved back before giving her full attention to the pastor.

"Ethan is our staff photographer at the magazine," she said.

Belatedly remembering his manners, Ethan stuck out his hand. "Sorry. Ethan Danes. It's nice to meet you, sir."

A large, freckled hand engulfed Ethan's. "Call me Charles David."

"Not Charles but Charles David," Ethan commented wryly, adding, "No one, but no one, calls me by my middle name, not even my mother, unless she's ticked off."

"Uh-oh," Abernathy said, grinning broadly, "now you've done it."

"He sure has," Heather confirmed, bumping her shoulder against Ethan's. "Just what is this middle-name-that-no-one-but-no-one-dares-call-you-by? Come on, give."

Ethan groaned.

"Armstrong," he confessed, knowing it was no more than he deserved for his quick tongue. "It's my mother's maiden name."

"Ethan Armstrong Danes," Heather mused. "I've heard worse."

"Man, if I ever heard Armstrong come out of my

mom's mouth, I knew I was in trouble big-time," he admitted.

"In my case," the preacher said, "I'm named after both of my grandfathers, and no one wanted to slight either, so I've always been Charles David."

"That reeks," Ethan said jovially, feeling quite comfortable with the other man. "How did you know when you were in for it?"

"Oh, it's in the tone," Charles David confided. "Definitely in the tone. My mother could make Cha-a-r-rles the longest noun in the English language, and my wife has the very same knack."

Ethan laughed, liking this man every bit as much as he'd felt he would.

He liked him even more when Charles David leaned back and said, "So you're a professional photographer. That was my number two choice of career. I love everything to do with photography. My wife claims it makes me real easy to buy for. In fact, you'll have to get Heather to bring you by the house sometime to take a look at my camera collection. I've got an old Brownie from the 1950s and a real Scovill Waterbury."

"Wow. Darlot lens?"

"Nope. The Instantane."

Ethan whistled. "Marketed about 1890, right?"

"1888."

"Sweet."

Charles David sat forward again. "So what do

you think of the new digitals? Or do you prefer 35 millimeter?"

"Depends on its use."

That resulted in a lively half-hour discussion, with Ethan showing off the thirteen-hundred-dollar digital SLR that he was carrying. Finally, an older woman came to pull Charles David away to judge an "Uncle Sam" look-alike contest.

"Why aren't you entering?" Tim asked Heather, tapping the top of her stovepipe hat.

"She'd get my vote for cutest Uncle Sam," Ethan said, pleased when she blushed. Tim gave him a puzzled look. Amy coughed behind her hand, and Heather announced that it was time to spend a little money for a good cause.

They got up and wandered around the booths as the lights strung through the tree limbs began winking on. Ethan put his camera to good use, catching scenes of pure Americana.

They played games of skill, had caricatures drawn and purchased some patriotic bookmarks. The money raised went to a variety of charitable causes, one of which had been spearheaded by Chris and a friend of his on the force.

They met up with Chris, in full uniform, near the lemonade stand, and Ethan learned more then about the program for at-risk youth which Chris and his buddy had developed. Ethan gathered that it was mostly funded by local churches and businesses. Intrigued,

Ethan would have liked to learn more, but Chris needed to get back to his duties and had yet to speak with his mother. They sent him off with a handshake on Ethan's part and a kiss on the cheek from Heather.

As evening deepened into true night, the temperature cooled. That, coupled with the breeze blowing across the surface of the broad Cumberland River, soon had Heather shivering in her silky top and Ethan jogging up to the parking lot to retrieve a light jacket that he kept tucked into a pocket behind the seat in case of rain. It was wrinkled from months of being crammed into a small space and it literally swallowed dainty Heather, but it got the job done.

When they returned to the blanket in order to watch the fireworks, Heather sat with her knees drawn up, huddled inside his much-abused windbreaker, and it was all Ethan could do not to wrap her in his arms, as well. His instinct to protect this woman seemed boundless.

He was grateful for the distraction when the fireworks finally began with a muted boom and whistle, followed by an explosion of breathtaking golds and greens. They were actually being shot off in Davis Landing, aimed over the lake in Sugar Tree Park and toward the river, but the church grounds offered a spectacular view. The river itself acted like a mirror to the clear black sky, intensifying the effect, and Ethan's long-range camera lens gave him an up-close-and-personal view, which he shared with Heather.

She even took a few snaps herself, and a couple of them were quite good.

Tim had disappeared just as the fireworks had started, mumbling something about wanting to avoid traffic. The sparkling red, white and blue embers of the grand finale were still sliding from the sky when Nora and Amy also rose to leave. Remembering his manners, Ethan got to his feet as Nora bent to hug Heather, explaining that it had been a long day, starting with a visit to the hospital in Nashville.

"We won't be far behind you," Heather assured her mother. "It shouldn't take long to load up this stuff."

"Don't rush on my account," Nora called, moving after Amy, who was already halfway up the hill. "Bye, Ethan. I hope you enjoyed yourself."

"Very much, thank you."

"I want some of those photos!"

"Absolutely." He reached down a hand for Heather, hauling her to her feet. All around them people were streaming upward toward the parking lot. Others were packing boxes and clearing away their trash. He gestured with one hand. "Shouldn't we help with this?"

"No, no. There's a committee. The volunteers have assigned tasks. We tend to alternate, and I did it last year."

"Ah." Disappointment niggled at him, and he ruefully admitted to himself that he hated for the day to end. He couldn't, in fact, remember a better one. "So what was your job last year?" he asked, just to have something to say, something to derail the moment of actual leave-taking.

She wrinkled her nose. "I coordinated the water-melon-seed-spitting contest. I recommended that we not repeat the performance again this year."

He laughed and snapped his fingers. "Just my luck. My one true talent outlawed."

Rolling her eyes, she began folding up chairs. "At least you wouldn't have chased and spit at me."

He felt instant, unreasoning anger. "Who did that?"

"A bunch of fourth-grade boys."

Boys. Of course. The anger slipped away, followed rapidly by something like panic.

What was wrong with him? Happy one minute, angry the next, worrying about things over which he had no control, like whether her father was going to be all right or if her brother had gotten in touch with her that day, and even how his apartment had looked to her.

Suddenly his heart was pounding emphatically inside his chest, and there was just no reason for it, not one logical reason, logical being the operative word.

He helped her fold the blankets, then gathered up the chairs and started toward the parking lot. She trailed along behind him with the blankets and a half-empty water bottle, calling out farewells to friends. After stowing everything and helping her up into his SUV, he got in line with everyone else leaving the parking lot.

Fortunately traffic moved pretty quickly. As he

drove, they spoke about the day, commenting on everything from the food to the fireworks and Pastor Abernathy, who wasn't what Ethan had expected.

"What did you expect?" Heather asked, sounding amused. "A bible-thumper in a black frock coat?"

"More like phony piety in an expensive suit."

She shook her head. "Charles David is the real deal and very down-to-earth."

"That's what I like about him."

"That's what I like about him, too, that and the fact that he can preach the stained glass right out of the windows."

"Yeah, I kind of got that feeling."

"Maybe you'd like to hear him sometime," she suggested. "Today hardly even counts, really."

"Maybe I would," Ethan admitted, as much to himself as to her. She went on talking about the pastor and his influence on her church for awhile. Apparently the minister was truly a man to be admired and her church had much to offer. She fell silent as they drew near her home.

The grand old estate pointed up the differences between them, and Ethan felt it keenly as he drove up the long drive toward the house. He'd stayed in hotels that were neither so large nor nearly so grand as the house in which she'd grown up. Yet, by some trick of fate, here they sat. He switched off the engine and bridged the space between their seats with his arm.

"It's been some day. Thanks for inviting me."

"Thank you for being there," she countered, sounding wistful in the dark shadow cast by the twin porch lights. "It really helped. Last year the family was all together. None of us could have guessed that it might be the last time."

"Hey, now, don't talk like that," Ethan urged. "Your dad's holding his own."

"Yes, but there's Melissa and Jeremy, too. I just don't know what's going to happen with either of them. I mean, Melissa will probably show up again eventually. Unless something happens." She shook her head, as if refusing to follow that path. "But Jeremy… He says he doesn't know who he is anymore."

"Whoever he is, he's still your brother," Ethan offered hopefully.

He heard the smile in her voice when she answered, "True." Then, a heartbeat later, she added, "You're a good friend, Ethan."

A frown tugged at the corners of his mouth. Was that really all he was, a friend? Even being a good friend seemed unexpectedly…sparse. It was too little, he realized suddenly, for what he felt, but that wasn't something he wanted her to know.

Or was it?

He let himself out of the vehicle, giving himself time to think while he walked around to open her door for her. She waited, and he was glad because he hadn't been sure that she would. It wasn't like this was the end of a date. But maybe he wanted it to be.

No, he definitely wanted it to be, though dating Heather wouldn't be like dating anyone else he'd ever known. He had to think about that as he took her by the arm and escorted her along the walk and up those broad front steps.

The funny thing was that he'd never expected to be thinking like this. He'd been "more than friends" with other women, but he and they had always known that it was a temporary situation. He was not the sort to stay in one place for very long. His parents' unhappy relationship and the constant upheavals of his childhood hadn't left him with any talent for permanence.

But Heather was a permanent kind of woman. Anything more than friendship with her would inevitably lead to commitment and putting down roots, roots as deep as this big old house was tall and wide, roots to hold for generations to come, the kind he personally knew nothing about.

Such a thought should have scared him stupid, and maybe it did because he heard himself asking, "What do you think about next Saturday night? Want to see a movie or something, maybe get some dinner?"

Heather stood there in that ridiculous stovepipe hat and stared up at him for so long that he began to wonder if she'd heard him, and then she blinked and tucked her hair back behind her ears with both hands.

"Um, sure."

He let out a breath that he hadn't even been aware he was holding.

"Okay. It's a date then."

A date. The words hung there between them like a big, glaring sign with blinking neon letters. For some time, it was all Ethan could see, all he could think about. Finally, he found something normal and sane to say.

"Check the listings and pick a movie. I'll take care of dinner."

"A-all right."

"We can go into Nashville, if you want."

"Oh. Yes, that probably would be best."

"And we could drop by the hospital, if you want, check on your dad, before the movie."

"That sounds good."

"Good," he echoed. "Sounds good. Sounds like a plan. We can decide later what time I ought to pick you up."

She nodded at that and sucked in a breath so deep she might have been about to take a plunge off a diving board. He knew the feeling.

"Well." She peeled off his jacket and handed it to him. "Thank you for letting me use your jacket."

He tossed the garment over one shoulder and took her hands in his.

"No problem."

"Guess I'll see you tomorrow at work."

"Absolutely."

She stood there uncertainly for a moment before flashing him a shy smile.

"Good night, Ethan."

That was his cue to walk away, get back in the truck and drive off. Instead, he stepped closer, knowing that what he was about to do would leave no doubt in anyone's mind where they were now headed. Unlike that last impulsive kiss, asking her out or even taking her out, this would be irrevocable. Dinner and a movie could easily come under the heading of friendship. This could not. No wonder it felt like such a solemn event.

Heather looked up, and Ethan swallowed before slowly bending his head to hers. She stood as still as a statue, her big, beautiful eyes widening as he brushed his lips across hers, once, twice. He closed his eyes before coming back to settle his lips over hers. He stood like that for a long, breathless while before stepping back, still grasping her hands with his.

"Good night," he whispered, slowly backing away until their hands parted.

She nodded, looking positively dumbstruck.

He was halfway home before it occurred to him to wonder if that was a good thing or a bad one.

Chapter Thirteen

Heather stared at her reflection in the mirror, taking in the stylish drape of her soft, dove gray, wide-leg pants and the trim pleated waistline of the short, matching jacket. Collarless, with a single button closure, the V-front of the jacket showed the pretty lace trim of her white camisole top. High-heeled sandals and pearl earrings completed her ensemble.

She let her gaze wander to her head, fluffing and plucking at strands with her fingertips until her hair wisped just so about her face and shoulders. Leaning in close to the mirror, she studied her makeup. Pale pink lipstick, mauve eye shadow and blusher, plus mascara made the most of her overlarge eyes and, in her opinion, too pointy chin.

It had been a busy week, every day seeming longer than the last, but every morning she was getting up just a little earlier than the day before in order to dress.

Confident that she looked her best, she backed off once more and gave herself a nod.

"Ethan will approve."

Realizing what she'd said to herself, Heather blanched.

It was not up to Ethan to approve or disapprove of her appearance. This was not for him. She hadn't gone to all this trouble on a work day to look her best for Ethan. This was for herself, for everyone around her, for... Ethan.

Closing her eyes, she faced a horrible truth: she didn't really much care what anyone else thought anymore. Somehow, at some point, she had started to groom herself, to dress, to look her best for Ethan, and Ethan alone.

Remembering the poignancy of his kiss again, she stared at her reflection.

"Little fool," she told herself. "What have you done?"

Gone and fallen for a handsome wanderer was what she had done.

Appalled, she lifted her hands to her head.

"You've been down this road before," she lectured to her image. "He won't stay in Davis Landing. He'll move on, just like Joshua, but this time if you let him, he'll take your heart with him."

Forlornly, she plopped down on the foot of her bed and tried to think through this dilemma. How had this happened? They had first been coworkers, aware of each other only peripherally. Then circumstance had thrown them together until they'd become friends. After a while, their friendship had deepened.

And then, a few nights ago, he'd kissed her, really kissed her, and changed everything.

At least, things had changed for her. She couldn't be certain about him.

Oh, he'd been attentive all week, fleetingly. He'd been just as busy as she had, but what did that really mean? She had no way to be certain.

No, that wasn't entirely true. She could be certain about a few things concerning Ethan Armstrong Danes.

He was a man on the move, the sort of man who could and would pick up and go at the drop of a hat. Everything she knew about him proved it. Moreover, his upbringing couldn't have been any more different from hers if he'd grown up on a different continent.

His relationship with his parents seemed extremely casual, not at all close, not like her own relationship with her mom and dad, at any rate. She was twenty-seven years old and still living at home! Ethan probably couldn't even name all the places he'd lived since he'd struck out on his own.

To make matters worse, Ethan had no personal relationship with the Lord. Most likely he had no idea how her own relationship with God dictated her values and actions. He probably thought she was as casual about romantic relationships as the majority of society seemed to be. And who could blame him for that, considering everything that was going on?

After all, everyone now knew that her brother was not her father's child, not that she blamed anyone for that. Her mother had made obvious mistakes before she'd yielded her life to Christ, and her father had not handled the revelation of that secret at all well, but considering the state of his health, it was probably understandable. Besides, it wasn't Heather's place to judge.

Nevertheless, someone who didn't know them well could get the wrong idea about the Hamiltons. That was what made seeing the story splashed across the front page of the rural newspaper so horrid.

Ethan could be forgiven if he'd gotten the wrong idea, but she had compounded that erroneous impression by letting him kiss her! She'd known what was going to happen, had sensed it with every bit of herself, and yet she'd done nothing.

The truth was, she hadn't even thought about backing away or turning aside. She hadn't thought at all. Some part of her had felt that it was about time, though, while another part had concluded that the kiss had been inevitable.

Why hadn't she realized what it would mean?

She should have known this would happen. All the time that she'd been leaning on him, coming to count on his support and his understanding and his kindness, trusting his friendship and his reliability, she'd been falling in love. Hopelessly so. Because Ethan was not the sort of man who could ever return her feelings in full measure.

Yes, he was clearly fond of her. Perhaps he was
even attracted to her, but she was not the sort of
woman who could inspire the kind of transformation
in a man that was necessary here if they were to have
any chance at a future together. Changing the *nature*
of a creature was not as easy as changing its *appearance*.

Ethan Danes simply was not a forever sort of man.

With a groan, Heather flopped back on the bed.

She had no one to blame but herself. She'd gotten
carried away.

The makeover had changed her outward appearance, and Ethan had responded. Then she'd allowed
her emotions to overwhelm her good sense, because
of all the men in the world, Ethan Danes was the last
one who might be meant for her.

He'd been nice to her, considerate, complimentary,
and she'd created a romance from that, a one-sided
romance, for surely Ethan would never allow a relationship to turn him into something he wasn't, not
when he could have his pick of women. Many of those
women would be content to settle for the kind of temporary romantic relationship that he was probably
used to. Heather knew that she could not settle for that.

She had to end this thing before it went any further.
That meant that she could not go out with him
tomorrow night.

A part of her yearned for just one real date with
him, but another part, a saner, more disciplined part,

knew that it was best not to go there. She would not make a total fool of herself, yearning for what could not, should not be.

Heather chewed the inside of her lip, thinking.

This was Friday, so she'd have to tell him *today*.

For a long while she lay there staring up at the ceiling in her room, mentally reaching toward God. She needed His strength for this. She needed His wisdom.

Pastor Abernathy often said that the choices were ours, that once a child of God made the choice to do the right thing, then the Holy Spirit would step in and empower us to follow through.

She needed that empowerment now. Closing her eyes, she asked for it, pleaded for it.

Then she got up and went to work. Sadly, her joy in the day had completely disappeared.

She stopped by Ethan's cubicle on her way to her office. Curious, knowing eyes seemed to follow her every move. Necks craned, and heads turned as she walked through the partitioned corridors, bringing the realization that she would have to speak to him in private. Unfortunately, he was not in his cubicle. She jotted a note, asking him to come by her office, and left it in the center of his blotter.

As she passed Brenda's desk on her way to her office, she paused long enough to ask nonchalantly, "Seen Ethan this morning?"

Brenda shook her head.

"Nope, but I heard there was some problem with releases on those last photos. The agency goofed up somehow. So they're reshooting with new models."

"I see. Well, when he comes in, would you let him know that I need a moment of his time?" Brenda looked at her oddly, and after a moment, Heather knew that Brenda was wondering why she didn't just call his cell phone. "I, um, don't want to bother him while he's working."

Besides, this was definitely something best done in person.

"I can leave a message on his voice mail, if you want," Brenda offered belatedly, but Heather shook her head. He'd see the note she'd left before he checked his office voice mail.

"Don't worry about it."

Thoroughly annoyed with herself, Heather went into her office and shut the door. Why did he have to be out of the office this morning of all mornings? She took a deep breath, telling herself that she must not lose her nerve. Surely, when the moment came, God would give her the words and strength to do what must be done. Meanwhile, she had work to do.

She sat down behind her desk and opened a file folder. One of the women profiled here would be the magazine's next makeover subject. Of course, if she'd found a new columnist for the Makeover Maven feature, she wouldn't have to make these decisions herself, but she'd had precious little time to search for, let alone interview, possible employees. Resignedly, she picked up the first report and began to read.

The hours crept by, second by torturous second, and if she actually accomplished anything, Heather wasn't aware of it. When she'd finished the last report, she couldn't remember a thing that she'd just read, let alone fix facts to the faces in the photos. Doggedly, she began organizing her notes on the computer and scanning in the photos in hopes that creating a spreadsheet of sorts would refine the process.

All the time she worked, however, she just kept thinking about talking to Ethan and wondering what she should say. Honesty was undoubtedly the best policy. Yet she balked at the idea of revealing her feelings. She didn't want to embarrass herself further, and she didn't want to put Ethan on the spot. What good would that serve? Still, she couldn't lie to the man, either.

Mentally, she tried several different tactics, but nothing sounded right in her mind. She kept telling herself that she would know what to say when the moment came, but gradually her confidence in that approach began to erode. She began to question her decision to end things with Ethan.

One moment she asked herself if it wouldn't be best just to let the thing play out to its inevitable conclusion. Why not enjoy Ethan's attention until the day, surely not too distant, when he would load up his SUV, wave goodbye and drive away?

The next moment she knew that if she spent one more hour in his company, her heart would surely break when he pulled up stakes and journeyed on. Better not to risk getting any closer, investing too much.

On the other hand, it felt wrong to back off now. Ethan had been such a comfort to her, such a support when it seemed that her father would surely die. Ending it with him now made it seem almost that she had used him. Yet, she dared not get in any more deeply with him, and mere friendship no longer even seemed possible.

Oh, why had she spoiled everything by letting him kiss her? It would have been far better to take a step back, smile and tell him quite firmly that she didn't want to ruin their special friendship.

She tried to comfort herself with the idea that the man for her was out there somewhere, a man chosen for her by God, someone with whom she had everything in common, a perfect fit. Sooner or later, he would stumble across her, as he was meant to do, and she had to keep her heart whole until he came. When he did, she promised herself, she would *not* be disappointed that he wasn't Ethan.

A rap at her door had her looking up sharply. Her stomach seemed to drop as she imagined Ethan standing on the other side. Then it opened, and Amy charged into the room.

"We need to talk."

Those were words that had been circling inside Heather's head for hours, words she meant to say to Ethan. Relieved that the moment had not yet arrived, she pushed thoughts of Ethan aside and gave her full attention to her sister.

"What about?"

Amy dropped down in the chair at the end of Heather's desk and folded her arms. Sighing, she slumped back.

"Mom called."

Heather sat up a little straighter. "Is Dad okay?"

Amy waved a hand. "Physically, he's still holding his own, according to this morning's report."

"But?"

There was definitely a "but." Heather saw it in the way her normally calm and collected sister held herself.

"He wants to see Jeremy."

Heather relaxed. "That's good. I think that's good. He's got to make it right with Jeremy for all our sakes."

Amy pressed her fingers to her temples. "But Jeremy won't see him. He says he's not ready."

Heather bit her lip. "Well, I guess that's…natural, if anything about this whole situation can be termed *natural*. He needs time. We've all said it."

Amy leaned forward and splayed a hand against the top of Heather's desk. "He says he may *never* be ready."

Never? That meant the family would never be mended, never be whole again. Surely that couldn't be.

For a long moment, Heather didn't know what to say. Finally, she came out with a weak pronouncement. "He didn't mean it."

"Have you ever known Jeremy to say something he didn't mean?" Amy asked gently.

Suddenly Heather's chest hurt. "No."

"You and I both know you can discount about half of what Tim says when he's in a temper, which is more than half the time these days," Amy went on drily, "but Jeremy and Chris are different. As hard as Chris tries to keep his distance, he's always sincere, always thoughtful, in what he says and does. He may tease and make droll pronouncements, but he doesn't bluster, just holds back. Jeremy, on the other hand, has always been an open book."

"He's always been up-front with his thoughts and opinions and feelings," Heather concurred. "Honest to a fault, that's our Jeremy."

"And sensitive," Amy added.

"I've always thought it one of his most endearing qualities."

"This must be killing him," Amy said softly.

Heather nodded and reached for her sister's hand, reading Amy's thoughts. What if Jeremy never got over this? How did the Hamiltons go on being the Hamiltons without him?

Heather suddenly felt small and self-centered for worrying so about her own silly feelings when Jeremy was obviously suffering such torment.

Ethan did not return to the office on Friday. Heather tried to tell herself that the better course would be simply to go out as they had arranged on Saturday evening and make it plain by her actions that they were not meant to be more than friends. She knew herself too well, however, to really believe that would work. Ethan would be his usual charming self, and she would forget that it was not wise to enjoy him so. The only recourse was to cancel the date.

After work she drove over to Ethan's apartment.

It seemed at first that he was not at home. She waited until she judged she'd given him long enough to answer the door. It was a small apartment, after all, little more than one room with a sleeping alcove and a kitchen that could be encompassed with outstretched arms. Just as she turned away, however, trying not to feel relief, he opened up.

"Heather!" He sounded surprised but not unhappy to see her. "Hey, come on in."

Her spirits plummeted even further, but she nodded and made herself step over the threshold.

"What's brought you out my way?"

"I thought we ought to talk."

"Okay, sure. Want some tea? It's cold. No, wait. The tea's sweet, and I know you don't like sugar in yours. Maybe a diet soda? I think I've got one." As he spoke, he moved toward the tiny kitchen tucked against the back wall.

"I don't need anything to drink, Ethan," she said quickly, stopping him in his tracks.

He seemed finally to understand that something important was afoot. As he turned toward her once more, she cowardly turned away, noting absently that the apartment had undergone something of a transformation. The boxes were gone. The shelving unit in the corner was filled with books, CDs and photo albums. He'd acquired a throw rug from somewhere and a potted plant. A pair of photography magazines had been arranged neatly atop the burnished metal coffee table and a coat rack had been mounted on the wall next to the door. Presently it held a pair of camera bags by the straps and a baseball cap.

"Sit down," he all but ordered.

She shook her head, glancing at the boxy sofa with its nubby, gray tweed cover. Finally she made herself face him. He brought his hands to his hips as if to say, "Get on with it."

"I can't go out with you."

His expression barely altered. After an instant he gave a little half shrug, almost as if he'd been expecting her to say that very thing. His tone when he spoke was bland, unconcerned. "Okay."

Feeling unaccountably deflated, Heather launched into the most logical and unassailable of the excuses she'd rehearsed that afternoon. "My family is in terrible turmoil just now, Ethan."

"I understand."

"Jeremy isn't himself, and—"

"Hey, no need to explain."

He stepped toward the door; she stood her ground. He might not need explanations, but she did.

"Dad still isn't out of the woods, and we don't know where Melissa is."

He lifted both hands as if warding off unnecessary information, as if he didn't already know all these things.

"Listen, it's no big deal. Don't worry about it. You've got enough on your mind."

"But—"

"It was just a movie, Heather. Nothing important. Don't give it a second thought."

She feared for a moment that she might cry. She'd stewed and agonized all day about this, and it was of no more importance to him than, well, than a movie. Obviously this confirmed her assumptions. Ethan was not the man for her.

She took a reluctant step forward. Ever the gentleman, he hurried to the door and opened it for her. Suddenly she couldn't get out of there fast enough. A terrible anger seized her, and a deep, crushing disappointment.

"See you Monday," Ethan called cheerfully as she stepped out onto the narrow stoop.

Not trusting herself to speak, she nodded and

hurried down the steep steps to the pavement below. He closed the door, and it was done.

Somehow it didn't seem possible that it had gone so easily, that it could be over so quickly, but she knew that it was. No matter how casually he had accepted its demise, her relationship with Ethan Danes, whatever it had been, was finished.

And that's as it should be, she told herself, hurrying to her car. As she drove away, she went automatically to that one perfect refuge in her life. She began to pray. Aloud.

"Thank You, Lord, for giving me the right words to say, for letting it end without angry words and recriminations. Thank You for bringing me such a good friend in the first place. F-Forgive me for trying to make it more when it so obviously wasn't meant to be." A sob escaped her, but she quickly forced it back into her chest. "Take care of him," she whispered. "Find a way to help him understand that You love him and that he needs You."

She focused her prayer on her family after that, lifting up Jeremy and her father and Melissa. After all, what better way was there to get your mind off your troubles than to concentrate on those of others? Their needs were surely greater than hers. God's guidance and healing and intervention should rightly be concentrated on more important problems than misguided romantic dreams.

It did occur to her that, like pain, God's care and

concern came in all shapes and sizes, and that sometimes the key to healing was simple, unglamorous endurance. Eventually, even a broken heart healed.

Ethan switched off the television and sat for a moment in lonely darkness, his feet propped comfortably on the coffee table he'd so carefully placed and arranged earlier that week. He should have known it wouldn't make any difference, and he had. On some level he'd always understood that Heather Hamilton wasn't for the likes of him. No doubt she'd wind up with some top-dog editor someday or a Pulitzer-winning reporter. Or a trust fund kid just like herself.

He hoped it was someone who'd grown up in church, someone who would see the sweetness and purity of her nature, not just its pretty package. Whoever it turned out to be, though, it wouldn't be him.

Dropping his feet to the floor, he leaned forward, rubbing his hands over his face. It was pretty stupid of him to think he might have found a real home here in Davis Landing. Guys like him didn't have real homes, none they didn't walk around in, anyway. The truth was, he should have moved on months ago. He'd only stayed on this long because Heather had seemed to need him.

What had made him think that he could actually fulfill her needs, though?

Shaking his head, he braced his forearms against his knees. He felt a great need to do something, *say* something. For a moment he was puzzled, but then he realized with a shock that what he was feeling was a compulsion to pray. He thought wildly that he didn't have a clue how to go about such a thing, but that wasn't really so. He'd watched and listened and even on some level participated as Heather and her family had prayed. He knew the basics, it wasn't all that different from talking to yourself.

"I don't know what to ask for," he said aloud, and he immediately had the uncanny feeling that Someone was actually listening. He figuratively backed up a step.

Heather always started with "Dear Lord" or "Father," but Ethan didn't figure he had the right to use such familiarity.

"Okay, God," he began, lifting his head and staring into the darkness of the night-filled apartment, "I don't know much about You, but I figure You know as much about me as You ought to."

Enough to know that I'm not good enough for Heather Hamilton, he thought.

"Which makes this pretty much useless," he muttered, rising to stride over to the apartment's only window, a large plate-glass square that looked onto the small car park in the alley. Lifting the blind away from the glass with one finger, he peered out, tilting his head back to catch sight of the night sky above the three-story building across the way.

"Look out for her," he whispered. "If You take her dad, she's going to need someone. I don't know Wallace well enough to know what he deserves, but she's due the best. The way I see it, she's never hurt another soul."

Except him.

"And that's all on me," he said, letting the blind fall and turning his back against the wall.

He should have known better than to let himself get drawn in by a daughter of the Hamiltons. After all these years of looking for someplace to belong, someone to belong to, he should have known better than to reach so high. If he hadn't kissed her, they could have gone on being friends, but then he'd have had to stand by and watch some other guy walk off with her one day. He didn't think he could take that.

Looked like it was time to move along again.

The thought depressed him. How odd. Usually the idea of a new assignment and a new place excited him. Maybe once he had a new job and town to go to the old enthusiasm would rise again. He'd start looking around tomorrow. By the end of next week, he'd be all set.

One week of pretending that nothing has changed, he thought bleakly. *One week of being nothing more than her friend.* Maybe he could manage if he could keep his distance.

"Please, God," he whispered into the darkness. Just that.

But he didn't have much hope that God would be merciful to a guy who had never before paid Him much mind.

Chapter Fourteen

"I think we ought to drop it," Heather said bluntly.

Every person around the table looked at her as if she'd suddenly sprouted a second head, but it was Tim who put words to their expressions.

"That's nuts!"

"It's not nuts," Heather insisted, flipping the folder in front of her closed.

"The Makeover Maven is one of our most successful features!" Tim argued.

"The Makeover Maven is a shallow, gimmicky sham of a project, and not one of this month's candidates holds the least bit of interest for our readers."

Brenda, whose job it had become to winnow some fifty-odd candidates down to the most promising half dozen for Heather's consideration, seemed shocked by Heather's pronouncement.

"B-but what about the mother returning from Iraq?" she asked. "Her husband wrote a moving plea about helping her make the transition from military to civilian life?"

Heather shook her head. "It's an eloquent letter, I'll give you that, but just take a look at her." She rifled through the photos in the folder and slid the appropriate one to the center of the table. "Blue-eyed, blond, fit. Even without makeup, the woman's gorgeous. What's to make over?"

Tim barely glanced at the photo before saying, "All the better. Slap on a little paint, she'll look like a movie star."

"What makes you think she wants to look like a movie star?" Heather demanded. "She's a mother."

Sounds of exasperation gusted around the table. Abruptly, Heather felt her resolve crumple. She'd walked into the room adamantly, passionately convinced that the makeover feature was an insult to the integrity of the magazine and its readership. Now, suddenly, she just didn't care.

"Fine," she announced, pushing back her chair and gathering up her materials. "The soldier it is."

She walked out of the conference room with her eyes smarting and headed straight for her office, where she closed the door and spun to lean against it. Her shapeless skirt ballooned around her with the violence of her movement. Her too-large and too-ruffled matching blouse sagged. The hair that she had ruthlessly tucked behind her ears fell forward around a face bare of all cosmetics.

It is a sham, she thought fiercely. The whole makeover thing was all a sham. Why couldn't they see it? Changing her looks had done nothing but get her noticed by the wrong man. And she was so angry about it.

She was shocked by how angry she was. She was angry at Ethan, angry at herself. She was even angry at her father and Jeremy and Melissa. She was angry and sad and confused by everything that was going on, even her own emotions. Ethan was avoiding her, and under the circumstances she should have been glad about that, grateful, even, but she wasn't. She was just angry.

A knock reverberated against her back.

"Heather?"

She cringed at the wounded uncertainty of Brenda's voice. Gathering her courage, she stepped away from the door and turned, expecting it to open. Instead, another timid knock came. Irritated, she stepped forward and yanked it open. Brenda literally drew back, and at once Heather's irritation evaporated in a wave of contrition.

"Sorry. Didn't mean to startle you."

Brenda seemed to relax a little. "Hey, no harm done."

Heather folded her arms, feeling oddly self-conscious. "Did you need something?"

Brenda held out a pen and a sheaf of papers. "You, uh, didn't sign off on the editorial decisions."

"Oh." Sighing inwardly, Heather flapped her arms in frustration. "I don't know what's wrong with me."

"You've got too much on your mind," Brenda said helpfully, "and I told the editorial board so. It's just not fair that you have to handle the beauty editor's job on top of everything else."

Heather tried to smile at her assistant's loyal defense of what she suspected was indefensible behavior, but the smile wobbled too much to maintain.

"We'll find someone soon," she muttered.

"Sure you will," Brenda said brightly.

Heather took the papers and carried them to the desk, putting her back to Brenda as she glanced over the editorial directives and added her signature in the necessary places.

"I apologize about this," she said, handing the papers back to Brenda. "I hope I didn't make work for you. And I wasn't implying earlier that you hadn't done your job, either. It's not your fault that none of the candidates impressed me."

Brenda nodded, head bowed. She shifted from foot to foot before glancing up at Heather.

"Is there anything I can do?"

Heather swallowed. *Can you make Ethan Danes care as much for me as I care for him? Can you make him want to put down roots and build a home?* Might as well ask God to change night to day.

"You can get those directives back to Amy," Heather said softly, but then as her intrepid assistant reluctantly turned away, Heather called out to her, "Thank you, Brenda. I don't know what I'd do without you."

Nodding, Brenda hurried away, her expression lightened somewhat.

Heather closed her eyes and leaned wearily against the door jamb.

She was dragging down everyone around her, and she didn't know how to stop. How was it that she suddenly couldn't seem to figure out how to go on living her life? A child of God shouldn't have this much trouble doing the right thing.

Make the choice, she told herself sternly, *and trust God to empower you.* Surely the God of miracles and healing would never abandon His children in a time of personal trial. She had to remember that and pull her mood out of this ditch she'd let her life career into.

Straightening, she squared her shoulders and opened her eyes, only to see Ethan across the sea of half walls and partitions. Their gazes locked, but then he looked away. After a moment, he turned and walked toward the exit.

Immediately Heather felt her spirits slide toward her toes.

"Heather, it's Friday. We have to make a decision. Now. Otherwise, we won't have everything ready in time for the shoot."

"How about Sugar Tree Park?"

"We did the end-of-summer fashion layout at the park," Amy pointed out.

Heather sighed. She'd forgotten about that.

"I told you the makeover feature was a bad idea, and I'm fresh out of new ones. I can't wait until we hire a new beauty editor."

Amy plopped down into the chair at the end of Heather's desk with a sound of exasperation. Heather picked up a folder on her desk and dropped it in front of Amy.

"Have you see this bunch of applicants?"

"Seen them? Heather, I sent those resumes to you, remember?"

"I know you sent them. I just wondered if you'd actually looked at any of them."

Amy tossed the folder back at her. "Of course I have. Why?"

"There's not one likely candidate in the bunch, that's why."

Amy pinched the bridge of her nose. "Okay, fine. Then there will be in the next group. Meanwhile, we have to decide on a venue for the shoot, a venue other than the park."

Heather bit her lip, trying to think. After a moment, she shook her head. It was just no use. She couldn't put together a coherent thought, let alone a workable idea.

"We should have gone with the teacher," she grumbled. "We could have shot at the school."

"We did that four months ago!" Amy exclaimed.

"Don't you remember? It was your idea. Ellen didn't want to do it, but you convinced her, and it worked out wonderfully."

"See? I told you. I don't have any more new ideas." Heather dropped her head into her hands. "I can't do this."

"Of course you can," Amy said encouragingly. "You're just stressed right now. Everything's catching up with you."

Nodding, Heather admitted that Amy was right. "I'm so tired. I'm so tired I can't even think."

"You don't have to," Amy told her gently. "Ethan has an idea where we can shoot, and I think we should just go with it."

Heather gulped at the mention of Ethan. Only by sheer strength of will did she prevent tears from flooding her eyes.

"Fine."

Ethan was the photographer, after all. His judgment could be trusted in such things.

"It's a restaurant down on the river in Nashville," Amy went on, "something out of the ordinary. He said you'd know the one."

Heather blinked, remembering the night of her father's transplant, the night she and Ethan had eaten dinner at that oddly picturesque little restaurant on the river in Nashville. They'd spent hours laughing and talking, full of hope.

He was right, it would be a great set for the shoot.

Yet, how could she go back there with him now for any reason?

She closed her eyes against a fresh onslaught of tears and covered her mouth with one hand. Amy reached across the desk top to latch her fingers around Heather's wrist.

"Honey, what is it? I've never seen you like this."

Blinking rapidly, Heather straightened and pulled her hand away. "I don't know what you mean. This is exactly what I looked like before that ridiculous makeover."

"That's not what I'm talking about, and you know it. This whole week you've been a different person, someone I don't even recognize. And *this* isn't the real you." Amy waved a hand, indicating Heather's appearance. "Why are you suddenly trying to look twenty years older?"

Heather leaned back in her chair, a bitter, scoffing sound crawling up the back of her throat.

"Look again, Amy. This is the real Heather. Remember her? Plain but sensible."

Amy shook her head. "No," she said, "this Heather is heartbroken, sad. But why? Dad's getting stronger every day. Okay, Jeremy's still keeping his distance, but at least he hasn't gone any farther away from us."

"And Melissa?" Heather asked cryptically.

"With Melissa, no news is good news, the way I figure it."

"I'm sure you're right," Heather muttered, sitting up again and starting to shift papers and pens, as if looking like she was busy would actually help her to *get* busy, when she hadn't been able to concentrate for ten minutes at a run for days and days.

"It's Ethan, isn't it?" Amy finally asked.

Raw pain ripped through Heather, but she kept her face turned away in hopes that her sister wouldn't see.

"What makes you say that?"

"Oh, maybe it's the way you're avoiding each other, the haunted look that comes over you any time he's mentioned by name and vice versa."

Heather tried for nonchalant denial, and failed miserably.

"We're just friends," she managed, her bottom lip trembling.

"Just friends?" Amy echoed softly. "That's not what it looked like to me."

"What else could we be?" Heather all but wailed.

"A lot more than friends, apparently."

Heather shook her head, tears rolling down her face.

"How can you say that? You know Ethan. You're the one who hired him, against your better judgement, I might add. 'He's a short-timer,' you said. 'We'll be looking for his replacement in six weeks,' you said."

"So I was wrong. That was, what, seven or eight months ago now?"

"Which only means he's due to bolt."

Amy tilted her head, asking, "Has he said as much to you?"

"No," Heather admitted, wiping her face with her hands, "but he wouldn't, would he?"

Amy sagged back against her chair.

"I don't get it. If he hasn't said anything about leaving and with the two of you getting so close…"

"Too close," Heather blurted, wincing when she realized that she'd said it aloud.

For a long moment, Amy made no comment, just stared at her sister as if finally seeing her. Heather knew the moment that Amy came to a conclusion.

"Something's happened. What is it? Tell me."

Heather shook her head, but then the tears started to flow again and she heard herself gasping, "He kissed me!"

Amy blinked, her spine suddenly ramrod straight. "Ethan kissed you?"

Heather nodded miserably.

"That's what this is all about? Ethan kissed you."

"On the Fourth of July." Heather sniffed and swiped at her eyes. "That night. When he took me home."

"I don't understand," Amy said after a moment. "You're obviously crazy about the guy. So what's the problem?"

"Nothing can come of it, that's the problem."

"What do you mean, nothing can come of it?"

"Don't you see? It's Josh all over again."

"Who?"

"Joshua. Joshua Calvecchio."

"Calvec— Oh! That guy you dated in college."

"Exactly."

Heather sniffed and folded her arms, but Amy just stared at her expectantly.

"Exactly what? I don't get the connection."

Heather dropped her gaze, murmuring, "Haven't you ever wondered why I didn't marry Josh?"

"Not really. I didn't know things were that serious with you two."

Gaze averted, Heather toyed with a pen on the edge of her desk blotter.

"Well, it was. Except he left. Don't you remember? We graduated, and he took a job in Florida."

"Right, and you stayed here in Davis Landing." Amy's words had the sound of question to them.

"Of course I did. What else would I do? The family is here. The business is here. This is my home, and that's a word I don't think Ethan even knows the meaning of!"

Amy stared for several moments before quietly venturing, "So, you didn't marry this Josh because he took a job in Florida."

"Yes."

"And you can't be more than friends with Ethan because he might move on, too."

Heather sighed with relief because it seemed that Amy finally understood. "Yes."

Amy narrowed her eyes. "Have you actually discussed this with Ethan?"

"Not exactly? Why would I? Everyone knows he never stays in one place for long. He told me so himself."

"But you're just assuming that he's not going to stick around."

"Safe assumption, don't you think?" Heather insisted. "Besides, we have absolutely nothing in common. He has no family ties to speak of, and the only time he'd been through the doors of a church before the Fourth was to attend a couple of weddings in the past." Heather shook her head. "I'm not an idiot, Amy. I know better than to pin my hopes on a rambling man who doesn't share my faith and can have any woman he meets along the way."

"But if you care for him—"

Heather looked down. "I never said I cared for him."

"I know. The two of you just seemed to be getting so close."

"Yes, well, I learned my lesson with Josh," Heather muttered, folding her arms adamantly.

"I never knew about Joshua," Amy said. "You never told me."

"I never told anyone. What would have been the point?"

"The point is, I could have been there for you. I could have helped you through that disappointment. You're always here for the rest of us, always ready and willing to listen to our problems. It's about time you did some talking yourself. Now, if you would just talk to Ethan, you might be pleasantly surprised."

"I have. More or less."

"And?"

"And nothing."

Amy sat for a moment longer, her eyes narrowed to slits, then she rose to her feet.

"I'm really sorry to hear this."

"There's nothing for you to be sorry about." Heather looked away. "Everything would be fine if Ethan hadn't kissed me. We could have stayed friends, then."

"Oh, come on. Make me believe you don't really want to at least date the guy."

"I'm not like you," Heather said softly. "I'm not the kind who can date casually and then just move on to the next thing. I don't know why, but I'm not."

"You make me sound flighty," Amy complained.

"Oh, no. Never that. Just the opposite, in fact. You don't fall in love with every guy who takes you to dinner."

"And you do?"

Heather didn't bother to answer her. She obviously didn't have the words to make Amy understand or the energy to try any longer.

Amy tapped her fingertips on the edge of Heather's desk, then she turned and departed.

Heather wondered dispiritedly what her sister was thinking, but she was suddenly too tired to ponder mysteries. Just functioning, and barely that, seemed to be all she could manage at the moment.

At least the family drama had calmed down enough that she could take the weekend to rest and recoup. By Monday morning, she was sure, she'd be back to her old self again.

For some reason, that thought did not comfort her as it ought to have.

Amy stood outside of Heather's office and considered.

You don't fall in love with every guy who takes you to dinner.

That statement said much more than Heather realized, because Heather herself was the last woman to tumble in and out of love. In fact, so far as Amy could tell, Heather had never acted like this over some guy. She certainly hadn't when Josh What's-His-Name had taken himself off to Florida! Maybe he'd disappointed Heather on some level, but not like this.

It was true that Heather had always been a quiet, private sort of person, almost shy, especially around men. Yet, she'd been different with Ethan, and everyone had seen it. She'd come out of her shell like never before, and unless Amy missed her guess, Ethan was thrilled. Or at least he'd certainly given the appearance of being thrilled. She couldn't help wondering what had really gone wrong. The real question, though, was what she should do about this situation.

Never before had she stuck her nose in her sister's business. In the past, Heather had seemed too private and too well adjusted to warrant interference, but maybe the time had come for a bit of meddling. Maybe she just wanted to be the serene, sensible one, for a change, Amy mused, or maybe this was her chance to really do good for her sister.

Heather had always been the keeper of the family secrets. Quiet, trusted, sensible, nonjudgmental, she was easy to talk to, easy to confide in. Only today had it occurred to Amy that Heather herself had never had anyone *she* could confide in, no one to take her side and offer her support. Until Ethan.

Amy had watched, first with some puzzlement and then with growing delight, as Ethan had stepped in time after time to offer her sister a strong shoulder and quiet companionship. The two had seemed to grow closer and closer, and Amy had assumed that they were becoming a couple.

She still wasn't convinced that wasn't the case. Otherwise, why had Ethan kissed Heather? Maybe he was the love-'em-and-leave-'em type, or maybe he'd just never had any reason to stick around before. Whatever his motivation, Amy felt reasonably certain that Heather's heart was much more engaged that she wanted to admit. Heather's demeanor this entire past week literally shouted her unhappiness to the world.

That being the case, how could Amy sit by and watch her sister lose a man about whom she obviously cared without at least trying to put things right? Ethan could be the wrong man for Heather, or he could be exactly who Heather needed, but one thing was certain: she wouldn't know unless she made it her business to find out.

Ethan heard the car door as he lined up the shot, but he didn't think much of it. He was set up on a sidewalk along a residential street in the middle of the afternoon, taking exteriors for the house chosen for next month's *Nashville Living* feature. The sound of a car door closing was only to be expected. Then he heard the brisk *tap-tap-tap* of high-heeled shoes behind him and inwardly groaned, expecting some gawker to wander into his shot momentarily. He snapped several exposures before pausing to make adjustments to his tripod position and give the interloper time to satisfy his or her curiosity. It was then that he heard a surprisingly familiar voice.

"Ethan, do you have a minute?"

He turned to Amy Hamilton with raised eyebrows. "Sure."

No one with an ounce of sense refused to make time for the boss, but his stomach did a flip as he considered the possible reasons she might have sought him out here in Nashville.

"Let's get out of the sun," she suggested.

Nodding to the senior editor, he left his setup and followed her to the base of a towering hickory that threw shade over the sidewalk, the street, and a pair of vehicles parked at the curb, his being one of them. Ethan ambled over to lean against the fender of his SUV, mentally preparing himself for what he feared would be a difficult conversation.

Looked like it was time to start packing again, after all. He'd been telling himself that he'd out-stayed his welcome for the past week but hadn't quite been able to make himself pick up and go. Apparently the Hamiltons were going to save him the effort.

Ethan folded his arms.

"What's up?"

"I've been talking to my sister."

Here it comes, he thought. Yet, he couldn't quite believe that Heather would have him fired.

"Does she know about this?"

Amy shot him a look, then shook her head. "No."

He relaxed, very glad that Heather wasn't behind this, at least not intentionally.

"You don't have to say anything else. I know I blew it and that it would be better if I moved on now."

"Blew it? Ah, you mean by kissing her."

He let his gaze slide away, not sure why that hurt to hear. He'd already faced the music privately. It just seemed out of character for Heather to discuss their business with anyone else. Then again, he reminded himself, they had no *business* between them.

"She's not comfortable around me now," he said as calmly as he could manage. "I understand."

"Well, I don't!" Amy exclaimed, yanking his gaze back to her. "Just tell me, Ethan, what were you thinking when you kissed her?"

Ethan turned away, placed his hands flat on the fender of his vehicle and swallowed in an effort to still the tremors inside his chest.

"What difference does it make?"

"It makes a lot of difference, actually," Amy said, and for some reason he believed her.

He stared at his hands, trying to put it into words.

"I thought she was the best thing ever to come into my life." He closed his eyes. "I thought I'd finally found a reason to—" He broke off, swallowing what he'd been about to reveal.

"To stay," Amy surmised softly. "The rambling man is ready to put down roots for our Heather."

Ethan sucked in a surreptitious breath. Then he shrugged and turned around, calling up every ounce of nonchalance he'd ever claimed.

"I wouldn't know a root if I tripped over it."

"And *that's* what's got her thinking the two of you aren't right for each other."

"Well, I can't argue with that. I mean, who am I to match up with a Hamilton, right?"

"Is that what you want, Ethan, to 'match up' with Heather?"

He smirked. "Are you asking me what my intentions are toward your sister, Miss Hamilton?"

Amy lifted one pale eyebrow. "I guess I am."

"I don't have any," he stated flatly, wincing mentally at the bitter edge to his voice. "I have no intentions whatsoever toward Heather, because she is not interested. Period."

"Oh, really?"

"She couldn't have made it clearer."

Amy shook her head. "I find that hard to believe, considering that I left her crying over you not an hour ago."

Ethan jerked as if he'd been poked. "Over hurting my feelings, you mean."

"No. She didn't say anything about your feelings, only that you were bound to pick up and take off again anytime now—just like her college boyfriend."

"What?"

"She didn't say anything to you about him?"

Ethan shook his head. He'd have remembered if Heather had mentioned another man.

"Well, apparently they were talking about getting married after they graduated," Amy told him, "but he took off for Florida, and she—"

"Could never leave Davis Landing," Ethan interrupted.

It was a given, a foregone conclusion. Heather belonged here with her big, messy family and the magazine, her church, her friends. He, on the other hand, had never belonged anywhere. Except maybe with her. But, no. He knew better than that.

"The truth is, I'm not good enough for her," he said as much to himself as to Amy.

"Oh, please," Amy scoffed. "You should know the Hamiltons better than that by now."

"It's got nothing to do with the Hamiltons," Ethan admitted. "It's me. It's Heather." He took a deep breath and bared his soul. "She's the best person I know. Her faith alone humbles me."

Amy smiled sympathetically. "I've often felt the same way, Ethan. Heather's capacity to trust God amazes me at times, and I grew up with her. But I've come to understand that she's as prone to self-doubt as the rest of us."

"Not Heather," he refuted, shaking his head.

"Yes, Heather. She's crazy about you. I know my sister well enough to know that much. But she's afraid to trust her own feelings, afraid it won't be enough to hold you when the wanderlust strikes again."

Wanderlust? he thought sourly. It wasn't wanderlust that always made him the outsider. It wasn't wanderlust that kept him looking for someplace to belong. It wasn't wanderlust that made him want to climb into his truck and drive away without looking back.

But he would look back. He'd always look back to this place. Still, that was better than staying around and disappointing Heather, wasn't it?

Except he already had disappointed her.

"I don't know."

"Will you do me a favor, Ethan?" Amy asked uncertainly. "Will you pray about this? Will you just pray about talking to her before you decide to leave?"

"I don't think she even wants—"

"Please, Ethan," Amy urged. "If anyone ever deserved to be happy, it's Heather, and I've seen how good you've been for her."

He shook his head. "No, I haven't. I don't even know how to be good for someone."

Amy stepped closer.

"Just consider it, then, and if you can find your way clear to pray about it, I think you'll realize that you have a lot to say and a lot to give. Someone has to help her now, and I'm not sure anyone but you can."

She left him standing there with his mouth open and nothing to say that seemed to make any sense. Finally, he just nodded. Whether or not she even saw him, he didn't know. It didn't really matter, because all that nod meant was that he had no choice, really, but to think about what she'd said.

Chapter Fifteen

Ethan dropped the box onto the coffee table and sat down on the sofa among stacks of books waiting to be packed. He reached for the nearest stack but in the end picked up only the top hardcover and turned it over in his hand.

It was a good book. He'd enjoyed it, but he had no intention of ever reading it again. He really didn't know why he'd kept it. For years he'd dragged this thing around for no good reason, yet he couldn't bring himself to throw it away. With a sigh of resignation, he tucked the book into a corner of the box then reached for another.

His hand never completed the journey.

Slumping back against the sofa, he rubbed both palms over his face. What was he doing? On the other hand, what else could he do? He didn't know how to do anything except move on when disappointment settled in. If this disappointment felt deeper, broader than any he'd experienced before, well, all the more reason to go. Unless… What if Amy was right and Heather did care for him? More importantly, what if she actually *needed* him?

Perhaps it didn't signify for a person like Heather, whose family obviously depended upon her quiet good sense and kindness, but Ethan had become painfully aware that no one had ever needed him before. He had felt honored, shocked and pleased that Heather had seemed to need him at times, which was exactly why he'd kept rushing to assist her every time a crisis had arisen.

It was more than that, though. He'd glimpsed a different kind of life with Heather. For the first time he'd really seen what it meant to be part of a family—and not just the troubles and disappointments this time. More, he'd seen what it meant to live the kind of life that one could look back on with pride. That was part of the problem.

He'd always thought of himself as a pretty good fellow, but he knew that he didn't measure up to Heather's standard. Her goodness, her utter lack of ego and self-interest, the inherent sweetness of her personality, her constant dependence on God, her ability to give thanks even in the midst of despair, all pointed out the shallowness of his own existence. Heather lived a kind of life that he wasn't at all sure he could fit into, and a perfect example of that was Amy asking him to pray about talking to Heather before deciding whether or not to leave town.

It wasn't that he was against praying, really, or even to discussing his feelings with Heather. It was more that he just didn't know how to begin. Was he supposed to ask God whether or not he should talk to Heather? And if so, how was God supposed to reply? Why should God listen to him, anyway?

Yet Amy seemed to feel that it was something he *could* and *should* do. Amy didn't know him, though. She wouldn't understand that he and God had never been on easy speaking terms. To Ethan, intentional prayer felt rather like imposing on a stranger.

If speaking to a stranger on the street made a difference for Heather's sake, Ethan knew he wouldn't have hesitated, but this wasn't quite the same thing. So what should he say? How presumptuous was it to think that God pay attention to someone like him?

Ethan rubbed his hands over his face again. He either had to get some answers to his questions or he had to load up his truck and get out of Davis Landing. Looking around him, he faced facts. Somehow he couldn't seem to make himself pack, so he guessed he'd better start trying to get some answers. But where?

He actually thought about Wallace Hamilton, then rejected the idea flatly. The last thing a sick man needed was a nobody whom he didn't particularly trust asking stupid questions. Christopher, as Heather's twin, was out of the question, as was Jeremy, for obvious reasons.

Leaning forward, Ethan braced his elbows on his knees and bowed his head, clasping his hands around the nape of his neck.

God, if You can hear me, I need some help here. What am I supposed to do?

God, of course, did not speak, or if He did, Ethan couldn't hear Him. And there lay the crux of the problem.

Suddenly Ethan remembered something that Heather had said the day he'd taken her to look for her brother Jeremy. That day had been the first time that he'd seen the church. They'd gone there because Heather had said that Jeremy had often stopped at the church to pray. Ethan remembered that they'd driven around the building to an entrance on the side where she'd hoped Jeremy's car might be parked.

Maybe, if he went there, he could get in that way. Surely God would be more apt to hear his prayer from church. Without even knowing why he thought that was true, Ethan rose and headed for the door. Ten minutes later, he was driving through town toward the river.

Since it was Saturday afternoon and the middle of July, people were out and about, biking, skating, jogging or just walking their dogs. He saw a couple with small children hiking toward the park with a kite and a couple going in the opposite direction trailing one. When he crossed the Cumberland bridge, he noticed several large motorboats anchored on the

Davis Landing side of the river. Folks in deck chairs were talking and laughing as they dropped lines into the water. In the distance he caught sight of a skier slewing around the bend, throwing up a shelf of white-caps as the skis cut into the surface of the water.

These people, he thought to himself, *are all home, or at least they know where they belong.*

The thought depressed him and woke a kind of envy he hadn't acknowledged since he'd been a child. It had been tough, always being the new kid in school, but he'd learned to act cool and confident, friendly but not too friendly. Consequently, nearly all his relation-ships had been only surface deep, with very few ex-ceptions. Realizing that fact left him feeling raw and lost.

Crossing over into the Hickory Mills area, he navi-gated streets largely empty in the business district near the river. Farther on, nearer his destination, the residen-tial avenues were lined with parked cars. His ears oc-casionally caught the puttering of lawn mowers.

Then he was driving along the lane that led directly to the church, the overarching trees putting him in mind of the ceiling of the central auditorium where he'd sat with Heather and her mother and sister on In-dependence Day. It was a peaceful drive, angling slightly upward until he reached the flat plane of the parking lot in front of the building.

Following a path made by memory, he skirted the stately white brick to the far side, nearer the river, and parked right up next to the building. He had the entire side lot to himself. There a glass door in the side of the building had been painted with the words "Prayer Chapel. All welcome." Figuring he had the place to himself, he got out and walked inside.

The door opened into a tiny vestibule, where a gold-edged guest book rested on a stand, a pen dangling from an attached ribbon. Removing his sunglasses, he glanced at the book but didn't sign it, moving instead straight ahead to a pair of pocket doors set between two panels of glass. A glance showed him that the tiny chapel was vacant.

Four or five rows of armless chairs padded with burgundy cushions to match the carpet had been arranged to leave a central aisle that led to a small altar covered with a white satin cloth trimmed in gold. Above the altar, against a dazzling white wall, rose a rough cross draped with a purple cloth and lit by a well-placed skylight rather than the brass lamps standing at the end of each row of chairs.

On either side of the cross hung colorful banners decorated with various symbols such as hands folded in prayer and a white dove clutching an olive branch in its beak. Another resembled a golden lamp with a flame at its tip. The one that caught his attention, however, was a circlet of thorny vines.

A crown of thorns. He didn't know how he knew that, couldn't even think where he might have heard it from, and yet somehow he recognized that symbol. It seemed to contain a message of both suffering and honor.

Ethan walked to the second row of chairs and sat down in the center, leaving a pair of empty seats on either side of him. He studied the symbols on the wall hangings and wiped his palms on the thighs of his jeans, wondering if he should have worn better clothing for this.

"Well, God," he said, staring at the cross, "here I am."

God did not speak a word, but again Ethan had an uncanny feeling that someone was listening.

Just then, a hidden door to one side of the altar opened, and Charles David Abernathy walked in carrying a big black Bible on a brass stand. His jeans and polo shirt calmed Ethan's fears about his own clothing, but the pastor's easy, welcoming smile made Ethan wonder if the prayer chapel was monitored.

"Hey, Ethan. Don't let me interrupt."

Ethan shifted uneasily, muttering, "No problem."

The big redheaded minister placed the Bible on its stand in the center of the altar and turned back to Ethan. He moved to the front row of chairs and leaned forward, grasping the back with both hands and placing his knee on the seat.

"You're looking pretty serious. Can I do anything for you?"

Even as he shook his head, Ethan heard himself saying, "I don't know."

Pastor Abernathy twisted to one side, sinking down

to fold his arms atop the back of the seat, one leg folded beneath him.

"Why don't you tell me what's bothering you, and let's see."

Ethan hitched his elbows up and hung them on the backs of the chairs next to him, trying to look relaxed.

"I don't quite know where to begin."

"Well, let's start with what you've you been doing since I saw you last."

Suddenly Ethan knew just what to say, and even as his cheeks reddened with embarrassment, he felt the words tumbling out of him. "I did something stupid that night after we left here."

It wasn't easy to tell, but eventually Ethan spilled everything to the genial pastor. He told Abernathy how much he'd come to admire Heather, how much he'd enjoyed her company, how she'd made him feel accepted, a real part of something that had seemed permanent. Ethan even admitted that he'd misread his relationship with Heather and ruined everything by kissing her good-night. Finally, he talked about her sister's request and how inadequate he felt to the task.

Abernathy surprised him by refuting at least one of his conclusions.

"I don't think you misread anything. I know Heather pretty well, and it seems to me that she has come to care for you a great deal. No doubt things changed between you that night, but they were already changing. That's often how it happens, you know," the pastor went on.

"You meet some halfway attractive woman who surprises you by being pretty easy to talk to. Then you realize that she's turned out to be a good friend, and as time passes she somehow looks better and better and friendship doesn't quite cover it anymore. Next thing you know you can't imagine living without her, and you start hoping she feels the same way."

"But that's where I misread," Ethan insisted. "She doesn't feel the same way. She all but told me so."

Abernathy shook his head. "I don't think so. I think Heather does care for you."

"Well, if she does, she doesn't know it," Ethan scoffed.

"Maybe she knows it, but she doesn't trust it," Charles David proposed.

"Doesn't trust me, you mean."

Charles Davis paused before answering. "Not necessarily. Maybe she thinks she's not supposed to feel that way about you."

Ethan dropped his arm, muttering, "Because I'm not good enough for a Hamilton."

Abernathy actually grinned. "If you'll think about it, you'll find that you're projecting your own assumptions onto Heather. She's the last one you'd expect snobbery from."

Ethan frowned, but after a moment he had to admit that the pastor was right.

"Actually, that's something I've always admired about her, the way she treats everyone with such dignity and fairness. She always seems to think the best of everyone and do the best thing for everyone. Even in the worst moments, she has this serenity about her, this sweetness. She's almost totally selfless, and the faith she has... It's like she *knows* that God will take care of her," Ethan went on. "She trusts Him to do what's best, even when what's happening hurts her."

He swallowed. "The truth is, I don't know how she does it, but I just know I can't. My whole life, it's been only me, and I think it's made me selfish and useless, when you get right down to it."

"Ah." Charles David Abernathy smiled and parked his boxy jaw atop his folded arms. "See, turns out I can help you after all. What you need, my friend, is a bit of grace."

"Grace?" Ethan furrowed his brow. "I don't follow."

"Let me explain it to you," Charles David said. "There's a whole ocean of grace that flows from the cross of Christ." He swung an arm around and pointed behind him. "And it's free for the taking by anyone willing to put aside the past and believe."

Ethan sat forward, intrigued and suddenly hopeful.

"What does that mean, putting aside the past?"

Pastor Charles David Abernathy seemed to smile with his whole being.

"I was hoping you'd ask."

Some time later—it might have been minutes or hours—Ethan rose from his knees at the end of the aisle in front of the altar. He stood for a moment in the quiet of that tiny sanctuary and assessed his feelings. The most acute was sheer relief, followed closely by awe and a sureness he'd never known was possible.

Charles David had left him earlier, though Ethan couldn't have said how long ago that might have been. After explaining that being "good enough" in God's eyes required asking for and accepting the grace that flowed from the sacrifice Christ had made upon the cross, he'd asked Ethan a few pointed questions designed to demonstrate his understanding of the concept. He'd then left Ethan to pray.

Ethan hadn't planned what had followed. He'd come there to pray about whether he should try to talk to Heather about his feelings for her. Instead, he'd found himself thinking of regrets, things he'd done and wished he hadn't or things he hadn't done and wished he had. Turned out that he'd had a lot to get off his chest, and by the time he was finished with that, he'd had some questions about how he could do better.

The funny thing was that as he'd prayed, he'd thought the answers himself. They'd just sort of popped into his mind, and the upshot of it was that he had to stop running and start investing some honest effort and emotion in others.

He was painfully aware that it might not make a difference in some cases, especially with Heather. But if his life was going to change for the better, he had to start taking some risks that went beyond simply being the new kid on the block. That might be frightening and difficult for some, but for him it was life as usual. That was his comfort zone. It was time to stop and make a permanent place for himself in this world.

All this time, he realized, he'd been looking for a place to belong, and suddenly he understood that belonging didn't always just happen. Sometimes it took real work. Sometimes it took staying put even when you wanted to run. Sometimes it meant being willing to lose, to endure, even being willing to have your heart broken.

Ethan looked up at the cross, backlit now by artificial means as the evening light had waned, and he understood a bit about what it meant to sacrifice for a love that might never be returned, might never be acknowledged or realized or might even be rejected. He gulped, both because he had been one of those who *hadn't* realized and because it might well be his turn to feel rejection, albeit on a much smaller scale.

Knowing that he was letting himself in for a kind of pain he'd always managed to avoid in the past, Ethan was willing to take that risk, to endure the disappointment that might well await him. It was in God's hands now, and he was content to let it rest there because he now understood that no matter what happened between him and Heather, he would never again be alone.

* * *

Heather pinched her nose with a tissue and sniffed. A summer cold was always the worst.

Except it wasn't a summer cold, no matter what she'd told Vera Mae earlier to explain the sweat suit, red eyes and tissues.

Or maybe it was. She certainly felt lousy enough to be sick. But she was sick at heart. And she didn't know why. She really didn't.

Doing the right thing was supposed to feel good on some level, even if it was difficult. On the other hand, maybe this was just the first time that she'd ever really given up what she wanted in order to live in God's will. Maybe before it had always been easy because there had been no real conflict. Which meant that confession would bring relief, right?

Except that it hadn't.

For the first time Heather was confused about her relationship with God, so much so that she didn't even know how to pray. She wanted God's will for her life; she really did, and yet she wanted Ethan, so much so that over the past week or more she'd prayed repeatedly to have that desire taken away. That hadn't happened yet, and the longer this went on, the worse she felt.

To her shame, she'd even taken to bargaining with God. She'd told God that she'd go right back to being her old self again, if that was what He wanted. Somehow, though, she couldn't seem to make that happen.

Oh, she'd washed her face and parted her hair in the

middle, tucking it behind her ears in as plain a style as she could manage, and she'd traded her stylish clothes for old ones. But all she'd accomplished was making herself feel strange and out of sorts. She just didn't feel like herself at all.

It wasn't about *feelings,* of course. It was about actions. She'd tried to do the right thing so far as Ethan was concerned.

Yet she found no peace, no certainty, and lately every time she sat down to pray she found herself on the verge of asking God to let her have Ethan in her life.

Was it possible that she was supposed to do that?

She didn't see how it could be. Everything she knew about the two of them told her that Ethan could not be the man whom God intended for her.

Perhaps God didn't intend her to be with anyone. It wouldn't be the first time she'd misinterpreted her own desire as God's will. She just didn't know what to think anymore.

The distant chime of the doorbell came to her, which was surprising since it was very nearly impossible to hear anything from the front of the house back here in the library, especially with the doors closed. Then again, the house was too often silent these days. Most of the time, only she and Vera Mae could be found in the place. Since Vera Mae worked Tuesday through Saturday, Heather kept her seat, assuming that the housekeeper would answer the door.

Curled up in the corner of an overstuffed leather

club chair, she lifted the book she'd been trying for hours to read and turned back to the beginning of the poem, unable to remember a word of the earlier verses.

The second time the bell chimed, she felt a spurt of exasperation. Who on earth could that be? She wasn't expecting company and wasn't particularly in the mood for any.

Glancing at the clock on the mantel, she was surprised to find that it was after nine. Vera Mae would be long gone to her own home. Heather uncurled her legs, but still she hesitated. It was late for someone to drop by.

The bell chimed a third time, and Heather sprang up with a huff of alarm. Surely if it was about her father or another member of the family, someone would have phoned. Puzzled, she got up to answer the door.

Eerie silence greeted her. Dismay shimmered through her and then away as the bell chimed yet again. Well, of course the house was quiet. She was the only one at home, although her mother should have come in by now. Heather vaguely remembered Nora saying something about dinner out with friends.

Maybe Nora had forgotten her key. Or maybe Melissa had at last come home and was unsure enough of her welcome not to simply walk in as usual. It could even be that one of the Andersons had read Jeremy's story in the newspaper and had come looking for him.

A flurry of other, more fearful possibilities filled

her head. Someone could have been hurt or, even
worse, killed in an accident. Chris might even have
been wounded on the job!

Heather headed toward the front door, her fuzzy
bedroom slippers scuffing along the hardwood floors
as she moved swiftly through the house. As she drew
nearer her destination, she realized that the porch lights
hadn't been switched on, so it was impossible to tell
who stood on the other side of the heavy, leaded glass.

Reaching for the light switch at the same time that
she reached for the doorknob, she flipped and turned
at the same moment, calling, "I'm here!"

She swung the door open to find Ethan Danes
turning around to face her, as if he'd given up and had
been about to go away. She wished that he had. Her
first impulse, in fact, was to close the door and pretend
he wasn't there. Unfortunately, good manners and the
habits of a lifetime wouldn't let her. Gulping, Heather
backed up a step.

"Ethan, what are you doing here?"

"We need to talk," he said softly.

Quickly, Heather considered her options. One, she
could refuse, politely, of course. That didn't seem likely
to be a successful ploy, however. He had a look about
him that she'd never before seen. It wasn't stubbornness
or determination. She'd seen both the day of her
makeover, and knew that he could be implacable when
determined on a course. This was something else,
something more like…*conviction.* Yes, that was it.

Whatever his reasons for coming, Ethan was utterly convinced that it was the right thing to do. That being the case, she didn't much think he was going to shrug and leave again if she asked him to.

That brought her to option number two. Get it over with as quickly as possible. That definitely seemed the most expedient course. In all likelihood, he'd come to tell her that he was leaving town, anyway.

She wasn't surprised, now that she thought of it. She'd been expecting this, after all. Her every instinct had told her that this would happen. It was decent of him to give her the news personally and in private. All that remained was to play out the final scene.

Resigned to a few difficult minutes in his company and the pain that it was sure to bring, Heather motioned him inside. After he stepped through the door, she closed it, then took a moment to steel herself. Briefly bowing her head, she reached for strength and solace.

So this was it. A mild sense of vindication crowded in with the myriad other emotions that filled her. She beat it back as unworthy of a child of God.

It wasn't about being right. Or wrong, for that matter. This was about being who and what God meant her to be, whether lovely or plain, fat or thin, short or tall, single or married. It was about acceptance of God's will and purpose. She believed with her whole being that this was the path to true happiness.

No one had said that it wouldn't be frightening. But her God was a god of miracles and power and wisdom, a god of love and caring and provision. Her job was to trust and obey, to hold tight to all that she knew of her Lord and accept whatever He deemed best, and that was what she was going to do.

Ethan stood in the center of the foyer, his arms crossed, blatantly taking in the place, while Heather decided where to put him.

Might as well stay right here, she decided. The formal living room felt too formal, the family room too intimate and the library too private. She walked over to the foot of the staircase and leaned against the newel post, waiting for him to face her. He finally did. She indicated a step on the staircase.

"Will this be all right?"

"Sure."

She slipped around the newel post and seated herself, drawing up her knees on the step below and leaning her forearms against them, hands linked.

"It's a nice house," he said, coming to brace one foot against the bottom stair.

"Thanks."

He tilted his head, studying her now, and she inwardly cringed, knowing how disheveled and unkempt she looked. Concern sparked in his dark eyes.

"Are you all right?"

She sighed, wishing she'd taken more care, and nodded. "I think so."

He seemed unconvinced. "You aren't sick, are you?"

She looked down, suddenly ashamed of the self-pity in which she'd been wallowing. "I'm not sick."

He shifted closer, folding his forearms atop his knees. "It's just that you don't look like yourself."

She chuckled at that. "Wrong. I look exactly like myself. This is the real me, Ethan—plain, colorless, even frumpy."

"You don't believe that," he said, but her level, un-wavering gaze seemed to shake him. "You *can't* believe that."

"I don't mind," she said softly. "I only want to be what God wants me to be."

He stared, narrowing his eyes as if trying to see what she did. "Why would you believe that God wants you to be less than you are?"

Her jaw dropped. "It's not that, Ethan!"

"Then it must be that you don't see what I do."

"Since the makeover, you mean. Before that, you didn't even *look* at me."

"That's not true. I've always looked at you, from the first day I interviewed with Hamilton Media, but you wouldn't give me the time of day. The makeover was just my first chance to get close to you. And yes, I was glad that you'd decided to let everyone else see how pretty you are, but so what?"

She stared at him, trying to wrap her mind around the idea that he might actually find the *real* her attractive. For some reason, that thought frightened her.

"This isn't supposed to be happening."

"I don't understand. What isn't supposed to be happening?"

"You're not supposed to like the real me."

"Why ever not?"

"Because I'm not pretty, and you know it."

He looked truly perplexed and more than a little impatient.

"Of course you are! In fact, you're beautiful, even more beautiful than I realized."

"Like this?" she demanded doubtfully, sweeping her hands downward, indicating her appearance.

"Yes, like this. Any way at all."

She just didn't know what to make of that. This was not the conversation she'd expected to have.

"So you prefer me in sweats and no makeup?" she challenged.

He straightened, his foot slipping off the step to land on the floor. "I'm not talking about appearance, Heather. I couldn't care less about that. I'm talking about inside, where it counts most." He stepped closer, bent down and tilted her face up, framing it with his long, artistic hands. "Inside, Heather Hamilton, you're the most beautiful thing I've ever known, and I thank God for that."

Heather went perfectly still, trying to understand what that might mean, and then a tiny flame flickered to life inside of her. The warmth and light of it spread steadily, until her whole being radiated with it.

"Ethan," she whispered, "what did you just say?"

He smiled with such genuine happiness that it took her breath away. "You heard me."

He dropped his hands to her arms and slowly lifted her to her feet. Standing two steps up from the floor brought her face level with his.

"Sweetheart, all that makeover did was show the world that you're almost as beautiful outside as you are inside," he told her, "but I know now that wasn't really the point."

"The point," she echoed, beginning to feel a bit lightheaded.

He nodded and said, "I know now that God brought me straight to you because *I* was in need of a make-over." He thumped his chest. "In here."

Her eyes grew large, as if they were trying to catch up to her heart. "Ethan? What are you saying?"

He slid his hands down her arms to her elbows. "I guess what I'm trying to say is that I've found something special here in Davis Landing."

"And you'll take that with you when you go?" she prompted.

He shook his head, one corner of his mouth crooked up in a wry smile that proclaimed he was surprised as she was to hear him saying, "I'm not going anywhere. Not unless God tells me to. At least not until I figure out just exactly what He has in store for me here. For *us.*"

Heather stared so hard that her eyes began to water,

and when she spoke, her voice was watery, too. "I didn't think there was an *us*."

He lifted a hand and brushed at her hair. One side fell forward, against her face, and he followed it with a gentle sweep of his fingertips.

"Well, God and I had a long talk about that this evening," he said matter-of-factly, "so you might want to rethink. Oh, and Charles David agrees with me. We had a long talk, too. Most of it didn't have a thing to do with you and me, but then I didn't need anyone to tell me what an idiot I'd be to walk away from you. I already knew that."

His smile revealed all about which he and the pastor had spoken. Heather saw it as plainly as if he wore a sign. The peace, the certainty, the rightness, it was all there. She saw that and more.

She saw the answer to prayers she hadn't even had the sense to utter, the broken, pointless shards of her own weak suppositions. It hit her then that she'd been looking at this through the cloud of her own insecurities. She'd been afraid to let herself believe, to hope, that this time it was right.

"Ethan!" she gasped, joy flooding her eyes with tears.

He laughed, and she knew it was because he was feeling the same thing she was.

"What?"

"Are you sure?"

"Never more sure," he vowed. "About a lot of very important things."

"It's just that Davis Landing isn't exactly the center of the universe."

"It's the center of *my* universe," he stated flatly. "Look, maybe it's not about *us*. I may not be the man of your dreams. I'm not even the man of *my* dreams, but that's not important anymore. What matters is what God intends me to be, what He intends *us* to be. That's all that counts. That's all I care about. And I just want you to know that I'm right where I want to be, where I'm *supposed* to be. I can't even imagine wanting to be anywhere else because, well, sweetheart, I guess the truth is, you're the woman of my dreams, sweats and all."

"Ethan! Oh, Ethan!"

Laughing, she threw her arms around him, and when his closed around her, she knew that they both wanted the same thing. Moreover, her every prayer had been answered in spectacular fashion. She understood it all then.

It wasn't that God wanted her to be plain or that she wasn't supposed to find her heart's mate. It wasn't about what she didn't have in common with Ethan or how handsome he was or how many places he had lived.

It was about two people finding God's will for their lives, about the wonder of shared meaning and hearts filled to overflowing. It was about getting all the junk out of the way—all the hang-ups and misconceptions and failures and disappointments and the self-limiting lies that people are so quick to tell themselves—

so God could make something truly wonderful from something ungainly and a little odd, like the caterpillar that becomes the butterfly. Beautiful.

Epilogue

The sound of tires on the gravelly pavement outside was exactly what those waiting in the formal living room of the Hamilton house had been listening for.

"Well, it's about time," Nora said, rising gracefully to her feet. Since Wallace had been deemed healthy enough to return to the hospital in Davis Landing, she almost looked her usual self again. She glanced at the watch pinned to the bodice of the sleeveless, tailored, salmon pink silk top that she wore with slim off-white slacks. "It's almost half past four already," she announced.

"Tim did call to say he'd be late," Heather reminded her.

"That doesn't explain Amy and Christopher," Nora insisted, moving toward the foyer.

Ethan wiggled an eyebrow at Heather, looking as perfectly relaxed on the antique sofa in her mother's formal living room as he had on the pew next to her in church that morning. Heather loved that she could tell what he was thinking.

"It's just that everything's changing," she explained softly. "A short while ago we were all together for our usual Sunday dinner, and now we're only five, not counting you."

"Is it a problem, my being here?" he asked.

She shook her head. "No, but it is significant."

He smiled. That morning after the service, as they were leaving the church with Nora and Amy, Nora had reminded everyone that it was the last Sunday of the month. Then she had turned to Ethan and informed him that he would, of course, be joining them. The shock on Amy's face must have mirrored Heather's own. Sunday family dinners were family-only events. Heather had known at once, though, that it was right for Ethan to be there, just as her mother obviously had.

Heather was a little surprised when her mother walked back into the room trailed by Tim, who was almost always the last to arrive. His hand fell on her shoulder as he passed her chair, then his gaze landed on Ethan, and he stopped dead in his tracks.

"Hello, Tim," Ethan said warmly, crossing his legs, looking for all the world as if he belonged right where he sat. And he did. Heather was convinced of that.

Tim glanced at Heather and then turned a significant look upon his mother, who smoothly stated the obvious, "Ethan's joining us for dinner."

Tim's eyebrows climbed. "So I see."

Before he could spill the question that obviously rode the tip of his tongue, Amy strode into the room. "I thought Chris would be here by now. Hi, Ethan."

Ethan smiled broadly. "Hello, again."

Heather craned her head at her older sister. "Did you ride over with Tim?"

"Yup." Amy dropped down into an elegant arm chair. "Well, we do live in the same building."

"But you didn't explain that Ethan would be here?"

Amy grinned. "I believe that's your explanation to make, sister dear."

"And here I thought you'd be taking credit," Ethan teased, and Heather laughed.

Amy airily waved a hand. "Oh, I do!"

Ethan dropped his foot to the floor and leaned forward. "I don't think I ever thanked you, by the way."

"Not necessary," Amy replied, smiling at Heather. "I'm just so pleased."

Tim glared at his sisters and said impatiently, "Would someone please tell me what's going on?"

"Isn't it obvious?" Amy asked.

At the same time, Heather said, "I don't know what you're talking about."

Just then they heard a car door slam outside.

"That must be Chris," she said, scooting to the edge of her chair and sending Ethan a pointed look.

He didn't misread her. Rising swiftly, he reached down a hand for her. She slid her palm against his and let him tug her to her feet. Together they turned and walked side by side into the foyer. She really wanted him with her when Chris came in, and she didn't miss the astonished look on their older brother's face when he realized that.

Heather and Ethan reached the door before Chris, and so it was standing open when her twin stepped foot onto the porch. Heather leaned forward, smiling, and lifted her cheek for her brother's kiss, feeling Ethan's hand at the small of her back.

"Hey, sis."

"Hey, yourself."

Chris looked past her, a knowing smile curving his lips. "Ethan. Somehow I thought I'd be seeing you here sooner or later."

"Better sooner than later in my book," Ethan said heartily.

"Speaking of later," Heather said, moving Chris aside with a wave and closing the door, "you're the last to arrive, and Mom's in a bit of a dither about it."

"Mom is not in a dither," Nora said from behind her. "Mom wisely put dinner back a half hour when Tim informed us he would be late, which is more than I can say for you." She walked to Christopher and patted his chest with one hand. "What kept you and why didn't you call?"

"One of my kids had me on the phone."

Everyone knew that he meant one of the kids in his youth program.

"Is everything all right?" Nora asked.

"As all right as it's going to be for now," Chris answered. "His dad got picked up last night for driving while intoxicated."

"Poor child."

"It's a good object lesson for him," Chris said, "and maybe for his father, too."

"I hope he sees it that way."

"I think he does."

"That's good. Shall we get it on the table then? Ethan, we could use your assistance."

"Sure thing."

He winked at Heather as he followed Nora into the dining room. Tim went after him, staring pointedly at Heather until he either had to look where he was going or walk into a wall. Amy strolled by, patting first Heather and then Christopher knowingly as she did so. It seemed that the family was conspiring to give the twins a moment alone.

"Well?" Heather asked, turning to her brother. If he had something important to say about her and Ethan, she was more than ready to hear it.

"Well," Christopher said. Then he smiled and hugged her. "I don't think I've ever seen you this happy."

Heather went up on tiptoe to hug him back.

"It's strange," she said, coming back down and looking up at him. "Dad's still so sick, and Jeremy's still so confused, and Mom's beginning to really worry about Melissa, but I've never been happier."

"It shows," Chris said. "You're absolutely glowing.

And I'm glad. This family needs some happiness right now."

Heather gripped his hands with hers. "Thank you for saying that, because at times I feel a little guilty."

"No, no. None of that. Your being miserable wouldn't fix anything, you know. You and Ethan be just as happy as you can be."

Heather laughed. "I know he's the last person you ever expected to fall for your sister," she began, but the look on Chris's face stopped her.

"Now why would you say that?"

"For all the obvious reasons, of course."

"I don't see any reasons, obvious or otherwise. Maybe you'd better explain these reasons to me."

Heather was surprised on one level and realized on another that her twin really didn't know Ethan all that well. She inclined her head.

"Our backgrounds are very different. He's an only child. His parents are divorced."

"Okay. But we've always known we were blessed in that regard."

She nodded in acknowledgment of that. "Ethan's never stayed in one place very long. His dad was in the military, and they moved around a lot even when he was small. In some ways, it's as if he's never really had a home."

"I see. So now he's decided this is his home?"

"Something like that."

Chris dropped his hands to his waist. "I'm still not hearing any reasons to be surprised that Ethan would fall for you."

"We didn't even share the same faith."

"Considering that he joined the church last Sunday, I'd say that was a moot point."

"Granted, but…" Heather threw up her hands. "Honestly, Chris, you can't expect me to believe that the first time you saw Ethan you thought, 'Now he and Heather would be the perfect couple.'"

"The first time I saw Ethan, he was with you, and I actually did think that the two of you looked pretty much like a couple even then."

"You didn't think he was, you know…" She wrinkled her nose, irritated that this still bothered her even a tiny bit. "Too good-looking for me?"

Her brother stared at her. Then he looked away. Finally, he stared at her again.

"I can't believe you even asked that. For one thing, I don't have opinions on whether other guys are good-looking. For another, there's no such thing as too good-looking, period. And for a third…" He shook his head. "Why would you feel that way about yourself? I know I'm prejudiced, but I'm not blind, and I see that all of my sisters are gorgeous."

Heather bowed her head, admitting, "I guess I just never felt that I could compete with Amy and Melissa in that way."

Chris clamped a hand around the nape of her neck

and shook her gently. "I always thought you just didn't *care* to compete."

"In some ways, I didn't," she admitted. "In other ways, I just…" She shrugged helplessly. "I don't know. Everyone's always said our mother is one of the most beautiful women anywhere, and Amy and Melissa are both so like her."

"And you're not?" Chris asked, obviously confused.

Heather made a gesture at her hair, feeling extremely foolish. He rolled his eyes.

"It'd be a real dull world if all the women were blond, Heather. And if Ethan Danes doesn't think you're the most beautiful woman in the world, I'll eat my shirt."

"You really think so?"

Chris bent down and put his nose to hers. It was a twin thing, something they'd done since he'd started to grow taller than her, like at about the age of *two*. It seemed to put them on equal footing and was his way of demonstrating that, appearances aside, they would always be two faces of the same coin.

"Take it from a guy, when a man looks at a woman the way Ethan looks at you, he *likes* what he sees."

Heather smiled, feeling the last shreds of doubt fall away. If there was another human being in the world upon whom she could count to be completely honest with her, it was Christopher.

"I wonder why I didn't talk to you about this before?"

Chuckling, Chris straightened. "Not our usual topic of conversation, is it?"

She parked her hands at her waist. "Tell me something, do you think it's faith that brings the love of one's life?"

For a moment, Chris looked taken aback. Then he shrugged. "Don't know." He thought a moment before shaking his head. "Not for me. Not yet, anyway. Maybe God intends some people to marry and has someone in mind for them, but even if that's so, I'm not sure I'm one of them."

"I thought the same thing not too long ago. I expect God will show you when your time is right."

"Oh, no," he said, "not me. I'm nowhere near ready for that. Really, sis, I don't think I'll ever be ready for romance."

"Famous last words," Heather said, laughing.

Nora appeared just then, widening her already enormous eyes at them.

"Will you two move it? Honestly, you forget the rest of us even exist if we leave you alone together too long."

"We're here," Chris said, pulling Heather with him into the dining room.

Heather laughed, that happiness her brother had mentioned earlier bubbling up and pouring out of her, as perfect and as beautiful as the newly spread wings of a butterfly.

* * * * * *

Dear Reader,

My grandfather, a wonderful Christian man, used to say that the only real difference between him and the worst of human monsters was Jesus Christ. As a child, I somewhat discounted that as an example of his great modesty. As an adult and a more mature Christian, I now understand what he was saying, that sin is sin in God's eyes, period, so we are all equally "dirty," but those of us whose faith is fixed on Christ are seen by God through Him.

Christians are, of course, just folks with all the warts and quirks normal to humankind. We sometimes devalue ourselves, forgetting that we are, after all, treasured by our Lord, or overvalue ourselves, when at best we can never measure up to Him. I firmly believe that as Christians we are empowered by the Holy Spirit to overcome, in the fullness of time, our personal warts and quirks. That's what the Christian life is, in large part, about, and that's why I became so fond of Heather and Ethan.

To me, Heather and Ethan epitomize in a small, very human fashion the true meaning of Christian romance, a definition that also comes from my grandfather. A Christian couple, according to George Absher, is meant to spur one another to greater and greater love, faith and perfection. Since no woman was ever more adored than my grandmother, no man ever more revered than my grandfather and no finer example of Christian romance ever found, I believe it. I hope you do, too, and that your own romance will prove it.

God bless,

Arlene James

QUESTIONS FOR DISCUSSION

1. How does self-image have an impact upon the way the world sees a person and why?

2. Heather deliberately, though perhaps not consciously, downplayed her looks. Why would a woman do that, especially a Christian woman? Is this humility or "false" humility? Is a fear of competition acceptable? An unwillingness to compete? Why or why not?

3. After her triumph at the awards ceremony, Heather muses that Ethan has helped her see who she could be, who God surely meant her to be and that it was much more than she'd ever dared to imagine she could be. Why would she place limits on herself? Should Christians place such limits on themselves?

4. Christian people suffer difficulties in this life. Ethan initially saw the difficulties experienced by Heather's family as undeserved punishment. How do you see it? Did poor judgment play a part in the difficulties the family experienced? Does poor judgment sometimes play a part in the difficulties that Christians experience?

5. Heather believes that God can and does use difficulties for the benefit of His children. If this is so, how was Heather, in particular, blessed through the difficulties that she experienced during the course of the book (her father's illness, family secrets being exposed, her sister's disappearance, her own uncertainty, etc.)?

6. Is Ethan's growing hunger for and interest in the things of God connected to his growing need for belonging and a real home? Or is it the reverse? Why or why not?

7. Ethan comes to believe that belonging doesn't always just happen, that it sometimes takes real work and real risk. Does this make sense to you? Why or why not?

8. Heather becomes confused about God's will for her life. Scripture tells us that God is not a god of confusion (1 Corinthians 14:33), so how can this happen to sincere, dedicated Christians?

9. When Ethan comes to her home in Chapter 14, Heather's silent prayer reveals the root cause of her confusion. What is it?

10. What's the difference between humility and a poor self-image? Can a physical transformation spur mental and/or spiritual transformation? How? Can the opposite occur? How?

The next Hamilton up for romance is Chris.
Look for his story, BY HER SIDE,
by Kathryn Springer,
coming out August 2006,
only from Steeple Hill Love Inspired.
Please turn the page for a sneak peek.

The telephone was already winking one red eye at her, letting her know she had some messages.

"Felicity, this is Tim. Push your nine o'clock appointment back to ten. My brother is coming to talk to you about the letter you got yesterday."

Felicity exhaled sharply. With Jeremy gone, the only brother Tim could possibly be referring to was Chris Hamilton. The police officer. She'd tried to play down her concern over the latest letter she'd received but obviously "Typhoon Tim" had taken matters into his own hands.

He'd gotten the nickname from the *Dispatch* employees and Felicity thought it certainly fit. With some of the new changes Tim had implemented, she was surprised half the staff hadn't jumped ship when he'd taken control.

Jeremy's leadership style had been as laid-back as his personality. The stress of a newspaper with never-ending deadlines had the potential to tie everyone in knots, but Jeremy had always been as calm as Sugar Tree Lake on a hot summer day. Tim was much more intense, which seemed to put everyone on edge. Still, she hadn't had a problem with him since Jeremy had left…

Until now.

She picked up the phone and tried to call Tim, hoping to change his mind. There was no response at his desk so she decided to track him down. Maybe he was on the second floor, terrorizing the employees who worked for *Nashville Living.*

Ducking down the hall, she headed toward the stairwell. Since the day she'd been hired, she'd been in a silent standoff with the ancient contraption most people referred to as the elevator. Fearless in most areas of her life, Felicity reluctantly called a draw when it came to enclosed spaces. She couldn't stand them.

Now, with every precious second counting, she paused at the elevator, tucking her lower lip between her teeth.

You're being silly, Felicity, she scolded herself. *You're a tough journalist, not a wimp. This is a three-story building, not exactly a skyscraper.*

She decided that whoever promoted self-talk as a good way to motivate a person hadn't been afraid of small spaces. It was a good thing she knew what *did* work.

Lord, You promised to give courage to the faint-hearted. I'm taking You up on it! Please give me courage.

The elevator's low, musical beep sounded and before Felicity could move, the door swished open.

She was trapped.

Not by the elevator, but by the man stepping out of it. For a second, the only thing in her field of vision was the color blue. Then the badge came into focus. Felicity wasn't petite but the man who took a step forward seemed to tower above her. When she lifted her eyes to his face, she saw a familiar combination of features—the chiseled features, firm Hamilton jawline and a pair of warm, intelligent eyes that happened to be the same shade of brown as the caramels she'd stashed in her desk drawer.

He stepped politely to the side and she could breathe again. Wait a second. Why was she holding her breath?

"Two or three?" he asked, holding the door for her.

"Neither." Felicity buried a sigh and extended her hand. "I'm Felicity Simmons and if you're Officer Hamilton, I believe we have an appointment. My office is just down the hall in the newsroom. I have several appointments this morning but I adjusted my schedule."

Chris barely felt the warm press of Felicity Simmons's hand before she pivoted sharply and moved away, her low-heeled shoes clicking against the marble floor. He fell easily into step beside her.

"I have to be honest. I wish Tim wouldn't have bothered you. I can't help but feel like we're wasting your time," Felicity went on.

Chris didn't answer right away. He was still suffering from the mild case of shock he'd been hit with when Felicity had introduced herself. He'd taken a few minutes to go up to the second floor to say hello to Amy and Heather, who were hard at work on the next issue of *Nashville Living*. It had been Heather who'd told him where to find Felicity, but when the elevator door had opened and he saw the young woman standing on the other side, his first assumption was that she worked in the accounting department.

She was younger than he'd expected. Probably close to his age. Even though she looked every inch the professional in conservative brown slacks and a matching jacket, with her auburn hair swept away from her face and anchored in place by an industrial strength copper clip, he never would have guessed she was F. Simmons, the reporter who had covered the last city council meeting. She'd written the piece with bold honesty, not attempting to soften the heated debate several councilmen had engaged in over some proposed budget cuts.

As they entered the newsroom, no one paid any attention to them as they weaved their way to Felicity's desk. Chris could sense the tension in the air and he was thankful he didn't have a deadline hanging over his head every day, although he knew his mom would have preferred he face a deadline instead of the wrong end of a gun.

"Please sit down," Felicity said, her voice brisk as she slid into the narrow space behind her desk. She motioned for Chris to take the chair across from her. "It isn't unusual for reporters to step on people's toes. Or to get letters from disgruntled citizens about an issue that ruffles their feathers."

"With all that's been going on lately, I'll have to admit I haven't read an issue of the *Dispatch* for the past few weeks."

Right before his eyes, the no-nonsense reporter changed. She suddenly seemed to see him as a person, not as a cop who was interrupting her schedule.

"I know this must be hard on your family." Her voice softened and it brushed against his defenses.

In the past few weeks he'd gotten used to people politely inquiring about Wallace and murmuring their surprise at the change in the hierarchy at Hamilton Media. Sometimes they asked questions that made Chris wonder if it wasn't simply idle curiosity motivating them, but he saw none of that now in Felicity's eyes.

We're doing all right. That was what he started to say. It had become his standard, by-the-book comment. Those words couldn't cover the sense of loss he'd felt when the family had gathered for their traditional monthly dinner not long ago. Not only had Wallace's chair at the head of the table been empty, but so were Melissa's and Jeremy's, too. Nor did they begin to express the helplessness he felt when he watched his mom try to be strong for everyone. Or that he couldn't make everything right.

"One minute at a time. Trusting God is the only way we're getting through it." He surprised himself by telling her the truth.

"That's the only way we can get through anything," Felicity murmured.

Adjustment number two. She was a believer.

"I'd like to read the letters Tim told me about." Back to business. He needed to dwell on the reason he was here instead of the way Felicity's eyes met his in complete understanding. And the fact they were the color of sweet tea. "He mentioned the last one seemed more threatening."

Felicity nodded but the way she lowered her gaze for a moment raised a red flag.

"You didn't destroy it, did you?" Chris asked, more sharply than he'd intended. It wasn't unusual for women who were being stalked to delete threatening e-mails or burn letters, as if getting rid of the threats was comparable to getting rid of the person making them. Without the necessary evidence, an investigation came to a grinding halt.

Felicity shook her head. "I still have it."

She leaned over the desk and wordlessly handed him some tear sheets from the two letters they'd printed in the newspaper.

Chris read the first one, a rambling commentary about the *Dispatch* being biased in their coverage but it was obviously directed at Felicity because the person who'd written it mentioned her. Felicity was the only female reporter on staff. The second one again mentioned an unfair bias and then ended with a veiled threat.

You'd better stop before it's too late.

Chris paused and looked up at Felicity. Body language was an important part of the interview process and he noticed immediately her hands were in a relaxed pose on the top of her desk. She didn't have her arms crossed. She wasn't fiddling nervously with a pen or shuffling papers. She was patiently waiting for him to finish so she could get on with her day.

"What do you think they want you to stop?"

"I have no idea." Felicity met his gaze evenly. "Since May, I've been covering city council meetings and attending court hearings. I've done the lead stories for two different jury trials. One was the drunk driver that pushed a car full of teenagers into the river, the other was a special interest piece on the mayor's vision to balance community development with economic development."

"Aren't they the same thing?"

"You wouldn't ask that if you'd been to the last council meeting." Felicity chuckled.

Felicity pulled out a piece of paper and handed it

to him. Reluctantly, Chris thought. "This one was delivered over the weekend. Addressed directly to me, not the newspaper."

> Things are different here than where you're
> from. If you keep it up, you'll find out that
> people take care of their own problems. In their
> own way. Just a reminder for you to watch your
> step.